THE FIRST MOUNTAIN MAN
PREACHER'S
SHOWDOWN

THE FIRST MOUNTAIN MAN
PREACHER'S
SHOWDOWN

William W. Johnstone
with J. A. Johnstone

PINNACLE BOOKS
Kensington Publishing Corp.
www.kensingtonbooks.com

PINNACLE BOOKS are published by

Kensington Publishing Corp.
850 Third Avenue
New York, NY 10022

PUBLISHER'S NOTE
Following the death of William W. Johnstone, the Johnstone family is working with a carefully selected writer to organize and complete Mr. Johnstone's outlines and many unfinished manuscripts to create additional novels in all of his series like The Last Gunfighter, Mountain Man, and Eagles, among others. This novel was inspired by Mr. Johnstone's superb storytelling.

All Kensington titles, imprints, and distributed lines are available at special quantity discounts for bulk purchases for sales promotions, premiums, fund-raising, educational, or institutional use. Special book excerpts or customized printings can also be created to fit specific needs. For details, write or phone the office of the Kensington special sales manager: Kensington Publishing Corp., 850 Third Avenue, New York, NY 10022, attn: Special Sales Department; phone 1-800-221-2647.

ISBN-13: 978-0-7860-1838-3
ISBN-10: 0-7860-1838-0

First printing: January 2008

10 9 8 7 6 5 4 3

Printed in the United States of America

One

Civilization stank.

As the man called Preacher paddled the canoe down the Mississippi River, he scented St. Louis before he ever came in sight of the settlement sprawled along the west bank of the stream the Indians called the Father of Waters. The smell was a mixture of wood smoke, tanning hides, boiling lye, rotting fish, burned meat, and a hundred other less-than-pleasant aromas. Preacher preferred to think of it as just the smell of civilization, and he thought it stank.

But then, he reckoned that after months in the wilderness, he was no fragrant flower. And the plews piled up in front of him and behind him in the canoe didn't smell too good neither. He chuckled. Soon enough, he'd be rid of the plews, since he planned to sell them first thing when he reached the settlement. Then he'd find a place to stay and maybe soak off in a tub full of hot water some of the months of grime that had collected on his body. Some folks claimed it was unhealthy to bathe too often, and the life Preacher had chosen to lead was already perilous enough as it was, but sometimes a fella just had to live dangerously.

Preacher was a tall, rangy man, although his height wasn't too evident while he was sitting in the canoe. His broad shoulders and muscular arms strained at the buckskins he wore and revealed the power in his body. His long, thick hair was black as midnight, save for a few silver strands, as was the bushy beard that concealed the lower half of his rugged face. His eyes, shaded by the broad brim of his felt hat, were dark and deep-set under prominent brows. His face and hands were tanned to the color of old saddle leather. He was in his early thirties, having been born as the eighteenth century turned to the nineteenth. He was no longer considered a young man in this day and age, but Preacher's active, outdoor life and iron constitution gave him the strength and vigor and attitude of someone younger.

He had left home at an early age, not really running away from the farm or his family, but rather running *toward* something—the lure of the unknown. He wanted to see the vast American frontier, and the best way to do that was to just set out on his own two feet.

Ever since then, he'd been wandering. After spending some time on the river, he had joined up with Andy Jackson's army and fought the British down at the town of New Orleans back in 1814. Then he had headed west with some mountain men, and except for occasional forays back to civilization in St. Louis or down yonder in Texas, he had spent the intervening years in the Rockies, making his living by trapping beaver and other animals and selling their pelts, and trying to stay out of trouble.

He hadn't been any too successful in that last goal.

But he'd spent the previous spring trapping and had a good load of plews, so he thought it would be all right to make a trip downriver to sell them, then head back up the Missouri for the fall season. The fur companies had begun to establish trading posts in the mountains where he could have disposed of his pelts, but Preacher had a hankering to visit the settlements again. He knew it was probably a mistake to do so. He wouldn't be happy once he got there and would be eager to get back to the frontier. But he had come anyway.

The river was narrower here than it was farther downstream, but it was still a pretty impressive thing, flowing as it did between high, wooded banks. Preacher figured he was still a mile or more above St. Louis. The south breeze would carry the smell of the settlement that far. His muscles worked with smooth efficiency as he dug the paddle into the water first on one side of the canoe, then on the other. The sleek craft, made of slabs of bark sealed together with pitch, cut through the water.

Preacher heard the dull boom of a shot at the same time as he saw the lead ball *plunk* into the water with a small splash just in front of the canoe's bow. His keen-eyed gaze went to the west bank of the river, where he spotted a puff of smoke floating in the air.

Some son of a buck had just taken a shot at him!

Come pretty damned close, too, considering the

range. Preacher's long-barreled flintlock rifle lay across the canoe slats in front of him. He put the paddle down and snatched up the weapon. It was already loaded and primed—an unloaded weapon wouldn't do a fella a lot of good if trouble came at him unexpectedly—so all he had to do was lift it to his shoulder and ear back the hammer. He figured the bushwhacker on the riverbank would have moved as soon as he fired that first shot. Question was, had he gone right or left?

One guess was just as likely to be correct as the other, so Preacher followed his gut and aimed just to the left of where he'd seen that puff of powder smoke. He pressed the trigger. The rifle roared and kicked back against his shoulder.

He didn't know if he hit the bushwhacker or not, but a moment later he heard the faint drumming of hoofbeats and saw a haze of dust rising in the air. Somebody was taking off for the tall and uncut over yonder, and Preacher figured it was the varmint who had tried to shoot him.

"Damn pirate," he said as his eyes narrowed with disgust. He figured the bushwhacker had a canoe hidden over there on the bank somewhere, and if the man had succeeded in killing him, he would have paddled out, tied a line to Preacher's canoe, and towed it back into shore with its load of furs.

Preacher couldn't even begin to understand why a man would rather steal and even kill than work for a living, but he knew that a lot of folks were that way.

He reloaded the rifle and placed it back in the bottom of the canoe, in easy reach in case he needed it again. Then he picked up the paddle and started back in with it—right, left, right, left, on down the river to St. Louis.

A number of keelboats and steamboats were tied up at the docks extending into the Mississippi from the settlement's waterfront. Not being fond of crowds, Preacher headed for shore before he reached that point. He found a place at the edge of town where he could pull the canoe out of the water, and put in there. A chunky boy about ten years old, wearing a coonskin cap, watched with great interest as the tall, rawboned, buckskin-clad man dragged the canoe full of pelts onto the shore.

Preacher turned and grinned at the youngster. "Howdy, son," he said.

In an awestruck voice, the boy asked, "Are you a mountain man, mister?"

"You betcha," Preacher replied, still grinning.

The boy pointed at the rifle in Preacher's hands and the pair of flintlock pistols bucked behind his wide belt. "Are them guns loaded?"

"They sure are. Wouldn't do me much good if they weren't, happen I should need 'em, now would they?"

"No, I reckon not. You ever shoot any Injuns?"

Preacher nodded, his expression solemn now. "Been known to," he said. "But only when they didn't give me no other choice. And I been good friends with a whole heap o' redskins, too."

"My pa says all Injuns are bad. He says they're all heathen savages."

"I reckon that's because he ain't never met the right ones. Indians is like any other kind o' folks.

Some are the best friends you'll ever find, and some are just low-down skunks. You'd do well to remember that, younker."

The boy nodded.

"You know a gent name of Joel Larson?" Preacher went on. Larson worked for one of the fur companies here in St. Louis, and Preacher had done business with him on several occasions in the past. Larson was honest and could be counted on to give him a fair price for his pelts.

"I know who he is," the boy said. "My pa works in the fur warehouses."

Preacher nodded. "Would you do me a favor?"

The boy's eyes widened. "Sure!"

"Go down to the docks and find Mr. Larson for me. Tell him that Preacher's waitin' up here with a load o' plews to sell to him."

The youngster's eyes bugged out even more. "You're the fella they call Preacher?"

"Yep. Last time I looked anyway." Preacher dug in one of the pockets of his buckskins and brought out an elk's tooth. "Here you go," he said as he tossed the tooth to the boy. "That's for helpin' me out."

The boy had plucked the tooth out of the air and now stood there for a second, staring at it in awe. Not only was the famous mountain man known as Preacher asking him for help, but Preacher was even willing to give him an elk's tooth as payment. Everybody knew that elk's teeth were good luck.

"Run along now."

"Yes, sir!" Clutching the lucky token in his pudgy hand, the youngster turned around and ran toward the docks and warehouses along the waterfront.

Preacher sat on a tree stump and waited. A short

time later, the boy returned, and following him was a dark-haired, mustachioed man in a swallowtail coat and beaver hat. The man smiled at Preacher and said, "I didn't expect to see you for a few weeks yet."

"Trappin' was good," Preacher explained as he shook hands with Joel Larson. Then he waved a hand toward the canoe full of pelts and added, "Reckon you can see that for yourself."

"Indeed I can. I'll look the furs over and make you an offer." Larson glanced over at the boy and went on. "Thank you for fetching me, Jake. Nobody brings in better pelts than Preacher."

"I was glad to, Mr. Larson," the boy piped up. "If you need me to do anything else, Mr. Preacher, sir, you just let me know."

"I'll do that, son," Preacher promised.

Over the next quarter of an hour, Preacher and Larson conducted their business, settling on a mutually agreeable price for the furs. "I'll have to meet you tonight to pay you," Larson said, "but if it's all right with you, I'll get some men up here with a wagon right away to load those pelts and get them in the warehouse."

Preacher nodded. "Fine by me. You ain't never given me any cause not to trust you."

A hard edge in Preacher's voice carried the unspoken warning that it wouldn't be wise to give him any reason for distrust.

Larson chuckled and said, "I certainly don't intend to start now. Where should I look for you?"

"I'll be at Fargo's tavern." Nearly everybody in St. Louis was familiar with the tavern operated by an old riverman named Ford Fargo. Preacher was sure Larson would know where the place was.

Larson nodded and said, "I'll see you later then. You'll keep an eye on those pelts until my men pick them up?"

"Won't let 'em out o' my sight," Preacher promised.

It took another half an hour for Larson's men to arrive with the wagon and start loading the furs. During that time, the boy called Jake pestered Preacher with seemingly endless questions. Preacher put up with it patiently for a while, but Jake was starting to remind him of a particularly annoying magpie by the time Larson's men arrived.

"Where you goin' now, Mr. Preacher?" Jake asked as Preacher headed for Fargo's tavern.

"Got some other things to do," Preacher replied. "And I done told you, boy, just call me Preacher. Ain't no need for the Mister."

"My pa says I ought to respect my elders, and you're pretty old."

Preacher's jaw tightened. "Well, I'll see you later, all right?"

"Can I come with you?"

"No, you run on back to the docks. Where I'm goin' ain't for youngsters."

"Where's that?"

"You know what a tavern is?"

Understanding dawned on Jake's face. "Ohhhh. You're gonna go get drunk and find yourself a whore."

Preacher frowned. "What the hell—I mean, what in blazes does a young fella like you know about things like that?"

"I know a lot," Jake said with a sage expression on his round face. "I listen when folks talk. Grown-ups don't always pay as much attention to what they're sayin' around kids as they should."

Preacher could believe that. He said, "Well, for your information, I ain't lookin' for no whore, and I don't plan to get drunk."

"Don't you like whiskey and women?"

Preacher gritted his teeth again and wondered if he was going to have to toss this little jackanapes into the river to get away from him.

It didn't come to that because, at that point, a man came along the riverbank calling Jake's name. "Shoot, that's my pa," the boy said. "Reckon it's time to go home for supper. Be seein' you, Mr. Preacher."

"Sure thing," Preacher said, thinking to himself that Jake wouldn't see him again if he saw the inquisitive little varmint first.

Now that he had gotten away from Jake, Preacher headed for the tavern again. He had told the boy the truth—he didn't intend to get drunk.

But a shot of whiskey would sure go down nice right about now.

"You sure that's him?"

"Yeah, I got a good look at him through the spyglass before you took that shot at him. That's the son of a bitch who put a rifle ball through my arm, all right. I got a score to settle with him."

The two men stood behind a run-down shack not far from the river's edge, peering furtively around the corner of the building. They had been watching for the past half hour or so as the dark-bearded mountain man waited for Joel Larson's men to arrive. The tall, sandy-haired one with the prominent Adam's apple wore buckskins and a floppy-brimmed felt hat. The shorter, stockier man was dressed in a shabby black suit and a gray shirt that had once been white. A battered beaver hat was crammed down on a mostly bald head. He had a dirty rag tied around his upper left arm to serve as a bandage. Blood had soaked through the rag in one place, leaving a small crimson stain.

Both men had gaunt, beard-stubbled faces and narrow, hate-filled eyes. Earlier in the afternoon, they had been perched in some brush along the western bank of the river about a mile north of the settlement, waiting for some pilgrim to come along who looked well-heeled enough to rob. The mountain man had certainly filled the bill with that canoe loaded with furs. If the tall man, Schuyler Mims, hadn't missed with his shot, the mountain man would be dead now, and Schuyler and his partner, who went by the name Colin Fairfax, would be selling those furs to Joel Larson.

Instead, Schuyler's aim had been just a little off. The same couldn't be said of the mountain man's aim. His return shot had nicked Fairfax in the arm as he and Mims were trying to get away from the riverbank. The ball hadn't actually gone through his arm as he'd said, but rather had grazed it, knocking out a tiny chunk of flesh. It wasn't a serious wound, but it had hurt like hell and Fairfax had bled like a stuck pig, all the while howling curses as Schuyler tried to patch up the injury.

Fairfax was still angry at his partner for missing, but he was more angry at the mountain man who had so coolly and accurately shot back at them.

During the ride back down here to St. Louis, Fairfax had vowed that he would find the man and get even with him for what had happened. The fact that the mishap had occurred while the two of them were trying to murder and rob the mountain man didn't mean anything to him.

Now they had spotted the object of Fairfax's wrath, and spied on him while he was arranging to sell his furs to Joel Larson. Schuyler and Fairfax knew Larson, and had tried to sell him some stolen furs in the past. Larson must have been suspicious, because he'd made such a low offer that the partners had turned it down. They'd wound up selling the pelts to one of the other fur traders, still for less than they were worth.

"No money changed hands," Schuyler pointed out as he and Fairfax withdrew around to the other side of the shack. "Larson's probably gonna meet him later and pay him then."

Fairfax nodded. "In that case, the wisest course of action would be to follow him and wait until our quarry has the cash in hand. Then we'll relieve him of it." An evil smile stretched across the man's face. "And of his life, too, of course."

Two

Preacher had told Jake the truth about something else, too—he wasn't looking for a whore.

But a whore had found him, and he wasn't quite sure what to do about it.

It wasn't that Preacher was morally opposed to prostitution or anything like that. Indeed, if he could be said to have had a love of his life, it would be the girl called Jennie. She had become a soiled dove at an early age, and had remained in that profession for the remainder of her too-short life.

But ever since Jennie's death, for the most part Preacher had steered clear of women. He had met a few that he had grown fond of, but his fiddle-footed nature had assured that nothing came of those brief relationships.

Now he had a buxom redhead named Abby perched on his lap, and she was being stubborn about getting off. She leaned closer and kissed on him and whispered sweet nothings in his ear. She wanted him to take her out to the crib behind Fargo's place where she plied her trade.

What she really wanted, of course, was some of the money she had seen Joel Larson giving him earlier in payment for those pelts.

Preacher had put away about a fourth of a jug of whiskey and a couple of thick steaks during the time he'd waited at Fargo's for Larson. He wasn't drunk, but the who-hit-John had caused a pleasant glow to spring up inside him, like the warmth from a campfire on a chilly night. The steaks had filled his belly. All of it combined to make him a mite drowsy.

Then Larson arrived and gave him a small leather pouch that was heavy with gold coins. They had shared a drink; then the fur company man had gone on his way. Preacher had already told Fargo he wanted to rent one of the rooms on the tavern's second floor for the night. He'd also asked the tavern keeper to haul the big washtub up there and see that it was filled with hot water. Fargo had agreed, knowing that Preacher was scrupulously honest and was good for any debts he incurred during his stay in St. Louis.

Preacher wasn't in the habit of thinking much beyond the present, but if anybody had pinned him down on the question, he would have said that he was going to hang around the settlement for a few days, buy some supplies for his next trip to the mountains, and then gamble and drink away whatever funds he had remaining. He'd planned to get started on that with a hot soak in the washtub, but before he got around to going upstairs, Abby had come over and plopped herself down on his lap.

To tell the truth, Preacher was thinking about asking her if she wanted to come upstairs with him and share that bath. It would be a tight fit for both of them in the washtub, but he thought they could manage, and having his arms full of wet, firm-fleshed woman sounded pretty damned good right now.

"Hold on, hold on," he said as he unwound Abby's arms from his neck.

She pouted. "I just want to show you some lovin', Preacher."

"And I reckon we might just get around to that. First, though, I told Fargo to haul that ol' washtub o' his upstairs and fill it with hot water. How'd you feel about gettin' in there with me?"

Abby giggled and said, "Why, that sounds like just about the dandiest thing I ever heard!" She pushed her large, plump breasts against him. "We can wash each other."

"All right, but you got to get off of me first."

She stood up and took his hand, eager to get on with the bath now that he had suggested it. "Come on!"

Preacher stopped at the bar to ask the burly, bearded tavern keeper if the tub had been filled. Ford Fargo nodded and said, "Yep, that boy o' mine just got through haulin' the last two buckets o' hot water up there. It's ready for you, Preacher. I ain't sure why you'd want to do such a thing, though. I hear that washin' too reg'lar ain't good for you."

"Well, since it's been months, I reckon I'll chance it," Preacher replied with a grin. He allowed Abby to tug him toward the stairs as he heard Fargo's knowing chuckle behind them.

Preacher had long since gotten over any guilt he felt about Jennie, and by the time he had followed

Abby up the stairs with her well-cushioned rump wiggling back and forth in front of his face, he had decided this was a pretty good idea after all. When they reached the room he was renting and went inside, he saw curls of steam rising from the water in the big wooden tub. Abby turned and came into his arms, lifting her face for him to kiss her. Preacher obliged.

After a moment, Abby pulled back. She was a little out of breath as she said, "Let's get these duds off and get in that tub."

Sounded like a good plan to Preacher.

Schuyler Mims and Colin Fairfax had followed the mountain man to Fargo's tavern. They hadn't been close enough that afternoon to overhear the conversation between the mountain man and Joel Larson, so they hadn't known where he was going and had to trail him. After he went into the tavern, they loitered across the street and waited for Larson to arrive with the money they were sure he would be bringing to pay for the pelts.

Dusk was settling down over the riverfront town when Schuyler nudged Fairfax with an elbow and asked, "Ain't that the kid who was talking to that mountain man earlier?"

Fairfax squinted at the boy who had ambled along the street and come to a stop in front of the tavern. "Yes, I believe it is."

"Why don't you talk to him, maybe see what he knows about that fella?"

Fairfax frowned. "You think it might help?"

"Can't hurt," Schuyler said with a shrug of his bony shoulders.

"All right. Stay here."

Fairfax strolled out into the street, seemingly just idling along. He came to a stop next to the boy and looked down at him as if he'd just noticed that the youngster was there.

"Hello, lad."

"Hey, mister."

"Say, didn't I see you earlier, talking to a friend of mine down by the river?"

The boy grinned. "You mean Mr. Preacher? He's a friend of yours, mister?"

"Yes. Yes, that's right," Fairfax said, while trying not to show the surprise he felt. He had heard of Preacher. People told stories about his exploits in the mountains, going all the way back to the time he had been captured by the Blackfeet as a young man and saved his life by preaching a marathon sermon that had convinced his captors he was touched in the head. Indians wouldn't harm someone they considered disturbed, believing them to have a special connection with the spirit world, so they had released him, and ever since then he had been known as Preacher. Fairfax had no idea what the man's real name was.

But he knew that Preacher was considered one of the most dangerous men west of the Mississippi . . . or east of it, for that matter.

"That's where he said he was goin'," the boy went on, indicating the tavern. "I heard him tell Mr. Larson. So I reckon he's in there, if you're lookin' for him."

"Perhaps I'll get together with him later," Fairfax

said. "We're old friends, but we haven't seen each other for a long time, so I'd like to surprise him. If you see him, don't mention that you spoke to me, all right?"

"Sure, mister. I don't reckon I'll be seein' him, though. My pa will be mad enough at me for slippin' out after supper like this. He'd tan my hide good if he ever caught me sneakin' into a tavern. He says that good, God-fearin' folks don't never venture into such places."

"How does one know which places to avoid if one never visits them?" Fairfax murmured.

"Huh?"

"Never mind, lad." He took one of the precious few coins he and Mims had to their names and pressed it into the boy's hand. "Here, take this and run along."

The boy bit the coin to make sure it was real, then beamed. "This has been a *good* day," he said, and then he hurried away through the gathering shadows.

Fairfax went back across the street to rejoin his partner. "I found out our quarry's name," he told Schuyler.

"What is it?"

"Preacher."

Schuyler's eyes widened. "Oh, Lordy. We better forget about it, Colin. Even them red savages don't mess with Preacher most of the time. He's all wolf and a yard wide."

"He's just a man like any other," Fairfax snapped. "And he shot me, damn his eyes. I've a score to settle."

Schuyler grunted. "Yeah, and once Larson brings

his money for them plews, he'll have a considerable amount of cash on him, I'm thinkin'. I ain't sure it's worth gettin' killed over, though. There's other ways to make money."

Fairfax glared and shook his head. "Preacher's never seen us before. We can walk right in there, and he won't have the slightest notion that we've a grudge against him. It's just a matter of waiting for the proper time to strike. Any man can be defeated if he's taken by surprise by an enemy who's ruthless enough."

"Well . . . maybe."

"I'll go after him by myself if I have to."

"Now, don't take on like that," Schuyler said. "We been partners for a good while, Colin. I ain't a'gonna desert you now." The taller man nodded. "We'll take him. Let's go on in and see what he's doin'."

They started across the street, but stopped as they saw Joel Larson approaching. Drawing back into the shadows, they waited while the fur merchant entered the tavern. Larson wasn't inside for long, and when he left again, Fairfax said, "He must have paid Preacher off for those pelts. That's what we've been waiting for."

Schuyler nodded, but he still looked nervous about what they were planning to do. He knew better than to suggest again that they give up on squaring the score with Preacher. Fairfax wouldn't stand for that, and he usually did the thinking for both of them.

Preacher was sitting at a table in the corner with a fleshy, redheaded young woman in his lap when the partners came into the tavern. Schuyler and Fairfax went to the bar and spent the last of their money on a couple of drinks they could nurse along for a while.

A short time later, Preacher and the whore went upstairs, pausing at the bar to speak to the proprietor for a moment. From the overheard conversation, the two men learned that Preacher was about to take a bath. That was good, because it meant that he would be naked. That wasn't exactly the same thing as unarmed, but at least he would have to take off his weapons and put them aside before he climbed into the washtub. When you were dealing with a man like Preacher, any edge was better than none, no matter how slight it might be.

Schuyler put his head close to Fairfax's and said in a low voice, "We can't just go traipsin' upstairs. Fargo rents them rooms out, and if we start up there, he'll holler after us and try to make us pay."

"I recall seeing some stairs in the rear," Fairfax said. "We'll make our entrance that way." He tossed back the little bit of liquor that remained in his cup.

Schuyler followed suit, and then the two men turned and left the tavern. No one paid them any mind.

They hurried around the building. Full night had fallen by now, and they had to find the back stairs in the dark. Schuyler tripped over something and nearly fell, and Fairfax cursed under his breath and told him to be careful. Then they came to the stairs and began a slow, careful ascent.

They reached the door at the top of the stairs and slipped inside. They found themselves in a narrow corridor with doors on both sides. The hallway was lit by a single candle stuck on a shelf at the far end, where the landing for the main staircase was. Thick shadows cloaked this end of the corridor.

Fairfax motioned for Schuyler to take the lead. Schuyler hesitated, then grimaced and started walking carefully along the hall, staying close to the wall. He paused at each door he came to and pressed his ear to the panel. Finally, at the third door on the right, he motioned for Fairfax to follow him.

"I can hear 'em splashin' around in there," Schuyler whispered in his partner's ear. "Sounds like they're havin' a fine old time."

Fairfax reached under his coat and drew out a short-barreled pistol. "It's about to get finer . . . for us," he said as he drew back the weapon's hammer.

Preacher took the two pistols from behind his belt and placed them on a chair near the tub, along with the heavy-bladed hunting knife in its fringed sheath and the tomahawk he also carried. His long rifle was leaned against the wall in a corner. Then he stripped off his greasy, dirty buckskins and tossed them in a different corner of the room.

By that time, Abby had peeled her homespun dress up and over her head, along with the thin shift she wore underneath it. That left her naked as a jaybird. She was cuter than a jaybird, Preacher thought. He stepped into the tub, wincing a little as his foot touched the hot water. He climbed the rest of the way in and sank down, motioning for Abby to join him.

Considering that she was a pretty solidly built young woman, her movements were a mite dainty as she got into the tub and lowered herself onto

Preacher's lap. They embraced and kissed again, shifting around to make themselves more comfortable in the close confines of the tub. Some of the water sloshed over the sides.

Preacher luxuriated in the heat, letting it soak away all the aches and pains he had stored up in his lanky body during the long months spent in the wilderness. Abby did a lot of kissing and playing around, but he was almost too tired to really get into the spirit of the thing. He was thinking about telling her that they ought to consider postponing the rest of their get-together until the next night, when he heard a floorboard creak in the hallway outside the door.

Preacher's thick, dark eyebrows drew down in a frown. The sound didn't have to mean anything. Just somebody else who had rented one of Fargo's rooms passing by in the corridor, that was all.

But the creak had been *right* outside the door, almost like somebody was standing there and had shifted his weight a little, and Preacher couldn't think of any reason why somebody should be doing such a thing.

Unless, of course, they were up to no good.

Now that he thought about it, he realized that he'd had a tiny feeling of unease ever since he had arrived in St. Louis. He had put it down to the fact that he was in a settlement again, with people all around, rather than out by himself on the high, lonesome plains or in the rugged, isolated mountains. He had figured that nobody was really watching him.

But maybe he'd been wrong about that. Maybe

that uneasy feeling had been a warning that trouble was lurking in those crowds.

Preacher sat up a little straighter in the tub and took his hands off Abby's heavy breasts. He reached for the butts of the pistols on the nearby chair instead, and she frowned and asked, "What's wrong, honey?"

Before Preacher could answer, the door to the corridor slammed open and two men rushed into the room, each of them brandishing a gun.

Three

Preacher filled his hands about as fast as it was possible for any man to do so, leaning to the side out of the washtub as he did so.

But at that same moment, Abby cried out in surprise and started to stand up, even though Preacher yelled for her to stay down.

The warning came too late. Both of the intruders fired, and as their pistols roared and powder smoke spouted from the muzzles, the heavy lead balls slammed into the young redhead's back.

Abby was thrown forward by the horrible impact. She crashed against Preacher, who was trying to stand up now that he was armed. The combination of the collision and the wet tub made his feet slip out from under him. He fell backward, out of the tub.

Images and impressions were jumbled together in his brain. He saw the blood spurting from the holes in Abby's chest where the pistol balls had gone all the way through her body and torn their way out. He saw the look of pain and shock filling her wide green eyes. He saw the two killers, one short, one tall, but that was all that had registered during the quick glimpse he had gotten of them. And he saw the ceiling of the room as he smashed down on his back on the floor.

Instinct saved his life then, causing his muscles to spring into action even though he was too stunned to think about what he was doing at that moment. He rolled to the side as another gun roared. At least one of the assassins had a second pistol. The ball chewed splinters from the floorboards near his head. He felt several of the little wood slivers sting his face. He came to a stop on his belly, the pistols in his hands tilted up but still unfired.

There was nothing to shoot at, Preacher realized. The two intruders were gone. They must have realized that to stand around and try to reload was to invite certain death at his hands. He heard swift footsteps in the corridor and knew they were fleeing.

As he leaped to his feet, he saw Abby draped over the side of the washtub. She had fallen to her knees and then pitched forward, so that the upper half of her body dangled outside the tub and the tangled strands of her long, wet red hair hung down and brushed the floor. Preacher had seen the extent of the terrible wounds she had suffered and knew she was dead. Nobody survived having a couple of fist-sized holes blown through their chest.

Ignoring the fact that he was still naked, he lunged toward the door and slid out into the hallway. Movement from the stairs caught his eye. He saw a beaver hat disappearing down the staircase and almost snapped a shot at it, but he held off on the trigger. He didn't want to waste powder and shot on a hat unless he could be sure of ventilating the head under it, too.

He hadn't known Abby for more than a couple of hours, but he was filled with rage at her useless death. He supposed the two bastards who'd interrupted his bath had been gunning for him and the girl had been killed by accident . . . but at the same time, he wasn't sure why anybody wanted to blow holes in him either. He hadn't had any run-ins with anybody since arriving in St. Louis earlier in the day.

Of course, there had been that attempt to bushwhack him while he was still on the river, he recalled. Maybe somebody held a grudge against him because of that. Or maybe some old enemy had spotted him. He had a few of them, although most of his enemies had a habit of winding up dead.

Those thoughts flashed through Preacher's brain in less than the blink of an eye as he broke into a run toward the stairs. He didn't know who the two men were, and he didn't really give a damn. They had killed Abby and tried to kill him, and he was going to settle those scores if he could.

Skidding a little because his feet were wet from the water dripping off his body, he reached the top of the stairs. Startled shouts came from the main room below. The tavern's patrons had heard the shots, and then they had seen the two murderers rushing out.

Now a tall, mostly pale, completely naked gent with long hair and a beard came charging down the stairs with a pistol in each hand. It was no wonder that the people in the tavern yelled in alarm and got the hell out of his way.

Preacher ran out into the street. St. Louis was pretty dark after nightfall. The light that came from the doors and windows of some of the buildings furnished the only illumination in the street. Preacher couldn't see the men he was pursuing, but he could hear them, running away to his right. He went after them. An occasional startled cry came from folks on the street as the naked, gun-toting mountain man charged past.

Preacher spotted a couple of running figures ahead of him as they passed through a rectangle of light that spilled from an open door. They were in sight only for a second, not long enough for him to draw a bead on them. He kept running.

But only for a moment, because muzzle flame suddenly bloomed in the darkness ahead of him. Something sledgehammered into Preacher's head, and he went backward as if he had just run into a wall. One of the men he was after must have reloaded on the run.

That was the last thought that went through his mind before a black tide claimed him.

Panting heavily, Schuyler Mims and Colin Fairfax paused in the stygian darkness of an alley. "Are you sure . . . sure you hit him?" Fairfax gasped.

"I saw him . . . go down," Schuyler replied as he bent over and rested his hands on his knees. "How could we have missed him . . . with all three shots in the tavern?"

Fairfax was getting his breath back now. "We couldn't have known that bitch would get in the way. And then I never saw anyone move as fast as Preacher did when you tried for him again. It was just bad luck all the way around, damned bad luck."

"Especially for that whore," Schuyler said.

Fairfax grimaced in the darkness. "That wasn't our fault. Blame Preacher for taking her up there."

That didn't make a whole lot of sense to Schuyler, but he didn't waste any breath pointing that out. Instead he asked, "What do we do now?"

"What do you mean?"

"Preacher's liable to come after us."

"You shot him, remember?"

"Yeah, but I don't know if he's dead," Schuyler said. "I got a feelin' he takes a heap o' killin'."

"Come along," Fairfax said. He led the way toward the far end of the alley, which was marked by a faint glow from the street. "Even if he's still alive, I doubt that he got a good look at us. He doesn't know who we are, so we don't have to worry about him finding us. In fact, we could make another try for him—"

"Not hardly," Schuyler said, for once standing up to his partner. "We've tried to kill Preacher twice, which is probably one more time than most folks ever get a chance to try. I ain't goin' after him a third time."

Fairfax scowled as they emerged from the alley onto another of St. Louis's hard-packed dirt streets. He didn't like it when anybody disagreed with him or refused to go along with his suggestions. But Schuyler sounded adamant about this, so Fairfax decided not to push the issue.

"I suppose it would be best to avoid the man from now on," he admitted in a grudging tone. "But we have to do something for money. We're almost flat broke now."

"We could go see Shad Beaumont. He's always lookin' for good men."

Fairfax fingered his rather pointed chin and frowned in thought as he considered the suggestion. "Beaumont's a dangerous man," he pointed out.

"Well, hell, so are we. Ain't we?"

Neither of them were too sure about that, considering how their last two endeavors had turned out. But they had to do something, unless they wanted to resort to begging or honest work, and those things didn't appeal to them at all.

"All right," Fairfax said with a decisive nod. "We'll go see Shad Beaumont, and even if that bastard Preacher *is* still alive, with any luck we'll never see him again."

Preacher was alive. His head hurt too damned much for him to be dead.

"Disgraceful! Utterly disgraceful! Why, he probably came straight from some harlot's bed before passing out in his besotted iniquity."

Preacher didn't know about his besotted iniquity, whatever the hell that was, but he had sure enough passed out in his birthday suit. He could feel a warm summer breeze blowing all over him. Might've been pleasant under other circumstances, but not here and now.

"Shameful!"

Whoever was doing all that yammering wasn't

helping matters either. In fact, Preacher thought it made his head throb even worse listening to the varmint. So he pushed himself up into a sitting position, blinked his bleary eyes open, and said, "Shut the hell up, why don't you, mister?"

Several people were standing nearby in the street. One of them carried a lantern, and even though its light was dim, Preacher squinted because it seemed like a glare to his eyes. His head spun dizzily from sitting up, but it settled down after a few seconds. There were four men and two women standing there, all of them soberly dressed in dark clothes. Probably on their way to or from a prayer meetin', he thought. And almost certainly they hadn't expected to run into a naked man along the way.

That thought reminded him that he was bare-ass, and he sort of hunched over trying to cover things up. His pistols lay nearby in the street. When he lifted a hand to his head and gingerly touched the spot on his skull that hurt the worst, the fingertips came away smeared with blood.

Mutters of disapproval still came from the little group of citizens. Preacher snapped, "Are you folks blind? Can't you see I been shot?"

"Oh, dear," one of the women said. "I do believe he *is* hurt. We have to help him."

The man who had been going on at length before said, "He was probably injured in some drunken brawl over a woman of ill repute, Martha." Preacher knew it was him because he recognized the shrill, hectoring tone.

"That doesn't matter, Walter," the woman insisted as she took a step toward Preacher. "The Lord said for us to do unto others as we would have them do unto us. The Good Samaritan stopped to help without asking who that poor man was or what had happened to him."

Preacher hunched over more as the woman approached. "Ma'am, I appreciate the sentiment, I surely do," he rasped, "but I'd be obliged if you and the other lady would move along and let your menfolks give me a hand. It'd be more fittin' and proper."

"Nonsense," she said as she reached his side and bent down to take hold of his arm. "Let me help you up."

She was a hefty woman, and Preacher didn't have much choice except to go along with her. With her supporting him, he climbed to his feet. The dizziness got to him again for a second, causing him to sag against her. He put a hand on her shoulder to steady himself.

"Here now! Stop that! Good heavens, sir, have you no shame?" That was Walter again. Preacher figured he was probably Martha's husband.

"Sorry, ma'am," he murmured as he straightened. "I was a mite out of my head there for a minute. Didn't mean to give no offense."

"That's quite all right," she told him. "How badly are you injured? Do you need us to take you to a physician?"

Preacher felt of the wound on his scalp again. It was just a short, shallow furrow where the pistol ball had barely grazed him. That had been enough to knock him down and make him pass out for a few minutes, but that seemed to be the extent of the damage.

"I reckon I'll be all right," he told the woman.

"That shot just nicked me, and this old skull o' mine is pretty darned thick."

Walter snorted, as if to say that he certainly believed *that*.

"At least take my husband's coat," Martha said.

This time Walter said, "What! Martha, you can't just offer my coat to this . . . this reprobate!"

Preacher's head felt steady enough now for him to bend over and pick up his pistols. As he straightened, he saw Walter peeling off the long black coat.

"Now we're being robbed!" Walter said. "Here, take the coat. Just don't hurt any of us, I implore you, sir!"

Preacher wanted to ask the fella if he was touched in the head, but he was tired of this whole encounter and just took the coat instead, saying, "I ain't stealin' your coat. You can come down to Fargo's tavern any time you want and get it back. I'll leave it with ol' Ford."

Walter swallowed hard and said, "That's all right. I . . . I've heard of that tavern. I wouldn't set foot in a place like that!"

"You wouldn't happen to have a little boy name of Jake, would you?" Preacher muttered as he shrugged into the borrowed coat. Walter was built sort of stout, so the garment hung pretty loosely on him, but it was long enough to cover the essentials.

"What? I don't have any children."

"More's the pity," Martha said.

Preacher wasn't so sure about that. If he was a kid, he wouldn't want a stiff-necked varmint like Walter for his pa. But folks didn't really get a choice about things like that, he supposed.

The important thing was that the two men who had killed Abby were long gone by now, and Preacher had no idea where to look for them. He wasn't even sure he would recognize them if he saw them again, although he thought there was a pretty good chance he would. While he was still in St. Louis, he would be keeping an eye out for a pair of gents, one short and one tall. He thought the tall one had been wearing buckskins, and the short one had sported that beaver hat he'd caught a glimpse of going down the stairs in the tavern.

He said good night to the folks who had found him and started back toward Fargo's, the tails of Walter's coat flapping around his legs. He felt pretty foolish walking into the tavern that way, but even though some of the patrons looked mighty hard at him, nobody snickered. In fact, an air of gloom hung over the place, and Preacher figured out why as a couple of men started down the stairs from the second floor, carrying a blanket-shrouded shape.

"Abby?" Preacher said to Fargo.

The burly tavern keeper nodded. "Yeah. I reckon you knew she was dead when you went chasin' out of here after those fellas. They the ones who shot her?"

"That's right," Preacher said. "They were aimin' for me. Abby just happened to be in the way."

Fargo shook his head as the men carried Abby's body on out of the tavern. "Damned shame. She was a fine gal, for a whore. Hell, she would've been a fine gal even if she hadn't been a whore."

"Did you see the two bastards who done it?"

"Yeah, but I never paid much attention to 'em.

Think I'd seen 'em somewhere before, but I ain't sure about that. And when they ran outta here, they were movin' so fast and everything was so confused I didn't get a good look at 'em even then."

Preacher bit back a curse. The two men had been close enough to him to fire at almost point-blank range, and yet they were still strangers.

Carrying his pistols, Preacher went back upstairs. Small puddles of water still lay on the floor of his room where they had splashed out of the tub during the ruckus. He grimaced at the sight of them, tossed the long black coat on the bed, and began pulling on his buckskins.

When he was dressed, he returned to the tavern's main room and asked all the other customers about the two killers. Nobody had gotten a really good look at them, but the questioning confirmed that the taller man had been dressed in buckskins and the smaller one wore a beaver hat and a black suit that had seen better days. Those descriptions didn't mean anything to Preacher, and they were vague enough that they might have fit almost anybody.

He had to wonder if the two men would try again to kill him. He hoped so.

Preacher was looking forward to making their acquaintance over the barrels of his guns.

Four

Preacher's sleep was restless that night, haunted by dreams of the stunned expression on Abby's face as the pistol balls tore through her and stole her life away. He had lost friends and even loved ones to violence in the past, like Jennie and the Shoshone woman Mountain Mist, and it never got any easier.

When he awoke the next morning, the pounding throb in his head had subsided to a dull ache, but it was still there, fueled by the bullet graze and the bad memories. He pulled on his buckskins and high-topped moccasins and stumbled downstairs, drawn by the smell of coffee.

The main room of the tavern was empty except for Ford Fargo, who leaned on the bar sipping from a steaming cup. "Pour me one o' those," Preacher said.

Fargo went over to the big iron stove where the coffeepot simmered, and complied with Preacher's request. He carried it back to Preacher, who grasped the cup eagerly and gulped down some of the contents. The coffee was hot enough to blister his mouth, but he didn't much care at the moment.

"Abby's service will be later today," Fargo said. "Couldn't find a preacher who was willin' to say words over a gal like her, so I figured on doin' it myself." He paused. "Unless you'd like to do it. You got the name for it and all."

Preacher shook his head. "You knew her a hell of a lot longer than I did, so any speechifyin' that's to be done, you need to do it. Besides, I ain't a real preacher."

"If I was, I ain't sure I'd claim it. Don't the Good Book say we ain't supposed to judge other folks? I figure Abby deserves to be laid to rest proper, but all the churchgoin' folks just turned their noses up at the idea. Good thing we got a public cemetery here in St. Louis now. They can't stop me from buryin' her there." Again Fargo paused. "I reckon she'd like it if you was there."

"Why? Because I'm the one who got her killed?"

"You don't know that."

"Yeah, I do. Those bastards were after me. I just don't know why yet, or who they were. But one of these days I'll find out."

Fargo shook his head. "I'll bet they're not even here in the settlement anymore. If I tried to kill you and botched the job, I'd be runnin' as far and fast as I could."

A chilly smile played over Preacher's face. "And it wouldn't do you any good."

"Yeah. That's what I'd be afraid of."

The tavern keeper fried up some salt jowl and flapjacks for his breakfast and shared them with Preacher. After eating, the mountain man said that he was going to see about replenishing his supplies before setting out for the wilderness again.

"I don't figure on stayin' here in town any longer than I have to," he added. "Bad things happen in towns."

He knew he was oversimplifying matters, but there was no disputing the truth of his statement. Of course, bad things could happen anywhere, but at least out there on the frontier, Preacher was better able to guard against them. He knew the dangers that lurked on the prairie and in the mountains better than he did the ones in the settlement.

"The buryin' will be at noon," Fargo told him as he went out. Without looking back, Preacher waved to show that he had heard.

He spent the morning visiting one of the general stores and telling the proprietor what he wanted. The man promised to gather the supplies together and have them ready whenever Preacher wanted to pick them up. Then Preacher went to the office of the fur company where Joel Larson worked.

"I heard about what happened," Larson said as the two men shook hands. "Sorry about the girl. Why do you think those men attacked you?"

Preacher shrugged. "Don't know. I've made a lot of enemies in my time. Also, somebody took a shot at me while I was still on the river yesterday afternoon, about a mile north of the settlement. Could be that whoever it was made another try for me."

Larson sat down behind his desk and clasped his hands together. "Here's another possibility. They might have seen us strike a deal for your pelts, or they could have been in the tavern when I paid you. It's possible that they were just thieves after your money."

Preacher frowned as he considered that suggestion. Of all the things to die for, money seemed just about the most ridiculous to him. But he knew not everybody felt that way. Not by a long shot.

"I reckon you could be right," he said with a nod. "I don't know for sure what those two fellas looked like, but I got an idea. Wanted to know if maybe you'd seen them around." He gave Larson as good a description of the killers as he had.

The fur company man listened carefully, but shook his head when Preacher was finished. "Sorry. That doesn't ring a bell. There are probably hundreds of men in St. Louis wearing buckskins or shabby suits and beaver hats."

"Yeah, I know." Preacher stood up and added with a decisive nod, "But I'll find 'em. I aim to settle the score for Abby. I ain't overly fond o' lettin' gents get away with shootin' at me neither."

Larson got to his feet and shook hands again. "Well, good luck to you, Preacher. If there's anything I can do to help, let me know."

"Sure will."

Preacher left the office. Something Larson had said had gotten him to thinking. That boy Jake he had talked to the day before, down by the river, had seemed like an observant little cuss. Maybe if the men who had killed Abby had been down there, too, and had seen Preacher strike the deal with Joel Larson, as Larson had suggested, then Jake might have seen the men who'd been watching Preacher. He had to admit that it was a long shot but he believed it was worth checking out.

All he had to do was find the boy.

* * *

Everyone in St. Louis who was of the less-than-honest persuasion knew Shad Beaumont, or at least knew of him. Schuyler Mims and Colin Fairfax didn't have any trouble finding the man, who was rumored to have a finger in every criminal pie in the region. They just asked around in the dives and whorehouses until a grossly overweight madam with hennaed hair pointed upward with a fat thumb and said, "Yeah, Shad's upstairs with two o' my girls right now."

"Two?" Schuyler repeated with his eyes widening.

The madam gave a bawdy laugh. "Yeah. Shad's got what you'd call well-developed appetites."

"Downright greedy, that's what I'd call it," Schuyler muttered.

"I wouldn't call it that to his face," the madam advised. "Not if you want to keep on breathin', my friend." She rubbed her hands together. "Now, could I interest you boys in some female companionship? Best-lookin' girls in town, and they're all clean as a whistle, too."

Schuyler and Fairfax both doubted the validity of those claims, and besides, they didn't have enough money to pay for even one soiled dove to smile at them, let alone to pay two for anything else. So Fairfax said, "Thanks, but we'll just wait for Shad."

"Not in here, you won't," the madam said with a frown. "This is a classy place. Can't have bums loiterin' around."

The brothel was one step up from a pigsty as far as Fairfax was concerned. With a sigh, he remembered some of the parlor houses he had visited back in Philadelphia, when he was a young man with money and connections.

Those days were long gone, of course. He said to his partner, "Come along. The street is still public."

"Just don't clutter up my doorway," the madam snapped. "I got customers who want to get in and out."

"Indeed," Fairfax muttered as he motioned for Schuyler to follow him and left the building.

They took up a position across the street and hoped that Beaumont wouldn't be inside the whorehouse all day. A man had to tend to his business sometime, even a criminal. Schuyler and Fairfax were both tired. They had slept in an alley behind one of the fur warehouses, since they couldn't afford anything better, and the night hadn't passed restfully for either of them.

"You watch for Beaumont," Schuyler suggested. "I'm gonna keep an eye out for Preacher."

"He doesn't know where to find us."

"Yeah, but he could come amblin' along the street and recognize us by pure dumb luck. We don't know how good a look he got at us."

"It couldn't have been much of one," Fairfax said. "The room was full of powder smoke, and that redheaded girl was between him and us."

"Yeah." Schuyler sighed. "I sure am sorry about what happened to that gal."

"It was an accident. We can't be held responsible for an accident."

"Yeah, but she'd still be alive if we hadn't tried to kill and rob Preacher."

Fairfax shook his head. "You can't be sure about that. Her next customer might have slit her throat, or beaten her to death. Whores get killed all the time. There's no point in wasting any sympathy on them."

"Yeah, I reckon you're right," Schuyler said, but he didn't sound like he was totally convinced of that.

An hour dragged by before a big man with a close-cropped brown beard came out of the brothel across the street. He wore a dark suit and a fancy vest and a beaver hat, and the summer sun glinted on the stickpin in his cravat. He really looked too good for such a place, but adaptability was one of the reasons for Shad Beaumont's success—he could make himself at home almost anywhere, from a cheap whore's crib to the drawing room of the finest mansion in town.

The other reason was that he was totally ruthless and would kill anybody who crossed him, and folks knew that.

Fairfax nudged Schuyler, and Schuyler nudged him back. "All right, all right," Fairfax muttered, and he started across the street with Schuyler trailing a pace behind him.

Before they could intercept Beaumont, a couple of burly men in rough work clothes moved swiftly to get in front of them. Fairfax had noticed them in the street earlier, and had even considered the possibility that they were waiting to talk to Beaumont, too, but now he realized they were Beaumont's bodyguards.

Fairfax stopped short and held up both hands, palms out. "Please, gentlemen," he said. "We mean your employer no harm. We just wish to speak with him on a business matter."

Beaumont didn't seem to be paying any attention to them as he strode past, but at Fairfax's mention of business, he paused and glanced over.

Making a motion for his men to wait, he asked, "What sort of business?"

Fairfax inclined his head toward Schuyler. "My partner and I would like to work for you. It's said that you're the sharpest man in St. Louis."

Beaumont chuckled and said, "If that's true, I didn't get that way by hiring just any broken-down bums who come stumbling along wanting a job, now did I?"

Fairfax's pale face flushed with anger. "We're not bums," he insisted, "and I wish people would stop referring to us that way. We're good men, smart and able to follow orders."

"And we can take care of ourselves," Schuyler added.

Beaumont lifted an eyebrow. "Is that so? We'll just see about that." He made a curt gesture again to his bodyguards. "Boys, hand these two their needin's." An ugly grin appeared on his face. "If they live through *that*, then we'll see about finding jobs for them."

Preacher headed for the fur warehouses. Jake had said that his father worked at one of them, and Preacher figured he would ask around until he found the boy's pa. Then the fella could tell him where Jake was.

It took a while for him to find the right place, but at the fourth warehouse, after asking the first man he saw if he had a son named Jake or knew anybody who did, Preacher heard what he wanted to hear. The fella pointed out one of the other workers who was bundling up dried pelts so they could be loaded on a riverboat and shipped back east. "I think Jonathan over there has a boy named Jake."

"Much obliged," Preacher said with a nod. He walked over to the man called Jonathan, who was a dark-haired, dour-faced gent with the heavy muscles that working in a warehouse gave a man. He scowled at Preacher as the mountain man came up to him.

"You need somethin', mister?" Jonathan asked in a brusque tone.

"I'm lookin' for a little fella name of Jake, about ten years old, I'd say. Got brown hair and sort of a round face. He's mighty inquisitive and likes to talk."

Jonathan's scowl deepened. "That sounds like my boy, all right. What do you want with him? What's he done wrong? If he's stolen from you or done something else sinful, I'll thrash him within an inch of his life."

"No, nothin' like that," Preacher said. "I just want to ask him a couple of questions. He seemed like a right nice little varmint, if you don't mind the chatterin'."

"He's like all children . . . full of sin. You have to steer them onto the right path as forcefully as you can. Do you have any children, sir?"

"Not that I know of," Preacher said.

Jonathan didn't care for that answer. "Don't make light of the Lord's commandments, sir."

"Didn't know I was," Preacher said, starting to grow impatient. He was surprised at how many holier-than-thou folks he was running into on this trip to St. Louis. But self-righteousness was something else civilization was good for, along with stinking up the air. "Look, I just want to talk to your boy. If you'll tell me where to find him, I'll go on and won't bother you no more."

"I don't know where the little scoundrel is, but if I was a wagering man, I'd say that he's getting into trouble, wherever he is."

"But you ain't a wagerin' man, are you?"

"Of course not. It's—"

"Sinful," Preacher finished for him.

Jonathan's face darkened with outright anger now. "Are you making fun of me?"

"I'm just tired o' gettin' a sermon instead o' answers. And even though it ain't none o' my business, I ain't too fond of the way you been talkin' about the boy. He seemed like a pretty good kid."

"He's my son. I'll talk about him and deal with him any way I see fit."

"Yeah, and one o' these days he's liable to run off, too."

"He wouldn't dare. He knows he would pay dearly for such an unholy act of defiance."

Preacher was sick of talking to this gent. With a disgusted shake of his head, he turned away. He would just have to find Jake some other way, he supposed.

A powerful hand clamped down on his shoulder. "Wait just a minute," Jonathan said. "If you think I'm going to tolerate such a show of disrespect from a reprobate who's probably as big a heathen as those filthy redskins you no doubt consort with—"

Preacher turned around fast, knocking Jonathan's hand off his shoulder. The warehouse worker was

just as tall as he was and heavier, but Preacher packed
an incredible amount of strength in his lean frame.

"Mister, I'm gonna give you one more chance
not to act like such a miserable human bein'," he
grated. "You may talk fancy and think that you and
the Lord are on such good terms, but to me you're
nothin' but a bag o' hot air."

"You can't talk to me like that, you sinner!" Jonathan shouted.

And with that he swung a big, malletlike fist
straight at Preacher's head.

Five

Jonathan was strong; anybody could tell that by looking at him. But he was also slow, and Preacher had no trouble weaving to the side so that the punch aimed at his head went past his ear without doing any harm.

Missing like that threw Jonathan off balance. He stumbled forward a step, and ran right into the short but powerful blow that Preacher snapped out with his right hand. Preacher's knobby-knuckled fist smashed into the middle of Jonathan's face. Blood spurted as cartilage crunched inside the man's nose. He howled in pain and flailed at Preacher.

Any of the wild, looping swings might have taken Preacher's head off if they connected, but the mountain man darted back a step, avoiding all of them. Then he moved to the side and went forward again, chopping another short blow at Jonathan's head. It connected just above the man's right ear and staggered him even more.

Jonathan must have realized that Preacher was too fast for him. He couldn't hope to stand there and trade punches with the mountain man, because Preacher was going to hit a lot more times than he *got* hit.

So with a roar of rage, Jonathan spread his arms and launched himself at Preacher, wrapping the mountain man in a bear hug that Preacher couldn't quite avoid.

Preacher felt himself going over backward, carried off his feet by Jonathan's unexpected tackle. They landed on the warehouse floor with Jonathan on top. His crushing weight drove the air right out of Preacher's lungs. A haze descended over his vision as he gasped for breath, and skyrockets that must have resembled the ones that flew over Fort McHenry during the War of 1812 exploded behind his eyes. Nobody was going to write a song about the red glare of these, though.

Over the roaring of blood in his ears, Preacher vaguely heard the shouts of the other workers in the warehouse. He couldn't tell if they were cheering Jonathan on or rooting for Preacher to get the best of him. Knowing that he was going to pass out if he didn't get some air pretty soon, Preacher groped upward and got his hand on Jonathan's face. He ground the heel of his palm against Jonathan's already busted nose.

Jonathan bellowed in pain and jerked back. That gave Preacher the chance to arch his back and heave the man off. Jonathan rolled across the floor, trailing strings of blood from his nose. Preacher went the other way.

He fetched up against somebody's feet and legs. Strong hands reached down and clamped hard around his arms. Before he could even start to fight back, he was hauled to his feet and set upright.

"Go get that Bible-thumpin' son of a bitch," a gravelly voice said in his ear. Hands slapped him on the back, encouraging him and propelling him toward Jonathan at the same time.

So Jonathan *didn't* have many friends here. Somehow, that didn't come as a great surprise to Preacher.

Jonathan had climbed to his feet as well, and now lumbered toward Preacher. The bottom half of his face was covered with blood from his pulped nose, which was grotesquely askew. His eyes looked like those of a maddened bull. But instead of charging ahead wildly, he took his time now, lifting his fists in a boxing stance as he approached Preacher.

"I am the strong arm of the Lord," he said in a thick voice. "I will smite thee, heathen. I will visit God's mighty wrath upon thine head."

"Mister, you're crazier'n a bedbug," Preacher said.

He blocked Jonathan's first punch, then another and another. Jonathan was more dangerous now that he wasn't fighting out of control, but he was still slow. Patiently, Preacher waited for a good opening, and when it came, he threw a hard right that landed solidly on Jonathan's jaw. That rocked the man back and set him up for a looping left that slewed his head to the side when it landed.

Preacher's fists were a blur as he stepped in and hooked a flurry of rights and lefts to Jonathan's midsection. Jonathan was gasping for air when Preacher finally stepped back. His heavy arms drooped with weariness.

Preacher shot in a stinging left jab, and then followed it with a hard right cross that caught Jonathan on the chin. Jonathan's head went the other way this time and his eyes rolled up in their sockets. His knees unhinged. He went straight down onto his knees, then pitched forward on his face, out cold.

The other men in the warehouse cheered.

Preacher was barely winded. He knew his hands would be a mite bruised and sore by the next morning, but he could tell he hadn't damaged them by banging them against Jonathan's hard head. As he looked down at the unconscious man, he muttered, "I got some Scripture for you, mister . . . God helps those who help themselves."

Suddenly sensing that he was being watched, Preacher turned and saw Jake standing just inside the door of the warehouse, silhouetted against the light from outside. The youngster's eyes were wide with shock and amazement as he stared at Preacher and at the unconscious form of his father.

Preacher took a step toward him and started to lift a hand. "Jake . . ."

The boy whirled around and dashed away.

"Damn it!" Preacher grated as he started after him. He didn't know how much of the fight the boy had seen, but it was pretty obvious Jake had seen Preacher knock his father out cold. No wonder the kid was scared of him.

The streets of St. Louis were busy this morning, as they nearly always were. By the time Preacher got out of the warehouse, Jake had lost himself in the crowd along the waterfront. Several riverboats were tied up at the docks, and passengers were loading and unloading. Workmen carried cargo off the boats and loaded other cargo. Jake could be anywhere, Preacher realized as he came to a stop. It would be just blind luck if he found the boy now.

Preacher bit back a curse. He didn't know whether or not Jake could have helped him find the two men who had killed Abby, but at least questioning him would have been worth a try. Now that opportunity had vanished along with Jake.

Might as well go on to the buryin', Preacher thought. He couldn't do any more good here.

One of Shad Beaumont's bodyguards was a big man with a bald, bullet-shaped head and an ugly grin made even uglier by the gaps where several teeth had rotted out—or been knocked out. The other man was equally large and sported a thatch of rust-colored hair and a handlebar mustache of the same shade. Both smiled in anticipation as they closed in on Schuyler Mims and Colin Fairfax. It was like they hadn't beaten anybody to death for a while and were looking forward to it.

But as Baldy swung a sledgehammer punch at Schuyler and Handlebar grabbed for Fairfax, the intended victims darted back with surprising speed. Schuyler had more strength packed into his lanky body than was apparent. He smacked home a punch into the bald man's face that landed with the sound of a meat cleaver striking a thick steak. Blood spurted from Baldy's crushed lips. He gave an incoherent roar of pain.

Meanwhile, Handlebar was still trying to get his hands on Fairfax, who danced away from each lunge with speed and agility. As Handlebar rushed forward again, Fairfax leaped to the side and stuck out a leg. Handlebar tripped over it and fell to the street with a startled yell, crashing down onto the hard-packed dirt with stunning force. He lay there gasping for air. The impact had knocked the breath out of him.

Angered by being hit, Baldy rushed at Schuyler, swinging his fists in wild, flailing blows. Schuyler ducked some of them and blocked others. The couple of punches that got through rocked him back on his heels, but he didn't lose his balance and stayed upright to slug it out with Baldy. Beaumont's bodyguard outweighed Schuyler by at least fifty pounds, but Schuyler offset that potential advantage by being a lot faster. He bobbed and weaved, peppering Baldy with swift blows that struck like a snake.

Meanwhile, Fairfax rushed forward while Handlebar was still gasping for breath and got hold of the man's arm, twisting it behind his back in a wrestling move. Fairfax didn't hesitate. Even though he wasn't a very impressive physical specimen to look at, he, too, was stronger than he appeared to be. And the dangerous, knockabout life he had led since being forced to flee from Philadelphia had made him ruthless when he had to be. He heaved as hard as he could on the bodyguard's arm, and heard the sharp snap as the bones in the man's shoulder came apart. Handlebar screamed.

That shriek of agony distracted his bald-headed companion, who looked over to see what was happening at just the wrong time. Schuyler's fists were blurs as he hammered them into Baldy's already injured face. Schuyler crushed Baldy's nose, and he thought he felt the man's left cheekbone shatter, too. Moaning, Baldy staggered back a step and then slumped to his knees. Schuyler's right foot shot out in a kick. The heel of his boot caught Baldy on the jaw, breaking it, too, and sending the big bodyguard flying backward to sprawl senseless in the street next to Handlebar, who was clutching his dislocated shoulder with his other hand and writhing in pain as he whimpered.

Schuyler and Fairfax were both out of breath as they turned to face an astounded Shad Beaumont. Schuyler leaned over and put his hands on his thighs as he drew in great drafts of air. Fairfax asked, "Was that enough of a demonstration for you, Mr. Beaumont? We told you we can take care of ourselves."

"I'd say you damned sure can," Beaumont replied as he jerked his head in a curt nod. "I wouldn't have guessed that anybody could handle those two bruisers like that. Can you shoot?"

"We're expert shots," Fairfax answered without hesitation, not mentioning anything about how Schuyler had missed Preacher on the river the day before or their failed attempt to kill the mountain man at the tavern. There was nothing wrong with their marksmanship there; they would have ventilated the son of a bitch if that whore hadn't jumped up and gotten in the way of the pistol balls.

"All right, I reckon maybe I *can* use you after all," Beaumont said.

Schuyler straightened, having recovered from his exertions. He waved a hand toward the fallen bodyguards and asked, "What about those two? I ain't sure we want to work for you if they're gonna be holdin' a grudge against us." He ignored the warning glance Fairfax sent in his direction. "I don't want to spend my days and nights havin' to watch my back for fear o' them tryin' to get even with us."

"Don't worry about that," Beaumont said. "Their services are too valuable for me to dispense with them, but I'll give strict orders that there won't be any reprisals. They followed my orders, and you two gents just defended yourselves. There's nothing there for anyone to be angry about."

Fairfax wasn't so sure. He'd be holding a grudge if he'd received a thrashing like that. But he supposed that with Beaumont's fierce reputation, the bodyguards would go along with whatever he said.

"You have any problem with following orders?" Beaumont went on.

Fairfax shook his head, and Schuyler said, "You just tell us what to do, Boss, and we'll do it."

"Even if it's against the law."

Schuyler shrugged. "I reckon if we didn't figure on breakin' the law, we wouldn't have asked you for a job in the first place."

Beaumont threw back his head and laughed. "No, I suppose not. All right, you're hired. I have a job in mind where I can use the two of you, if you're interested."

"Oh, we're interested, all right," Fairfax said. "Just tell us who you want killed."

Abby's funeral at the public cemetery on the outskirts of the settlement was surprisingly well attended. Ford Fargo was there, of course, and so were the half-dozen girls who worked at his tavern. Fargo must have closed the place down for the funeral, Preacher thought, which was an indication of just how highly the tavern keeper thought of Abby. In addition, several roughly dressed rivermen were there at the cemetery. They were probably tavern customers who had been with Abby and were fond of her.

Preacher didn't feel guilty about what had happened. He had never been one to blame the victim. Abby's death was the fault of the two sons of bitches who shot her, and nobody else. But he regretted that she had lost her life by being in the wrong place at the wrong time.

Fargo, who stood beside the open grave where the crude wooden casket had already been lowered, was talking when Preacher sidled up to the rear of the little group of mourners. Fargo was reminiscing about what a cheerful and enthusiastic worker Abby had been. "She was a gal who would do just about anything you asked her do," he said.

One of the rivermen snickered, and looked like he was about to make some ribald comment about Fargo's choice of words, but Preacher tapped him on the shoulder before he could say anything. When the man glanced around and saw the cold, dangerous stare Preacher had fixed on him, he swallowed and ducked his head, making it clear by his attitude that he would keep his mouth shut after all.

Fargo gave Preacher a grateful glance and went on. "All of us will miss Abby, who had a smile and a kind word for just about everybody. She was one sweet little gal, that's for sure." He bowed his head and started to pray. "Lord, some would claim that folks like us don't have any right to ask any favors of You. But I recollect what it says in the Good Book about how when Your Son was down here on earth, he spent quite a bit of time in places like mine, talkin' to folks like us. I'm hopin' that you'll bear that in mind when I ask that You have mercy on poor Abby and let her into Your house up there in Heaven. She may not have been what folks would call a good girl, but I can promise You, there wasn't a smidgen of evil in her. She had a good heart. Amen."

Several of the mourners muttered, "Amen," including Preacher.

Fargo picked up a handful of dirt from the pile of it beside the grave and dropped it onto the casket. The clods thudded against the lid. One by one, the women came forward and did the same, followed by some of the men. The rest looked uncomfortable with the idea, and started to drift off toward the river. The sun was high overhead, and the air was hot. At this time of day, folks wanted a drink, or something to eat. That was true of Preacher, too, but he wasn't going to leave just yet. He lingered while the others all walked, and after a few minutes only he and Ford Fargo were left standing beside Abby's grave.

Preacher picked up a shovel he saw lying on the ground nearby and began filling in the hole. While Preacher was working, Fargo asked, "Did you have any luck findin' those bastards who done this?"

"Afraid not," Preacher said with a shake of his head. "I didn't turn up anybody who knew them."

"Those skinned-up knuckles of yours look like you might've asked the questions sort of emphaticlike."

Despite the grim circumstances and surroundings, Preacher had to chuckle at that. "One fella took exception to tellin' me what I wanted to know."

"I'll bet he was sorry he did that."

"Wouldn't know. He was sorta quiet when I left."

Fargo laughed, too, then grew more solemn as he said, "At least Abby got a proper send-off. I think that's important. I hope wherever she is, she knows that we done all we could for her."

"I reckon she does," Preacher said. He finished shoveling the dirt into the grave, leaving it slightly mounded. It would settle with time. The wooden headstone on which Abby's name had been carved would stand for a while, but eventually it would be gone. The time would come when nobody even remembered Abby, and people might not even be able to tell that there had ever been a grave here.

That was the fate of most folks, Preacher reflected, but at least Abby would be remembered for a while and her bones would rest together in one place. He figured that when he crossed the Great Divide, his body would probably lie unattended on the prairie or in the mountains until scavengers came along and disposed of it, scattering the bones to kingdom come, where sun and wind and weather would strip everything from them and polish them until they were all that was left of him, not even a memory.

But to a man like him, who lived so close to the earth, that didn't sound like such a bad way to go.

He was just tamping down the mound of dirt with the shovel when a footstep sounded behind him, and a voice said, "Excuse me. I'm looking for a man called Preacher."

Six

Preacher turned, still holding the shovel, and saw a man in tight gray trousers and a black swallowtail coat standing there, holding a beaver hat. The man was about Preacher's age, clean-shaven so that it was apparent he had a rather heavy jaw. His hair was dark and thick. There was nothing of the frontier about him, but he was sturdily built, as if he had done at least some hard work in his life.

"I'm Preacher," the mountain man said. "What can I do for you?"

The stranger made a vague gesture that took in their surroundings and said, "I hate to intrude on your grief, sir, but it's rather important that I talk to you. My name is Corliss Hart, and I have a business proposition for you."

Preacher frowned. "I already sold the load of plews I brought in to Joel Larson."

"I don't want to buy your furs," Corliss Hart said with a shake of his head. "I'd like to hire you."

"To do what?"

"I'm in need of your services. I should say, my cousin and I are in need of your services."

Preacher wasn't in a very good mood, but he managed to restrain the impatience he felt. "Services as what?" he asked, wishing that Hart would get to the point.

"As a guide for a party heading west," Hart said. "I'm told you've performed such a function in the past."

"Yeah, but not always of my own choosin'," Preacher said, thinking about how he had gotten roped into helping out those troublesome pilgrims a couple of winters earlier when a bunch of angry Arikara warriors were after them. Then, just a little more than a year ago, he had been forced by circumstances to help out an artist fella from back East who had come to the frontier to paint portraits of the Indians, only to wind up in a whole heap of trouble.

"We're prepared to pay you, of course, and I think you'll find that my cousin and I can be quite generous."

"It ain't a matter of money. I got things to do here in St. Louis." Preacher was thinking about the two men who had killed Abby. Even though he'd had no luck in locating them so far, he was far from ready to give up. In fact, when the Good Lord made him, He hadn't put much "give-up" in Preacher's nature.

"Well, our wagons aren't leaving for a few days yet," Corliss Hart said. "Perhaps that would give you time to conclude whatever business you have here, and then you could go with us."

"Wagons?" Preacher repeated with a frown. "You

ain't talkin' about immigrant wagons, are you?"
More and more people were heading west to settle,
and Preacher didn't like that trend. There was talk
that big wagon trains full of immigrants would start
rolling toward the Pacific Northwest in the next
few years. The whole frontier was going to fill up
before you knew it, he thought.

"No, Jerome and I are businessmen, not coloniz-
ers like Stephen Austin down in Texas. We have six
wagons full of supplies that we brought out here
from Chicago. We plan to travel to the Rocky
Mountains, find a suitable location, and set up a
trading post. We need an experienced man not
only to guide us, but also to advise us on the best
location for such a business venture."

Preacher didn't know whether to laugh or curse.
There were some trading posts in the mountains
already, but they were few and far between and
had all been set up by tough men who knew what
they were doing. The chances of a couple of
greenhorn merchants from Chicago succeeding at
such a venture—or even surviving for very long,
for that matter—were slim.

But everybody had to start somewhere, Preacher
supposed. When he had set out on his own as a
boy, he was a greenhorn, too. All he'd had going
for him were his grit and determination and will-
ingness to work and learn. He had been lucky
enough to fall in with some fellas who could teach
him how to get along on the frontier. Maybe
Corliss Hart and his cousin Jerome would be fortu-
nate in that regard, too.

But they might have to find somebody besides
Preacher to give them a hand, because he figured

on being busy, at least until he found the men he was looking for. After that, if Hart and his cousin hadn't already left with their wagon train, maybe he would consider hiring on with them. Their money would spend as good as anybody else's.

"Sorry," he said with a shake of his head. "I might be done by the time you're ready to leave, or I might not, so you'd best find somebody else."

"Are you sure? We were told that no one knows the mountains, and the area between here and there, better than you do." Corliss Hart fidgeted with the hat he held in his hands. "And we were also told that you're probably the toughest man between the Mississippi and the Pacific Ocean."

Preacher had to chuckle at that. "I wouldn't know. I ain't fought everybody between the Mississippi and the Pacific Ocean. Leastways, not yet. Gimme time."

"You won't reconsider?"

"Nope."

Fargo put in, "You might as well give up, mister. Preacher's the stubbornest man on the frontier, that's for sure."

"I reckon I'll take that as a compliment," Preacher told the tavern keeper with a smile.

Hart sighed. "Very well. If you change your mind, we're staying at the Excelsior Hotel."

"All right," Preacher said with a nod. He didn't think it was very likely that he would be visiting the cousins.

Hart turned and trudged back toward the main part of the settlement, putting his hat on as he did so. Fargo watched him go and said, "That fella looked like he had plenty o' money, Preacher. Job might've paid pretty well."

"Time enough to worry about that after I've settled the score with the two skunks who did for Abby."

"Once you sink your teeth into something, you don't let go easy, do you?"

"Not hardly," Preacher said.

He spent the rest of the day circulating through the waterfront taverns, and there were plenty of them along the river. In each place, he nursed a beer and bought drinks for anybody who was willing to talk to him and answer his questions. But he didn't find anyone who recognized the admittedly vague descriptions of Abby's killers.

Irritated by his lack of success, he was on his way back to Fargo's place late that afternoon when he heard a voice behind him say, "Hey, Preacher! I been lookin' for you."

Preacher stopped short and turned around. He recognized the voice as Jake's, and sure enough, the round-faced youngster stood there a few feet away.

"Good Lord, son," Preacher said. "I been lookin' for you, too. I reckon we must've kept on missin' each other." He stepped over to Jake and placed a hand on the boy's shoulder. "I'm sorry you had to see that ruckus between me and your pa this mornin'."

"I'm not," Jake said as he looked up at Preacher. "I was glad to see you whip him like that. I just couldn't believe it at first. I never seen anybody knock him down before. But he had it comin'. He thrashes me all the time on account of I'm sinful, he says. Seems to me like beatin' on somebody smaller'n you would be just as sinful as anything I ever done, though. Maybe even worse. I reckon I hate him."

Preacher frowned and said, "You don't want to go talkin' like that about your own pa."

"Why not? It's true."

"Well, maybe what he does to you ain't right, but I'm sure it's because he loves you and thinks that's what he oughta do to help you grow up proper."

"Yeah, but that don't make it hurt any less when he takes a strap to me."

Jake had a point there, Preacher thought.

"If that's the way you feel, how come you run off like that?" he asked.

Jake hung his head and didn't meet Preacher's eyes. "It made me feel so good every time I saw you wallop him that I reckon I was ashamed of myself. I mean, a boy ain't supposed to like it when he sees his own pa bein' whipped, is he?"

"I guess it depends on the circumstances, and how that pa treats his boy," Preacher said with a shrug. He wasn't used to having conversations like this, and didn't feel too comfortable with it himself.

"Yeah, that's what I finally decided, too. So then I figured I ought to find you and thank you for what you done, and ask you a question."

"What sort o' question?"

"Are you goin' back to the mountains?"

Preacher nodded. "Yeah. Not right away, but sooner or later I will."

"When you go . . . can I go with you?"

That question took Preacher by surprise and made his thick, dark eyebrows rise into twin arches.

"Go with me?" he repeated. "You mean to the mountains?"

"Yeah. I'll make you a good partner if you'll just give me a chance. I can pull my weight, I swear. I know how to shoot a rifle already, and I'll bet if you'd teach me, I could learn how to handle a beaver trap with no trouble. I'm pretty smart, if I do say so myself."

"I'll bet you are," Preacher said, "but that don't mean you're ready to go to the mountains. Hell, you ain't but what, ten years old?"

"I'm eleven, nearly twelve."

"Well, that ain't anywhere near old enough."

Jake gave him a shrewd look and asked, "How old were *you* when you left home, Mr. Preacher?"

"I told you, you can forget about callin' me Mister," Preacher said. "And it ain't any o' your business how old I was when I went out on my own. I was older'n you are now, I can tell you that much for damn sure."

As a matter of fact, he'd been only two years older, but he wasn't about to tell Jake that. The boy already had too many damn fool notions in his head.

"It ain't fair," Jake complained. "If I stay here, my pa's just gonna beat me worse an' worse. He'll be mad 'cause you whipped him, and he'll take it out on me from now on."

Preacher scowled. "Maybe I need to have another talk with him and let him know that wouldn't be a good idea. I reckon he might listen to me."

"Yeah, for a while, because he'd be scared of you. But you said it yourself, Preacher. You'll be goin' back to the mountains. Once you're gone, Pa won't be scared no more, and then he'll thrash me within an inch o' my life if I do the least little thing wrong or do somethin' that he considers a sin. And you won't be anywhere around to stop him."

Preacher's scowl darkened. The little varmint had another point.

But even so, the frontier was no place for him. Preacher had to find another solution.

"Tell you what," he said. "I'll take you to see a friend o' mine named Ford Fargo."

"Is that Mr. Fargo who owns the tavern down by the river?"

"Yep, that's him. Maybe he could hire you to give him a hand around the place. If he does, he might find a place for you to sleep."

"You mean I could live in a tavern?" Jake sounded astonished by the idea.

"Well, yeah."

Jake grinned. "Where all those nice-lookin' young women work?"

"You're too young to be concernin' yourself about things like that," Preacher told him in a stern voice. He wasn't sure he was right about that, however. Jake seemed plenty interested in the idea of being around the soiled doves who worked at Fargo's place.

Keeping a hand on Jake's shoulder, Preacher steered him toward the riverfront. As they walked, he said, "Now I got a question for you."

"I ain't sure I ought to answer it, seein' as how you won't let me to go to the mountains with you."

Preacher reined in his impatience and said, "You can go back to your pa if you want."

"No, no, what is it you want to ask me, Preacher?"

"Yesterday, when I got to the settlement and was makin' my deal with Mr. Larson to buy my furs, you were watchin' pretty close, right?"

"Yeah. You were carryin' a rifle, two pistols, a knife, and a tomahawk, and you looked about as savage as a Injun."

"Did you notice anybody else watchin' me and Larson?"

Jake looked puzzled. "You mean like somebody skulkin' around like a Injun?"

"That's right."

Jake thought about it for several seconds, making faces as if that much mental activity made his brain hurt, before finally shaking his head and saying, "Sorry, Preacher, I don't recollect nothin' like that."

Preacher tried to jog the boy's memory by saying, "These fellas I'm talkin' about, one of 'em was tall and wearin' buckskins, and the other one was shorter and had on an old suit and a beaver hat."

"Nope, I just didn't see 'em."

Preacher swallowed his disappointment. "All right. I'm obliged to you anyway for answerin' the question."

So this trail was yet another dead end. Preacher didn't get discouraged. He knew that sooner or later Fate would lead him to the two men he sought.

The tavern was already busy when they reached it. Dusk was settling down, and men who had finished their work for the day were eager to quench their thirst and maybe play a little slap-and-tickle with the serving gals. Nobody paid much attention to Jake when Preacher took him inside. While it wasn't that common to see a kid in a tavern, neither was it unusual to come across somebody Jake's age guzzling down a shot of whiskey. A lot of youngsters were on their own because their folks had died or abandoned them or the kids had run away. They fended for themselves. It was a hard life. The ones who toughened up quickly were the ones who survived.

"Who's your friend?" Fargo asked when Preacher brought Jake up to the bar.

"His name's Jake," Preacher said.

Fargo reached across the bar to shake hands. "Well, I'm mighty pleased to meet you, Jake," he said. "What're you doin', associatin' with an old scoundrel like Preacher here?"

"Preacher's gonna teach me how to be a mountain man," Jake declared.

"Now dad-gum it!" Preacher burst out. "I never said any such thing. Jake got some crazy idea in his head that he was goin' back to the mountains with me, but I never said he could. I thought maybe you could find a place for him here, Ford."

"Here at the tavern, you mean?"

Preacher nodded. "Yeah. Got to be some chores around here he could do to pay for his grub and a roof over his head."

Fargo scratched at his jaw and frowned in thought. "There's always plenty o' work around the place, that's for damn sure. I might could use a boy to help out." He looked at Jake. "Where are you from, son?"

"Right here in St. Louis."

Fargo gave Preacher a surprised glance. "Is that so? You got kinfolks here?"

"Just my pa. Jonathan Brant. He works in one of the fur warehouses by the river. You wouldn't know him, though. He'd never set foot inside a tavern. He says they're all dens of iniquity, whatever that is."

Churchgoers must like that word, Preacher thought, remembering how one of the men who had found him the night before after he'd been knocked out had used it.

Fargo started shaking his head. "Sorry, Preacher," he said. "I can't take the boy."

"Why not?"

"You heard him. He's got a pa right here in town. Hell, the fella works just a few blocks away! If I kept the boy here and he found out about it, he'd have the law on me, sure as shootin'."

"You heard what Jake said. His pa wouldn't ever find out, because he'd never come in here."

Stubbornly, Fargo continued to shake his head. "Somebody might recognize the boy and tell his pa that he's here. Then I'd be liable to be thrown in jail for child-stealin'! Nope, I'm sorry, Preacher, but I just can't do it."

Preacher glared at Jake. "Now what in blazes am I gonna do with you?"

"I told you," Jake said, grinning up at him. "Take me to the mountains with you."

Seven

Shad Beaumont's house on the southern edge of town was one of the nicest dwellings in St. Louis, as befitted his status as the leading figure in the settlement's criminal underworld. The big white-washed building had two stories and columns holding up the porch roof over the front door. The place reminded Schuyler Mims of some plantations he had seen down in Louisiana, although not quite as fancy, of course. Beaumont's illicit activities had made him well-to-do, but he wasn't as rich as those cotton planters down South.

Beaumont brought Schuyler and Fairfax to the house after sending his two battered bodyguards off to seek medical attention for their injuries. Baldy and Handlebar had glared at Schuyler and Fairfax before limping off together, helping each other hobble along the street, but Beaumont again assured his two new associates that no one would seek reprisals against them.

Now he led them into a well-furnished parlor that looked fancy enough to Schuyler to have come out of a high-class whorehouse. If Beaumont lived in a place like this, Schuyler wondered, then why did he patronize dives like the one they had seen him coming out of earlier?

Because he must like places like that, Schuyler realized, answering his own question. He'd probably spent a lot of time in them when he was younger and poorer, and they still held some appeal for him.

Beaumont went over to a sideboard and said, "Would you gents like a drink?"

Schuyler licked his lips thirstily and looked at Fairfax, who nodded and said, "That would be fine, thank you."

"Brandy?"

"Whatever you're having."

Beaumont poured amber liquid from a decanter into three crystal snifters that had to have come from New Orleans. He handed one to Fairfax and another to Schuyler, then raised his own.

"To our new association, gentlemen," he said.

"Hear, hear," Fairfax replied as he clinked his snifter against Beaumont's. Rather clumsily, Schuyler followed suit.

The brandy was smooth as it could be. At first he didn't think it had much kick to it, but then his insides started to glow warmly, as if the stuff had kindled a nice little fire in his belly. He took another drink, guzzling down more than he intended to. He knew it made him look like some kind of bumpkin to be drinking that way when Fairfax and Beaumont were sipping their brandy like fine gentlemen, but Schuyler didn't care. It had been a long time since he'd had anything this good.

"You said something about having a job for us,"
Fairfax prodded.

"Yes, of course," Beaumont said. "Several wagons
were ferried across the river from Illinois yesterday.
I was curious about them, so I asked around. I have
quite a few sources of information about what goes
on along the riverfront."

Fairfax murmured, "I'll bet you do." He and
Schuyler both knew that a lot of people would be
eager to help out a powerful man like Beaumont,
in hopes that he would return the favor later on.

Beaumont ignored the interruption as if it hadn't
happened. "There are half-a-dozen wagons in the
party," he went on. "They're loaded with all sorts of
supplies and trade goods, and they're owned by a
pair of cousins named Hart, Corliss and Jerome
Hart."

"And you've got your eye on those wagons and
the goods inside them," Fairfax guessed.

Beaumont smiled and took another sip of
brandy. "That's right. I've discovered that the
Harts plan to head west with their little wagon
train and establish a trading post somewhere in
the mountains."

"What about Indians?" Schuyler asked. "Ain't
there a bunch o' Indians out there that like to
scalp and kill white folks just for the fun of it?"

"Not all the savages are hostile," Fairfax said. He
looked at Beaumont. "Or at least, that's what I've
heard."

"That's right," Beaumont confirmed. "If you
know which areas to avoid, you're relatively safe
from Indians. Some of the tribes are even willing
to trade with white men. And with the fur indus-

try continuing to grow, more and more trappers are heading west. A trading post like the one the Hart cousins want to establish could do a lucrative business."

"But you plan on taking those wagons, and all the goods in them."

"Exactly. There's no reason why I shouldn't reap the profits from that trading post." Beaumont tossed back the rest of his liquor. "But I'll need a couple of good men to run the place."

"You want *us* to do that?" Schuyler asked.

"I think you could handle the job, from what I've seen of you so far. Some of my men would be working with you, of course."

"How do we know we can trust you?" Fairfax asked.

The blunt question didn't seem to offend Beaumont. He said, "We'll have to trust each other. The arrangement will be of benefit to all of us, so none of us will have any reason to double-cross the others." He paused. "Besides, there's something else you'll have to do before I'd turn such an important operation over to you."

"What's that?" Fairfax wanted to know.

"You'll be in charge of getting the wagons and their cargo in the first place," Beaumont said. "That means you'll have to kill Corliss and Jerome Hart and everyone who's traveling with them. Can you handle that?"

Schuyler looked at Fairfax. Taking a potshot at a fella in a canoe on the river was one thing. So was accidentally shooting a whore. But carrying out cold-blooded murder on at least half-a-dozen people and probably more, well, that was something else entirely.

Fairfax looked like he was up for it, though, so Schuyler sighed and nodded. Fairfax grinned, tossed back the rest of his brandy, and held out the empty snifter for a refill.

"Let's drink to success, shall we?"

Jake's bottom lip trembled as he looked at the shack. The flickering glow of candlelight showed through the oilcloth tacked over the single window.

"He's gonna be mad because I wasn't there when he got home," the boy said. "If you make me go in there, Preacher, he'll beat me. I swear he will."

"I can stop him if he does."

"But if he sees you with me, he's liable to be so crazy that he'll kill me as soon as you're gone. I reckon he hates you even more'n the Devil right now, and my pa's got a powerful hate for the Devil."

Preacher muttered a curse. Circumstances had put him in one hell of an awkward situation. Living the life he led, he couldn't take on the responsibility of caring for a kid, even a smart little whippersnapper like Jake. But he wasn't sure he could live with himself either if he left Jake here and then discovered on his next trip to St. Louis that Jonathan Brant had indeed beaten the boy to death. Even if that didn't happen, Jake might run away and take off for the mountains by himself. Preacher didn't figure the youngster would last a week on the frontier without somebody to look after him.

There was an old saying about a rock and a hard

place. That was where Preacher found himself now, stuck smack-dab between them.

But maybe there was another answer, he realized suddenly. Frowning, he looked down at Jake and asked, "You really don't want to go back to your pa?"

Without hesitation, Jake shook his head. "No, Preacher, I don't. I'm scared of him."

"If you're gone for a few days, will he come lookin' for you?"

"I don't know. I don't think so, at least not for a while. He's sort of stove up after that whippin' you gave him. He ain't gettin' around all that well. I reckon any time he's not workin', he'll lay around the cabin and read his Bible and feel sorry for hisself."

"All right, then," Preacher said. "I got an idea. You'll have to lie low for a few days here in St. Louis, but then you'll be able to leave, and you won't never have to come back if you don't want to."

"Where am I goin'?" Jake's face brightened with excitement, even in the gloom of falling night. "With you?"

It might come to that, Preacher thought. "We'll see," he said.

He turned Jake away from the cabin and went looking for the wagons belonging to Corliss and Jerome Hart.

It didn't take long to find them. Preacher asked a few questions along the riverfront and was directed to a field on the western edge of the settlement. As he and Jake approached, Preacher saw the half-dozen wagons drawn into a rough circle with the oxen that would pull them gathered inside. Even though here on the edge of St. Louis there was no reason to circle the wagons other than to contain the livestock, it was good that the members of the party had already gotten into the habit. Out on the plains, the formation would be vital for protection in case the wagon train was attacked by Indians or outlaws.

"Who do these wagons belong to?" Jake asked.

"Some folks I know," Preacher replied, even though the only one of the party he had actually met was Corliss Hart.

"What're we doin' here?"

"I thought maybe you could stay with them for a while. They're headin' west to the mountains to start a tradin' post. I figure they might be able to use a smart, hardworkin' youngster like you."

"Really?" Jake sounded excited by the idea. "You think they'd take me along?"

"We'll see about it," Preacher promised.

No one challenged them as they walked right up to the wagons, and that was worrisome. Guards should have been posted, even here in town. There were dangers lurking in St. Louis, too, as Preacher knew all too well.

A cooking fire burned inside a circle of rocks, but no one was tending it. Preacher called out, "Hello, the wagons! Anybody home?"

The canvas flap over the back of one of the vehicles was pulled aside, and a hand thrust a flintlock pistol into view. "Don't come any closer," a voice commanded. "Who are you, and what do you want?"

"Take it easy, mister," Preacher said with a scowl. He didn't cotton to having guns pointed at him. Never had and likely never would. "We're lookin' for a fella named Corliss Hart, or his cousin. I disremember what his name is."

The gun lowered, and the canvas flap opened wider. A small, wiry man climbed over the wagon's tailgate and dropped to the ground, still holding the pistol although he wasn't pointing it at Preacher and Jake anymore. The man wore high-topped boots, whipcord trousers, and a leather vest over a white shirt. He had a sharp, foxlike face and slightly wavy brown hair.

"I'm Jerome Hart," he introduced himself. "What business do you have with us, sir?"

"They call me Preacher, and this here is Jake," Preacher said, not answering Jerome Hart's question just yet.

Jerome's interest perked up. "Preacher," he repeated. "You're the one my cousin went to talk to." It wasn't a question.

Preacher nodded. "That's right. He asked me to take on the job of guidin' you folks to the mountains and helpin' you set up a tradin' post."

"But you refused," Jerome said. "Have you reconsidered your decision?"

"No, not really."

"Then why are you here?"

Preacher rested a hand on Jake's shoulder. "I was hopin' you folks could find a place for the boy here. He's a hard worker, and he's smart as a whip. I reckon he'd be good to have along on a trip like the one you're takin'."

"You think so?" Jerome lowered the hammer on the pistol and stuck the weapon behind his belt. He looked at Jake and asked, "Well, boy? What do you have to say for yourself?"

"I'd sure admire to go with you to the mountains, Mr. Hart, sir," Jake replied. "I been wantin' to see such things for a long time. Ain't no mountains here in St. Louis."

"There *aren't* any mountains here in St. Louis."

"Yes, sir, that's what I just said."

"No, you said, 'Ain't no mountains.' That's incorrect."

Jake took off his hat and scratched his head. "Yeah, but it's the same thing, ain't it?"

"Not at all. Have you ever been to school?"

"A little. Have you?"

"I *taught* school for several years," Jerome said.

Preacher tried not to wince. He hadn't known that he might be saddling Jake with a schoolteacher for a boss.

Preacher didn't have anything against book learning. He could read and write and cipher, and figured those were good things to know. A surprising number of mountain men were well educated and well read. Some of them could quote vast stretches of the Bible or ol' Bill Shakespeare's plays from memory. But in Preacher's experience, schoolteachers were often priggish and hard to get along with. Corliss Hart had seemed to be a much more easygoing sort than his cousin. Preacher supposed he had expected Jerome Hart to be the same way.

"If you went with us," Jerome went on, "and I'm not saying that you can, I'd expect you to show some initiative and try to learn some things, Jake."

"Oh, I don't mind learnin'," Jake said. "It was sittin' in a schoolroom on a pretty day that I didn't like."

"Well, there are no schoolrooms where we'll be

going, I expect, or at least there won't be any time soon. Perhaps once the trading post is established, I might think about starting a school, too. Some of the Indian children might like to be educated."

Again, Preacher had to hide a grimace. Jerome Hart would get his hair lifted if he started trying to mess too much with the Indians and their ways. Most of them just wanted to be left alone to live the way they had always lived. Trying to change them had probably caused more trouble between the white men and the red men than anything else.

"Well, how about it?" Preacher asked. "Think you might be willin' to take the boy along? He'd earn his keep."

"Before I agree to anything, I need to know a few more things," Jerome said. "What relation is Jake to you?"

"No relation. We're just friends."

"Does he have any family here? How do they feel about sending him west with our wagon train?"

Preacher hesitated. He hadn't said anything about the problem with Jonathan Brant, and he had warned Jake not to mention it either. The Harts wouldn't want to take Jake along with them if they thought they might get in trouble with the law for doing so. Once the wagon train reached the mountains, though, Preacher figured it wouldn't really matter that much. There would be nothing Jake's pa could do about it anymore.

Before Preacher could reply, Jake spoke up. "I ain't got no family," he said. "I'm a orphan."

Jerome gave him a stern look. "You don't have any family. You are an orphan."

Jake sighed and shook his head. "You sure do like repeatin' everything folks say to you, Mr. Hart."

Jerome's mouth tightened and he said, "We'll discuss that later. For now, I'm tempted to say that yes, we'll take the lad along with us. But there are two conditions."

"What might those be?" Preacher asked, his eyes narrowing with suspicion.

"One is that my cousin agrees. Corliss and I are equal partners and we each have a say in every decision, even the small ones."

"And what's the other one?"

Jerome said exactly the thing that Preacher didn't want to hear.

"That you accept the job as our guide and come with us, too, Preacher."

Eight

Jake turned to look up eagerly at him. "Yeah, Preacher," he said. "You can come, too!"

"No, I can't. I got business here in St. Louis—" Preacher began.

"We're not leaving for a couple of days," Jerome pointed out, echoing what Corliss had told Preacher that afternoon at the cemetery. "Perhaps you could conclude your business by then."

Preacher scratched at his bearded jaw. "Well, maybe," he allowed. "But I can't be sure about that."

"Let me ask you this . . . were you going to be returning to the mountains anyway?"

"Sure. The fall trappin' season will be comin' up, and I plan to get another load o' pelts."

"Then doesn't it make sense to travel with a large party like ours? I'm sure it much safer for you that way than being by yourself."

Preacher wasn't at all sure of that. He'd always figured that he could take care of himself just fine, and it would be easier if he didn't have a bunch of pilgrims to look after. But of course a city-bred fella like Jerome would think it was safer to have a bunch of folks traveling together. In most cases he'd even be right.

Still, if it wasn't for wanting to find the two men who'd killed Abby and tried to kill him, Preacher would have accepted the offer without hesitation. The Harts and the men who worked for them would have a better chance of survival with Preacher going along to guide them and keep them out of trouble. And now there was the matter of Jake's future to consider, too. It was a damned dilemma, all right, and Preacher was on the horns of it.

"Where's that cousin of yours?" he asked Jerome, stalling for time. "You said he'd have to go along with the plan."

"Corliss is staying at the Excelsior Hotel, along with his fiancée."

"Oh, yeah, I recollect him sayin' something about that. I thought it was you and him stayin' there, though. He didn't mention any fiancée when he was talkin' to me." Preacher frowned. "The gal ain't goin' along with the wagon train, is she?"

Jerome's mouth tightened. "Not that it's really any business of yours, but no, Miss Morrigan won't be accompanying us. She'll be waiting for Corliss here in St. Louis. When the trading post is well established, he intends to return here, and they'll be wed. Corliss will then run this end of our business enterprise."

"Makes sense. There're damn few white females out there where you're talkin' about goin', and there's a good reason for that. The frontier can be a mighty dangerous place."

"And yet you'd send a young lad there," Jerome said with a gesture toward Jake.

"That's different," the boy said before Preacher could reply. "I can take care o' myself."

"We shall see." Jerome turned his attention back to Preacher. "What do you say to my proposal? Will you come along with us?"

"Can't tell you one way or the other right now," Preacher replied. "Give me a day or two to see what I can work out. In the meantime, you reckon Jake can stay here with you folks?"

Jerome nodded. "I think that would be all right. There are chores to do around the camp while we're getting ready to depart. He can help with them, in exchange for his food and shelter."

"I'm obliged to you." Preacher stuck out his hand.

Jerome took it rather gingerly, as if he were afraid that Preacher would try to crush his fingers with his grip, but Preacher didn't do any such thing. A strong man didn't need to go around proving it.

Preacher patted Jake on the back and said, "Be seein' you, son." He turned and started to walk away, but he had gone only a few yards when Jake ran after him, calling his name. Preacher stopped and turned back, dropping to one knee because he could tell by the look on Jake's face that the youngster was upset about something.

Keeping his voice pitched low enough so that only the two of them could hear, Jake said, "Preacher, I . . . I got to thinkin' about my pa. I know I said I hate him, but he's liable to worry about me when I don't never come back. He might think somethin' bad happened to me. I don't know that I'd want him thinkin' that, or never knowin' what become of me."

Preacher thought it over and nodded. "I reckon I can understand that. Bad as he is, he's your pa. Tell you what . . . if I don't go with the wagon train, then after you're gone, after enough time's gone by so that he can't do anything about it, I'll go see your pa and tell him where you went. I'll tell him that you're all right and there ain't no need for him to worry about you. How'd that be?"

"I reckon it'd be all right," Jake said. "But he's liable to be awful mad at you for helpin' me get away."

Preacher smiled. "I ain't worried overmuch about whether or not your pa gets mad."

"Yeah, you already whipped him once. I reckon you can do it again if you need to." Jake thought some more. "But what about if you come with us? I'm hopin' you do."

"Then before I go I'll write a letter for your pa, explainin' everything. I'll give it to Mr. Larson to give to him later, after we're good an' gone. How's that?"

Jake grinned and bobbed his head. "Yeah, that'll work. Thanks, Preacher."

"Sure thing." Preacher stood up and ruffled the boy's hair. "You run on back to Mr. Hart now, and do what he says, hear?"

"Yeah." Jake sighed and added, "He's gonna try to learn me a bunch o' stuff, ain't he?"

"More'n likely. You're just gonna have to put up

with it, though. Gettin' educated's just part o' the price of bein' free."

"Free," Jake repeated. "I like the sound of that."

So did Preacher. Always had, and always would.

The dull, faint headache that plagued him all day because of the pistol ball that grazed his head was gone by the next morning. Preacher was fast to recover from most injuries, and this one was no different.

He spent the day combing the town for anybody who knew or had seen the two men he was looking for. Without names or more detailed descriptions, though, it was difficult. St. Louis had grown by leaps and bounds in the decades since it was founded, and now more than six thousand citizens lived there. It wasn't difficult for two men to lose themselves in that many people, if they didn't want to be found.

Preacher made no secret of the fact that he was looking for them. He spread the word far and wide, all up and down the riverfront and in other areas of the settlement, in hopes that if the killers heard that he was on their trail, *they* might come to *him*, instead of the other way around, and try to kill him again. Preacher was more than willing to take that chance in return for another shot at them.

But nothing came of those efforts either, and as another evening settled down, Preacher had to admit that he didn't seem to be any closer to the men he sought than he had been when he started. He headed for the wagon camp on the outskirts of town, figuring at least he could find out how Jake was getting along with Jerome Hart and the other members of the party.

When Preacher got there, Jake was carrying a couple buckets of water to fill a trough for the oxen in the center of the circle. The boy spotted him, grinned, and called, "Hey, Preacher!" He started to set the buckets down, obviously intending to run over to the visitor.

Preacher motioned for him to stop. "Finish what you're doin'," he said. "A fella don't get very far in the world by neglectin' the chores he's been given."

Jake grimaced, but went on with his work. Preacher walked into the circle of wagons. More people were moving around the vehicles than he had seen there the night before. Preacher spotted Jerome Hart talking to a couple of brawny, roughly dressed men. Preacher pegged them as drivers that the Hart cousins had hired to handle the wagon teams. He didn't know if Jerome and Corliss planned to drive any of the wagons themselves, or if they had hired help for all of them.

Jerome saw Preacher and lifted a hand in greeting. He finished his conversation with the two men and then came over to greet the mountain man.

"It's good to see you again, Preacher," Jerome said. "I hope this means you've decided to accept the offer to come with us."

"Just came to check on the boy," Preacher replied with a nod toward Jake, who was emptying the buckets into the water trough. "My business is still hangin' fire."

"I'm sorry to hear that. We're going to be pulling

out day after tomorrow, first thing in the morning. Perhaps your business will be concluded by then."

Preacher just grunted. He didn't know what was going to happen. He'd never been much of a hand at predicting the future.

Jake had finished with his chore. Carrying the empty buckets, he hurried over to Preacher and Jerome. Preacher grinned at him and asked, "How're you likin' it here?"

"I like it just fine," Jake said. "Mr. Hart's been nice to me so far. He gives me chores to do, but he don't beat me and yell at me and call me a sinner if I don't do 'em exactly right the first time."

Jerome frowned. "Beat you and call you a sinner? Who in the world would treat a boy like that?"

Preacher could tell by Jake's sudden expression of alarm that the youngster realized he might have said too much. But Jake recovered quickly, replying in an offhand manner, "Oh, just a fella who looked after me for a while."

"Well, that's no way to be," Jerome said with a sniff of disapproval. "You did well to get away from that individual, I'd say."

"Yeah, I'd say so, too," Preacher agreed.

Face flushed with excitement, Jake told Preacher, "Mr. Hart says I can have a rifle o' my own to use durin' the trip, if I can show him that I know how to use one. Ain't that great?"

"Isn't that great," Jerome corrected.

"Yeah." Jake nodded. "I meant, isn't that great." From the sound of it, he was beginning to understand that he was going to have to put up with Jerome correcting his language and grammar if he wanted to go west with the wagon train.

Preacher felt a twinge of worry. The cousins' party might well run into trouble out there on the plains or in the mountains. Was he taking too great a chance with Jake's life by sending the boy along?

On the other hand, Jake seemed to be convinced that his life wouldn't be worth a plugged nickel if he stayed here in St. Louis with his pa. Preacher figured Jake would know more about the truth of that situation than *he* ever could.

Anyway, all of life was a risk, no matter where you went or what you did. Misfortune could strike without warning at any time, often with tragic results. But if a man dwelled too much on that, he'd drive himself plumb loco. You had to just hope that everything would be all right and forge on ahead.

It never hurt to try to stack the odds in your favor, though.

Jerome looked past Preacher and Jake and said, "Here comes my cousin now."

Preacher turned and saw Corliss Hart coming toward the wagons. A woman was with him. Preacher supposed she was Corliss's fiancée. She wasn't stunningly beautiful, but she was very pretty, with a sweet, heart-shaped face and thick dark hair bound at the back of her neck.

Another man trailed behind Corliss and the woman. He was tall and heavy-shouldered, his muscles stretching the buckskin shirt he wore. His broad-brimmed felt hat was thumbed back on a thatch of red hair, and he had a spiky beard of the same color. A long-barreled flintlock rifle was tucked under his arm, and a pistol and a knife had been stuck behind his belt. He looked vaguely familiar to Preacher, but the mountain man couldn't place him.

"Hello, Preacher," Corliss said. "I didn't expect to see you here."

Preacher inclined his head toward Jake. "Came to check on the boy."

"Yes, of course, the boy." Neither Corliss's expression nor his voice were very friendly this evening. "We're not good enough for you to accept our job offer, but you don't hesitate to stick *us* with the job of caring for a brat."

"Corliss!" Jerome said. "Jake is not a brat. He's been very helpful and cooperative."

Jake didn't seem offended by Corliss's words. In fact, he said, "That's all right, Mr. Hart. I been called a whole heap worse in my time."

"Still, there's no need to be rude," Jerome insisted.

"I quite agree," the woman said with a stern frown at Corliss. "I know you can be a perfect gentleman when you want to be."

"Sure, sure," Corliss grumbled. "Sorry, I guess."

The woman prodded him with an elbow as she smiled at Preacher. "Aren't you going to introduce me?"

Still grudgingly, Corliss said, "This is my fiancée, Miss Deborah Morrigan. Miss Morrigan, this is the man known as Preacher. I'm afraid I don't know his real name."

It was Arthur, but Preacher never used it anymore. He took off his hat, nodded politely to the woman, and said, "Preacher'll do fine. It's an honor to make your acquaintance, ma'am."

"And I'm pleased to know you, Mr. Preacher. Or do you prefer not to be addressed as Mister?"

"That'd be best," Preacher said, glad that for

once he didn't have to explain how there was no need to call him Mister.

Jerome gestured toward the red-bearded man who accompanied Corliss and Deborah and asked, "Who's this?" The question surprised Preacher a mite, because he had figured that the man was another of the wagon drivers. Evidently, though, he was a stranger to Jerome.

"Oh," Corliss said, turning toward the big man, "this is Merrick Foster. I've hired him to be our guide."

Jerome's eyes widened with surprise. "I thought we agreed that we wanted to hire Preacher."

"Preacher had his chance to take the job," Corliss snapped. "We can't wait any longer for him to make up his mind."

"But we're not leaving until the day after tomorrow."

"Yes, and if we wait until then and Preacher still doesn't want to go, we'll be faced with either starting west without a guide—which would be an incredibly foolish thing to do, I think—or accepting another delay while we try to find someone then. Time is money, Jerome."

A smirk appeared on Merrick Foster's rugged face as he looked at Preacher. He looked like he thought he had just come out on top in some sort of competition, but a race took two people, not just one, and Preacher hadn't been competing for anything.

Jerome frowned as he mulled over what his cousin had said. After a moment, he looked at the mountain man and asked, "What do you think, Preacher?"

"I reckon your cousin's got a point," Preacher answered without hesitation. "It'd be a mighty foolish thing for you folks to start off without a guide." He had recalled now where he knew Foster from, so he went on. "But there're other things you could do that'd be just as foolish, maybe even more."

"Oh?" Corliss challenged. "Like what?"

Preacher nodded toward Foster. "Like hirin' this fella here. I wouldn't trust the varmint as far as I could throw him."

Foster's smirk disappeared as his face darkened with fury. "You got no call to talk about me like that!" he said as he took a step toward Preacher. His free hand balled into a fist, and the other one tightened on the rifle he carried.

"No?" Preacher said, his voice cool with disdain. "What happened to your partners the last time you went trappin', up in the Tetons? Seems to me like they got ambushed on the Snake River and wiped out by Sioux because you went and messed around with one o' those Indian gals when she didn't want no part of you. How is it you were the only one who survived, Foster? You figure out what was gonna happen and slip away first, leavin' your partners there to distract the war party?"

"You lyin' son of a bitch," Foster grated.

"Prove it," Preacher said.

With a roar of rage, Foster whipped the rifle to his shoulder, earing back the hammer and tightening his finger on the trigger.

Nine

Moving with blinding speed, Preacher sprang toward Foster. His left hand shot out and grabbed the flintlock's barrel, wrenching upward so that when the rifle exploded, the heavy lead ball flew harmlessly into the air. At the same time, Preacher swung his right fist in a powerful punch that crashed into Foster's jaw. The big, red-bearded man stumbled backward.

Preacher tore the rifle out of Foster's hands and rammed the stock into the man's belly. Foster doubled over in pain. Preacher dropped the rifle, grabbed Foster's shoulder, and brought his knee up into Foster's face. Foster toppled onto his back and lay there groaning as blood welled from his broken nose.

Preacher hooked a toe under Foster's shoulder and rolled the stunned man onto his belly. "Leave him layin' on his back and he'd be liable to choke on his own blood," Preacher exclaimed. He wouldn't have lost a lot of sleep over it if Foster died. The man had attacked a woman, and he had deserted his partners and left them to die. Either of those things would have damned Foster in Preacher's eyes. Put 'em together and there was no doubt in Preacher's mind that the fella was one no-account son of a bitch.

But it was bad enough already that that Deborah Morrigan was standing there with a horrified expression on her face because of the violence that had occurred. She had delicate sensibilities, not those of a woman accustomed to life on the frontier, and Preacher was just chivalrous enough not to want to shock her anymore by standing by and allowing Foster to strangle to death on his own blood.

Corliss Hart grabbed Preacher by the shoulder. "You had no right to do that!" he said. "You've injured our guide!"

"Blast it, Corliss!" Jerome burst out. "Didn't you hear what Preacher said? This man's not trust-worthy!"

"Oh, no? How do you know that Preacher's telling the truth?"

Preacher looked down at the hand on his shoulder and said in a low, dangerous voice, "I don't cotton much to bein' grabbed, Hart. I like it even less when the fella doin' the grabbin' hints that I'm a liar."

Corliss let go of Preacher and took a hasty step back, his face paling a little in the light from the cooking fire. "That's not what I meant and you know it," he said. "I just mean that we don't know you any better than we do Foster here. We've no reason to distrust him and yet accept everything you say."

"You got the best reason in the world," Preacher

said. "He's a no-good, lyin' skunk, and to top it off, he don't know the mountains that well neither. Even if he didn't double-cross you, he'd be liable to get you lost or wind up with a war party chasin' you, wantin' to lift your hair."

Deborah shuddered. "Do things like that really go on, Preacher, or are they just stories to scare small children?"

"You'd better believe they go on, ma'am, and it ain't just youngsters that need to be scared. A little fear's a mighty healthy thing when you're dealin' with the frontier."

Merrick Foster groaned and tried to push himself onto his hands and knees, succeeding after a moment's effort. He shook his head groggily. Strings of blood dangled from his smashed nose.

Preacher gripped Foster's arm and hauled the man to his feet, lifting Foster's weight without any noticeable effort. "Get on outta here," he said as he gave Foster a shove and sent him stumbling back toward the settlement.

"Damn it, you can't just waltz into this camp and start giving orders!" Corliss complained.

"He can if he's going to work for us," Jerome said. "As our guide, Preacher would be in charge of the wagons and everything to do with our journey. Isn't that right, Preacher?"

Preacher grimaced as he looked around. He saw the eager expressions on the faces of Jake Brant and Jerome Hart and the keen-eyed interest of Deborah Morrigan. He saw as well the irritation on Corliss's face and the outright hatred blazing in the eyes of Merrick Foster.

Circumstances had reared up and walloped him

yet again. He hadn't found the men he was looking for, but after revealing Foster's true colors, he almost felt an obligation to help these greenhorns. If he didn't, then there was a chance Foster would worm his way back into their good graces, or in their inexperience they might hire somebody else who would be just as bad as Foster or even worse.

Well, it wasn't like he was never coming back to St. Louis, he told himself. He would be back in the fall with another load of pelts. And just because he hadn't found the men who killed Abby didn't mean that he never would. They were obviously hiding out, and if he was gone for a while, they might let their guard down so that it would be easier for him to find them when he got back.

Anyway, he had a long memory. The grudge could still be settled four or five months from now.

"All right," he said. "You've got a deal. I'll take you to the mountains."

Jerome grinned, and Jake let out an excited shout. Foster shuffled off, cursing. Corliss just glared until Deborah led him away, talking softly to him as she tried to calm him down.

Preacher shook hands with Jerome. "You won't regret this decision," the man from Chicago said, "and neither will we."

Preacher hoped he was right about that.

Shad Beaumont had advanced Schuyler and Fairfax enough money to rent themselves a room in a run-down boardinghouse where nobody asked any questions and nobody paid any attention to the tenants' comings and goings either. For a few extra coins, the slatternly landlady had agreed to bring their meals up to their room on a tray, so they didn't have to come down to the house's dining room. With Preacher looking for them, the fewer people who knew where they were, the better.

According to Beaumont's information, the wagons belonging to the Hart cousins were leaving in a couple of days, early in the morning. That gave Schuyler and Fairfax time to figure out exactly how they were going to get their hands on the wagons. Actually, Colin Fairfax would do the figuring out. He handled most of the thinking chores for the partners, and that was the way Schuyler liked it.

It would be best if they and some of Beaumont's men could lie in wait somewhere and ambush the wagons. They could kill all the drivers, or at least most of them, before anybody knew what was going on. That ambush would be easier to set up, though, if they knew exactly which trail the wagons were going to follow.

That realization prompted Fairfax to come up with an idea. Arranging the ambush would be even easier if they had someone with the wagon train working with them.

Schuyler was the one who suggested Merrick Foster. He had known Foster casually for a while, and knew that the man was game for almost anything if the price was right. Foster already had sort of a bad reputation among his fellow mountain men, but those greenhorns from Chicago wouldn't know that. And since the exact details of the fate that had befallen Foster's former trapping partners were unknown, folks tended to keep their mouths shut about him, even though they might suspect him of deserting his companions.

Schuyler got word to Foster through the landlady, and he came to the boardinghouse, climbing the back stairs to visit Schuyler and Fairfax without anybody else seeing him. Foster had agreed readily to the arrangement. He would try to get the job as guide for the wagon train full of supplies, and if he did, he would lead the wagons with their valuable cargo right into the ambush set up by Schuyler, Fairfax, and other members of Beaumont's gang. All he had to do was insinuate himself into the cousins' party somehow.

Schuyler and Fairfax were waiting to see what the results of Foster's efforts would be. Schuyler was restless. Hiding out like this was a tiresome, difficult business. He was bored. He wanted to go to a tavern. They had a jug of whiskey, so Schuyler could take a slug from it any time he wanted, but he craved company, maybe a friendly game of poker, definitely a pretty serving gal hovering over him, bumping into him from time to time with a plump breast or a nicely curved hip. Instead, he was stuck here in this little room, staring at the walls.

So he was glad for the diversion when a soft knock came on the door. Fairfax went over and leaned close to it, clutching a loaded pistol in his hand. "Who's there?" he asked in a harsh whisper that disguised his natural voice.

"Foster," came the reply, and Schuyler thought there was something wrong with the man's voice. It was thick somehow, as if he were having trouble talking.

Fairfax swung the door open, and when Foster came in, Schuyler saw why he sounded that way. Foster's lips were swollen, his face was bruised, and there was dried blood in his beard. Somebody had walloped him several good ones.

"What the hell happened to you?" Fairfax asked as he closed the door behind Foster.

Schuyler added, "You look like you been kicked by a mule."

Foster gave an angry grunt and said, "A mule named Preacher, damn his eyes!"

Fear welled up inside Schuyler as he looked at Fairfax, who appeared to be equally startled by Foster's words. "Preacher?" Schuyler practically yelped.

"What are you talking about?" Fairfax snapped. "What does Preacher have to do with this?"

"You know who he is?" Foster asked.

Fairfax nodded. "Of course we do." He glanced at Schuyler. "Everyone in St. Louis, ah, knows of Preacher."

Schuyler realized that Fairfax didn't intend to tell Foster about their problems with Preacher. That wasn't anybody else's business. Certainly not Shad Beaumont's. Beaumont probably wouldn't have hired them if he'd known that Preacher was looking for them.

"Yeah, well, those damn pilgrims have hired him as their guide," Foster went on.

Fairfax winced, and the worry inside Schuyler grew stronger.

"I managed to get in good with Corliss Hart. Him and his cousin tried to hire Preacher first, and he put 'em off, claimed he had some business here in St. Louis to take care of."

Schuyler and Fairfax exchanged another glance. They knew all too well what that business was. Preacher was looking for *them*.

"Corliss was tired of waitin' for Preacher to make up his mind," Foster continued, "so he hired me and said he'd get his cousin to go along with it. But when we got out to the wagon camp, Preacher was there, and he started tellin' 'em all sorts of lies about me. Said they shouldn't hire me, and that little weasel Jerome believed him."

"So you got in a scuffle with Preacher," Fairfax guessed.

Foster's eyes narrowed. "He hit me while I wasn't lookin'."

Schuyler doubted that; Preacher had no reputation for such treachery. On the contrary, he was known far and wide as an honorable man.

"So he gave you a thrashing and sent you slinking away with your tail between your legs," Fairfax said with a scornful glare. "And then he accepted the job with the Harts after all, I take it."

"He took the job. I hung around outside the camp long enough to hear that. But I didn't slink away, damn it! I'll settle the score with that son of a bitch if it's the last thing I do!"

"Well, I'm glad to hear that anyway." Fairfax rubbed his chin. "Perhaps we can make use of you. The wagons aren't leaving until the day after tomorrow. If something were to happen to Preacher between now and then, the Harts might not have any choice but to give you the job after all."

Foster's eyes narrowed. "You reckon?"

"What can it hurt to try?" Foster asked with a

smile. "And at the very least, you'll have the satisfaction of revenging yourself on Preacher."

Foster's eyes burned with hatred as he nodded. "Damn right." He smacked his right fist into his left palm. "I'll do it! You care how?"

Fairfax shook his head. "As long as we don't have to worry about Preacher interfering with our plans, that's all we care about. Isn't that true, Schuyler?"

"Uh, sure," Schuyler said. "Just get rid of him, Merrick, and we'll owe you one."

"Don't think I won't collect." An ugly grin stretched across Foster's face. "There was a really pretty gal with those cousins. I don't know if she's goin' along on the trip or not, but if she is, I claim her, you hear?"

"She's all yours," Fairfax assured him. "All we care about are the wagons and the goods they'll be carrying."

After a few more minutes of ranting about Preacher, Foster left. When he was gone, Schuyler looked at Fairfax and asked, "You really think he can get rid of Preacher for us?"

"He's your friend. You tell me."

Schuyler shrugged. "Merrick's tough, and it don't bother him to shoot somebody in the back or any other way he can. But goin' up against Preacher . . . I just don't know. Lord, when we got that job with Shad Beaumont, I thought we'd be gettin' away from Preacher!"

"So did I. Fate takes some mysterious turns, my friend. But with any luck, Foster will kill Preacher, and we won't have to worry about him any longer. And if he doesn't, well, we haven't lost anything."

Maybe not, Schuyler thought, but that wouldn't

be true of Merrick Foster. Foster stood to lose a lot if he tried to kill Preacher and failed.

Most notably, his life, because in that case, Preacher would sure as hell kill *him*.

Preacher spent the evening at the wagon camp, getting to know Jerome and Corliss Hart and getting a better idea just where it was they wanted to go. Once he knew that, he was better able to figure out which trail would be best for them to follow. He told them some of the obstacles they would face, both natural and in the form of possibly hostile Indians, but the cousins seemed unfazed by the potential for danger. Preacher would do his best to keep them safe, but sooner or later it was likely they'd have to fight. Corliss nodded almost eagerly when Preacher said that, but Jerome looked a mite nervous.

When they were through talking, Preacher said good night to Jake and headed back toward Ford Fargo's tavern. He hadn't given up on finding the two men he was looking for before the wagon train left St. Louis. Since the wagons wouldn't be rolling out until the day after tomorrow, Preacher intended to spend one more day searching the settlement for his quarry. If he didn't find them then . . .

Well, vengeance would just have to wait, he reckoned.

The life he had led since leaving the family farm a little more than two decades earlier had taught him to always be watchful. When a stray cat suddenly dashed out of the black mouth of an alley Preacher was just about to pass, he stopped short, thinking that the cat must have been spooked by something else in that alley. Preacher twisted away from the dark maw of an opening and reached for the butt of the pistol stuck behind his belt.

Before he could grasp the gun, a large, dark shape hurtled out of the alley, mouthing curses, and the gloom of night was split open abruptly by the glare of muzzle flame spurting from the brace of pistols the attacker thrust at Preacher.

Ten

Even as the guns roared, belching flame and lead, Preacher was twisting and falling away. He heard the heavy hum of a pistol ball passing through the air, close beside his ear. He didn't know where the other shot went, but he was sure it hadn't hit him.

He landed on his shoulder and rolled, and as he came up he drew his own pistol and eared back the hammer as he lifted it. The weapon bucked in his hand as he pressed the trigger and its charge of black powder ignited.

Most of the time, Preacher double-shotted his pistol, but since St. Louis was a crowded place and he didn't want to spray lead around where it might strike an innocent person, tonight he had just one ball rammed down the pistol's barrel atop the powder charge. Even as he fired, the man who had ambushed him was already ducking back into the alley. Preacher growled a curse as the varmint vanished without breaking stride. His return shot had missed.

But that didn't mean Preacher was going to let

the bastard get away. He sprang to his feet and dashed after the ambusher, shoving his pistol back behind his belt as he did so. The man had fired both of his pistols, so his guns were empty, too. Preacher wasn't going to take the time to reload when he had a perfectly good knife and tomahawk on him as well.

Of course, the fella could have a rifle or another pistol stashed back in the alley, in which case Preacher might be running right into the face of another shot . . . but the mountain man would rather risk that than take a chance of the man getting away. It had already occurred to Preacher that the ambusher might be one of the two men he had been looking for. He had been hoping that they would come after him.

Then there was the possibility that the second man could be lurking in that alley, too. A savage grin touched Preacher's mouth as that thought crossed his mind. He didn't care how many enemies were waiting for him. Bring 'em on. As long as his cause was just, that was all that mattered.

The running footsteps he heard belonged to only one man, though. The fella was fleeing, rather than staying to put up a fight. Typical of somebody who would strike from hiding like that. Preacher's keen eyes could see almost as well in the dark as those of the stray cat that had run out of the alley to inadvertently warn him. He picked out the shape of the running man up ahead as the varmint dashed through the shadows.

Preacher plucked his tomahawk from behind his belt, paused, and then let fly with the Indian weapon, putting a lot of strength behind the throw. The 'hawk revolved through the air, turning over and over with blinding speed. With a solid, meaty *thunk!* it struck the man who had tried to kill Preacher. With a yell of pain, he went down. A clatter filled the alley, probably from garbage the man had knocked over as he fell.

Preacher ran forward again. The ambusher struggled up to his feet, surprising Preacher a little. The man had a lot of strength and stamina. Most fellas would have stayed down after being hit by a tomahawk like that.

But not this one. He reached behind him, ripped the 'hawk from his back with a gasp, and slashed it through the air at Preacher's head. Preacher had to jerk away from the blow to keep the keen-edged blade from cutting his throat.

Missing with the tomahawk caused the ambusher to stumble a little. Preacher drove in low, tackling him around the waist and bearing him over backward. Both men crashed to the ground. Preacher got his left hand on the man's right wrist, clamping the fingers around it to keep the man from slashing at him with the tomahawk again. With his other hand he reached for the man's throat.

The ambusher threw his arm up to block that move, and then went for Preacher's eyes with his clawed fingers. Preacher pulled his head back. The man's fingernails raked down his cheek.

They rolled over in the dirt and garbage of the alley as they grappled. It was dark as a pit in here, and the man's breath stank as he panted in Preacher's face. To Preacher, it almost seemed more like he was wrestling with a demon than with a man, but he knew his opponent was human. He got confirmation of that when he drove his knee into the man's groin and the man screamed.

The ambusher didn't stop fighting, though. If anything, the agony he had to be in gave him the strength of a madman. He got a hand on Preacher's throat and closed it with crushing force. They rolled again, and Preacher came to a stop with his back pinned against the wall of a building. He had no room to maneuver, and the roaring in his head and the flashing lights behind his eyes told him that he would pass out in a matter of moments. He knew that if he lost consciousness, his attacker would choke the life out of him. He had to take a risk or die.

Preacher let go of the hand that held the tomahawk. Moving with all the speed he could muster, he cupped both of his hands and slapped them against the ambusher's ears as hard as he could. The man cried out again as pain burst inside his ears, filling his head, Preacher hoped.

Grabbing the front of the man's buckskin shirt, Preacher heaved him aside. Preacher heard something fall, and as he scrambled up, he put his hand down for balance and felt the handle of the tomahawk under his fingers. He snatched up the deadly weapon and dove toward his opponent, landing with his knees in the man's midsection as the man writhed in pain on the floor of the alley. Preacher's left hand drove against his chest, holding him down. The tomahawk rose in Preacher's right hand. He didn't hesitate. This son of a bitch had called the tune. Now he could dance to it.

Preacher brought the tomahawk down with devastating force.

The sound of the blade striking home and the

way the man's body jerked violently told Preacher that the blow had found its target. That single spasm was the last move the man made. He lay there limp and motionless as Preacher wrenched the tomahawk free.

A little out of breath from the struggle, Preacher climbed to his feet. It was too dark to see back here, and he wanted to know who he'd been tussling with. He bent down, found one of the man's legs, and dragged the corpse toward the street, where there was a faint glow from lamps and lanterns in nearby buildings.

Preacher stopped and let go of the leg when he reached a spot where he could make out the man's features. The lifeless limb dropped with a thud. Preacher knelt and studied the gory wreckage of the ambusher's face. The tomahawk had hit him between the eyes and cleaved his head wide open. Despite that terrible damage, Preacher recognized Merrick Foster.

He was somewhat surprised that the attacker turned out to be Foster, but not too much. Foster certainly had a grudge against him after their encounter at the Harts' wagon camp earlier that evening. Preacher had thought that the ambusher would turn out to be one of the men he was looking for, but this made sense, too.

And he felt a grim sense of satisfaction that the Indian woman Foster had assaulted and the partners he had left to die had been avenged. If anybody ever deserved such a grisly fate as Foster had received, it was him. He'd had it comin', Preacher thought.

With that, he cleaned the blade of the tomahawk

on Foster's shirt, then rose from his kneeling position and slipped the weapon behind his belt. He left the body where it lay, just inside the alley mouth. St. Louis had a constable, Preacher supposed, and he could have reported the incident to that official, but he had no desire to deal with the law. That was another of civilization's trappings that Preacher had little use for.

Instead, he walked away, heading for Fargo's tavern and a good night's sleep.

When the boardinghouse landlady brought breakfast up to Schuyler Mims and Colin Fairfax the next morning, she could hardly wait to tell her reclusive boarders all about the latest gossip.

"Chopped wide open, his head was," she said with a grin. "The fella that found him said he looked like somebody took an ax to him."

"You're sure it was Merrick Foster?" Fairfax asked, frowning.

"Oh, yeah. The undertaker came and got him, but not before quite a few people saw the body. Lots of folks along the riverfront know Foster." The coarse, middle-aged woman got a cunning look on her face. "Includin' you two. Why, it was just yesterday that Foster come up here to pay you a visit. I'll bet that whoever chopped his head open would like to know about that."

Fairfax's face hardened into a dangerous mask. "You're playing a dangerous game, woman," he snapped as he took a step toward her.

She cringed away, but even as she did so, she reached into a pocket of her apron and brought out a wicked-looking knife. "Come any closer and I'll cut your jewels off," she threatened. "You don't have to worry. I ain't gonna tell nobody that Foster was up here."

"Do you know what we talked about with him?"

The landlady shook her head. "What d'you think I do, lurk around with my ear up against the door?"

"I wouldn't put it past you," Fairfax sneered. "What do you want from us?"

"Just a little extra coin when you leave," the woman said. "Whatever you think is fair. I reckon I can trust you, just like you can trust me."

Schuyler and Fairfax exchanged a glance that showed they didn't trust her at all, but neither man really wanted to go to the trouble of killing her, let alone having to deal with the questions that her death was liable to raise.

"All right," Fairfax said after a moment. "Go ahead and keep your mouth shut, and if you do, there'll be something in it for you."

The landlady smiled, but she didn't put the knife away. "I knew you two were gentlemen," she simpered. "I'll be goin' now."

When the door had closed behind her, Fairfax waited a minute, then jerked the door open again, just to make sure the woman wasn't eavesdropping. He looked back and forth along the corridor and saw that it was empty.

With a sigh, he shut the door and turned to Schuyler. "Foster failed us."

Schuyler nodded. A sad expression played over his face for a second. Foster had been more of an acquaintance than a friend, but even so, Schuyler wouldn't have wished such a horrible fate on him. Or on anybody else, for that matter.

"We knew there was a chance Preacher would get him," Schuyler said. "Poor bastard."

Fairfax snorted in disgust. "We're the poor bastards. Now we have to go through Preacher to take over that wagon train."

"He's only one man. If Beaumont gives us enough men to ambush the wagons, Preacher won't be able to stop us."

"Of course not," Fairfax said, "but it would have been easier without him along." He sighed. "Ah, well, I suppose one can't have everything. Now that Foster's dead, maybe that will lull Preacher's suspicions. Perhaps he won't be expecting any more trouble."

Schuyler said, "I got a feelin' that Preacher's the sort of gent who *always* expects trouble."

Preacher didn't lose any sleep over killing Foster. When he rose the next morning, he set out to spend one final day searching St. Louis for the men who had murdered Abby.

Not surprisingly, he had no luck. Those two bastards had either left town or found themselves a hole and pulled it in after them.

He stopped by Joel Larson's office at the fur trading company, and borrowed a pen and a sheet of paper to write the letter to Jonathan Brant, as he had promised Jake. Then he sealed it and gave it to Larson, who said, "Don't tell me what's in this letter, Preacher. I have a feeling I wouldn't want to know. But I'll see that it's given to Brant in a few days."

"I'm obliged," Preacher said with a nod. He didn't really care if Brant ever found out where Jake had gone, but he had given the boy his word.

When evening came again, he paid another visit to the wagon camp just outside the settlement, to make sure that the Harts and their men would be ready to leave at first light the next morning.

All the preparations for departure had been made, but a new and unexpected problem seemed to have developed. Preacher heard angry voices coming from inside one of the wagons, and when Preacher asked Jake what was going on, the boy grinned and said, "Corliss and Miss Deborah are havin' a spat. A big one, sounds like."

That was true enough. Preacher recognized the raised voices. They belonged to Corliss Hart and Corliss's fiancée, Deborah Morrigan.

Preacher jerked a thumb toward the wagon where Corliss and Deborah were arguing and asked, "What are they squabblin' about?"

"I can answer that," Jerome said as he came up to Preacher and Jake. "Deborah has decided that she wants to come along with us, and my cousin had totally forbidden it." Jerome shook his head sadly. "Corliss doesn't realize that it's unwise to attempt to forbid a woman to do anything she has her mind set on."

"Damn right," Preacher muttered. He didn't have a lot of experience with women, but at least he knew that much.

"How come?" Jake asked.

Preacher looked down at him. "How come what?"

"How come you can't tell a woman what to do? The man's supposed to be the boss, ain't he?"

"Well, yeah, but, uh, a lady's got certain arguments she can use that are hard for a fella to get around."

"What sort of arguments?"

Preacher looked at Jerome, who shook his head as if to say that he wanted no part of this discussion.

"Well, she can cry and suchlike," Preacher said. "Most fellas can't hardly stand to see a woman cry, especially if they cares about her. You didn't like it when your ma cried, did you?"

"I don't hardly remember my ma," Jake said. "And I don't remember her ever cryin'. What else does a woman do when she's arguin'?"

Preacher scratched at his beard. "If she's mad at a fella, she won't . . . uh, she won't let him . . . she don't want to . . . well, be friendly to him, I reckon you'd say."

"I wouldn't want a woman to be my friend. From the sound of it, they're all a mite crazy."

"You feel that way now," Preacher said, "but chances are there'll come a time when you don't."

"No, I'm pretty sure I'll always feel that way," Jake said with confidence.

"We'll see," Preacher said. Corliss and Deborah were climbing out of the wagon now, and he wondered if they had solved anything. From the tense, strained expressions on their faces, Preacher sort of doubted it.

"Ah, there you are, Preacher," Corliss said when he spotted the mountain man. "I was hoping you'd stop by tonight. Please, inform Miss Morrigan that she can't come along with us."

Preacher looked at the young woman and said,

"It can be mighty dangerous out there on the frontier, ma'am."

Deborah pointed at Jake. "You're taking a little boy with you. How dangerous can it be?"

"Hey!" Jake protested. "I can take care of myself."

"It's different where women are concerned, ma'am," Preacher said.

"What about the women who come west with their families to settle?" Deborah countered. "I've heard it said that within a few years, there may be thousands of immigrants heading for the Pacific. That means women and children, too, and they'll be crossing the same plains and mountains that Corliss and Jerome are traveling to now. What about those women?"

In a grim tone, Preacher answered, "I reckon we'll just have to wait and see how that goes. But if it was up to me, I'd say it'd be a whole heap better if all those folks stayed back East."

"But the march of civilization isn't up to you, is it?"

Preacher shook his head. "No, ma'am, it ain't. It sure ain't."

"This argument is pointless," Corliss said. "You're my fiancée, Deborah, and I say you're not going. That's the end of it." He shook his head. "I don't know why you got such a crazy idea in your head to start with. The plan all along has been for you to stay here in St. Louis until Jerome and I have the trading post well established."

"And how long is that going to be?" Deborah demanded.

"That's difficult to say," Corliss replied with a shrug. "A year, maybe two. I can't imagine that it would take any longer than that."

"So it doesn't bother you for us to be apart for that long?" Tears began to roll down her cheeks. "That doesn't bother you in the least?"

"I never said that—!"

Jerome caught Preacher's eye and angled his head away from the arguing couple. Preacher nodded and followed Jerome toward the other side of the camp, putting a hand on Jake's shoulder and taking the boy with him.

"I told you," Jake said with the air of one wise beyond his years. "It just don't pay to have a woman as a friend."

Eleven

Preacher said good-bye to Ford Fargo that night because he intended to gather his gear and take it out to the wagon camp, spending the night there to insure that there would be no delays the next morning.

"What about those two fellas you been lookin' for, Preacher?" Fargo asked as they stood at one end of the bar, lingering over cups of beer.

"I'll find 'em," Preacher said. "I'll settle the score for what they done to Abby and what they tried to do to me. But it'll have to wait a while. Those Hart cousins need a good guide to get them where they're goin'."

"And you're the best there is at things like that," Fargo declared. "Still, I hope the whole bunch of you don't get your hair lifted."

Preacher grinned across the hardwood at the tavern keeper. "You and me both, Ford. I've talked to all the drivers the Harts hired. They're a mite short on frontier experience, but they seem like tough enough fellas, and they'll be willin' to fight

if they have to. They know what they're gettin'
into. And they've got plenty of rifles and powder
and shot. Unless we run smack-dab into some
damn big war party, I reckon we'll be all right."

Fargo lifted his cup and said, "Here's to luck
then."

Preacher hoisted his own cup and responded
with a grin, "We can always use plenty o' that, too."

He left the tavern a few minutes later with his
rifle cradled in one arm, his possibles bag slung
over his shoulder, and his pistols, knife, and tomahawk in their accustomed places behind his belt.
Armed for bear, he was—and for any other trou-
blemakers, too.

The argument between Corliss Hart and Deborah Morrigan was long since over by the time he
got back to the wagon camp, which lay quiet
under the stars in the black, arching summer sky.
Deborah, unhappy with the outcome of the argument, was back in her hotel room, Preacher supposed. One of the sentries confirmed in a
low-voiced conversation that Corliss had taken her
back into the settlement earlier, then returned to
the camp and turned in for the night. Everyone
seemed to be asleep except for the two guards
who had been posted to watch over the wagons.
Preacher heard loud snores coming from several
of the vehicles. He spread his soogans under one
that was quiet and stretched out to get some sleep.
As was his habit, he dropped off quickly. On the
frontier, a man learned to sleep when he could.

Sometime later, far into the night, Preacher
rolled over and was instantly awake. He didn't
know what had disturbed his slumber, but he

trusted his instincts and knew he wouldn't have roused unless there was a reason. Picking up one of the pistols he had placed close beside him, he slid out from under the wagon and got to his feet. He stood there for a long moment, looking and listening.

Nothing unusual seemed to be going on. Preacher had taken off his boot-topped moccasins when he turned in for the night. Now he padded across the camp in his stocking feet. He circled around the dozing oxen and stepped over a wagon tongue. One of the drivers was supposed to be standing guard right in this area. He was the one Preacher had talked to earlier, a tall, wiry-haired man named Gil Robinson. Preacher's eyes narrowed as he realized that he didn't see Robinson anywhere.

Then he spotted a dark shape against one of the big wagon wheels. Preacher's jaw tightened in anger. He stepped over to the wheel and knelt down. His free hand clamped over Robinson's mouth and nose as the man leaned his head back against one of the spokes and snored softly.

Robinson jerked and tried to flail his way up at Preacher's unexpected touch. Preacher dug the barrel of the pistol into the soft flesh of Robinson's neck under his chin. That made Robinson freeze.

"If I was an Indian or a highwayman, you'd be dead right now, mister," Preacher whispered in Robinson's ear. "Because this would be a knife instead of a pistol, and your throat'd be cut from ear to ear."

Preacher eased off the pressure on the gun and took his other hand away from Robinson's mouth and nose. The man gasped for air. After a minute, he managed to say, "I . . . I'm sorry, Preacher. I never meant to go to sleep."

"Most folks don't mean to die from bein' careless neither, but it happens," Preacher said.

"It won't happen again. I swear it." Robinson let out a little groan. "Are you gonna tell Corliss and Jerome? They'll fire me if you do."

"I ought to," Preacher said, "but I reckon I won't since that'd mean they'd have to find another driver to hire, and that would be another delay." Now that he had made up his mind to return to the mountains with the wagon train, Preacher found himself surprisingly eager to get back to the frontier. "I won't say nothin', but you'd damned well better not let your guard down again, Robinson."

"I won't. You can count on that, Preacher."

Preacher straightened to his feet and hauled Robinson up, too. "Stay here while I take a look around," he ordered. "Somethin' woke me up, and I want to make sure nobody came skulkin' around and got up to mischief while you were sleepin'."

"I can come with you—" Robinson began.

"No, do like I said and stay here."

Preacher left the man there and started cat-footing his way around the wagons, stopping often to listen intently and search the darkness with his keen-eyed gaze. He looked into each wagon and saw nothing except the crates and piles of supplies and trade goods stacked in the wagon beds under arching canvas covers. Some of the drivers were asleep in the wagons, and their snoring told Preacher that nothing had disturbed them.

A frown creased his rugged face as he concluded his search. Nothing seemed to be amiss in the camp. There were no intruders, and as far as Preacher could tell, nothing had been messed with or stolen. And yet something had alerted his instincts and tugged him out of a sound sleep.

He wondered if he had somehow known that Robinson had fallen asleep on guard duty. That possibility seemed mighty far-fetched, but Preacher couldn't think of anything else.

Shaking his head, he went back to the wagon he had been sleeping under. He crawled onto his blankets and rolled onto his back to stare up at the bottom of the wagon. The night was quiet and untroubled.

Despite that, it was a long time before Preacher dozed off again.

He was up the next morning by the time the eastern sky had barely begun to turn gray with the approach of dawn. After poking the cook fire back to life, he put the coffeepot on to boil and then went around the camp waking everyone. Jake groaned as he climbed out of a bedroll that he had spread on some boxes in one of the wagons.

"It's awful damn early," the boy said.

"Don't cuss," Preacher told him.

"Why not? You do."

"I'm a man full-growed, not a boy. And when I *was* a boy, I respected my elders and done what they told me to."

"I thought you said you ran away from the farm

where you was raised when you just a couple o' years older'n me."

"Yeah, well, up until then I respected my elders anyway." Preacher gave Jake a little push toward the livestock. "Go tend to them oxen. They're gonna be hitched up and workin' hard pretty soon."

He went back to the fire, and using supplies from the wagons, soon had a big breakfast of flapjacks and bacon cooking. Even in mid-summer like this, the early morning air held a welcome hint of coolness. That, along with the smells of coffee and bacon, invigorated Preacher and made him eager to hit the trail.

Corliss Hart was rubbing sleep out of his eyes as he came stumbling up to the fire a few minutes later. Preacher glanced up at him and said, "If you want to go say so long to that gal o' yours, you'd better go and do it now."

"Miss Morrigan and I said our farewells last night," Corliss replied. A short laugh came from him. "Besides, I wouldn't dare awaken her this early. My life wouldn't be worth a plugged nickel if I did. Deborah can be a real harpy when she wants to."

Jerome came up behind his cousin in time to hear that comment. With a frown, he said, "You shouldn't talk about her that way, Corliss. Deborah's always struck me as a very sweet girl."

Corliss grunted. "You don't know her as well as I do."

"No, of course not, but still—"

Corliss turned back to Preacher, ignoring his

cousin. "How many miles a day do you think we'll be able to travel?"

"With heavy wagons like this . . ." Preacher shrugged. "We'll be doin' good to make eight or ten miles a day. It'll be slow goin'."

"Good Lord, at that pace it'll take us a month or more to reach the mountains!"

"More probably," Preacher agreed, "because some days we'll run into problems and won't be able to move that fast. But don't worry. That'll get us to where we're goin' while the weather is still good, and you'll have a few weeks to get your tradin' post built before it starts to turn bad. Even then, it'll be a month or two before winter really sets in. You ought to be set up in good shape by then."

"But once winter begins . . . ?" Jerome said.

"You won't be goin' anywhere," Preacher replied. "The snow will block the passes, and you wouldn't want to get caught out on the plains in a blizzard anyway. That happened to me a couple o' winters ago. It ain't too pleasant."

"So it will be next spring before we can get back here to St. Louis," Corliss said.

"Yeah. Maybe even early summer, dependin' on how the weather is."

"It really *will* be a long time before I see Deborah again then."

"That's why I said that if you wanted to go say so long—"

Corliss stopped Preacher by shaking his head firmly. "No. We've made our farewells. Seeing her again would just make things worse. She'll be fine, and so will I."

"Suit yourself," Preacher said as he moved bacon around in a big cast-iron frying pan.

The camp was soon filled with the hustle and bustle of preparations as the group made ready to move out. Once the oxen had been given grain and water, they were separated into teams and led out to be hitched to the wagons. The drivers climbed onto the high boxes attached to the front of the vehicles. Using long whips, they got the lumbering beasts to move, and the wagons broke the circle and formed up into a line, one behind the other.

The common practice was for men who drove ox teams like this to walk alongside the massive creatures, lashing them with bullwhips. These bullwhackers, as they were called, could also be counted upon to fill the air with a near-constant stream of colorful profanity. The addition of seats on the wagons so that the bullwhackers could more properly be called drivers was a fairly new innovation. That made it a little easier on the men, although the oxen didn't really have it any better.

Jake climbed to the seat on the lead wagon, where he perched next to Jerome Hart. Jerome looked down at Preacher, who stood beside the vehicle, and asked, "Where are you going to ride?"

"Not on one o' these big ol' wagons, that's for danged sure," Preacher replied. "I figure on bein' out in front. I'll walk it for now, but we're gonna be stoppin' at an Indian village where I left my horse and dog a while back."

"An Injun village?" Jake repeated. "Does that mean we're gonna see Injuns?"

Preacher smiled. "You'll see your fill of 'em before this trip is over, Jake. Once we leave St.

Louis, there's a good chance all the new faces you'll see for the next month or more will be red."

Jake looked excited by that thought, and maybe even a little scared. One thing was sure—before this trip was over, the youngster would experience a lot of things that he had never experienced before.

Preacher could only hope that would be a good thing.

He walked along the line of wagons, checking each one of them. Corliss Hart was handling the team on the second wagon. Gil Robinson was on the driver's seat of the third vehicle. The other teamsters were stocky, sandy-haired Pete Carey, towheaded Swede Lars Neilson, and a scrawny but strong, middle-aged man with a black patch over his left eye, known only as Blackie. He looked sinister, but was actually quite soft-spoken and mild-mannered . . . except when talking to the oxen. Then he could be every bit as loud and profane as the other drivers. Neilson called out to his team in Swedish, so Preacher couldn't understand the words, but from the tone of them he assumed the Scandahoovian was cussin' up a storm.

The sun had barely started to peek over the eastern horizon when Preacher waved the wagons forward. The popping of whips and the yelling of the bullwhackers filled the air. With wheels creaking, the wagons lurched into motion. They rolled forward. Even on foot, Preacher had no trouble staying ahead of them. He strode out some fifty yards in front, calling back over his shoulder to Jerome, "Follow me!"

They headed due west from the settlement,

guided by Preacher's near-infallible sense of direction. He knew that by late that afternoon or early the next day, they would reach the Missouri River, which made a great curve west of St. Louis, arcing up to join with the Mississippi north of the town.

Once they hit the Big Muddy, they would follow the stream across the state of Missouri to the settlements of Independence and Westport, which served as jumping-off points for the Santa Fe Trail. From there, instead of angling southwest toward the Mexican territories, Preacher intended to head northwest. That was the route people were talking about most often when they discussed the seemingly inevitable wave of immigration that was bound to happen soon.

Folks back east wanted to travel overland to the rich Pacific Northwest country, and to do that they would have to follow trails that had been used for the past two decades by mountain men and fur traders. A few missionaries had taken wagons through that way already, making it through the Rockies by way of South Pass, but it remained to be seen whether the big prairie schooners could make such a trip on a regular basis.

If they could, then a trading post established in the vicinity of South Pass could prove quite lucrative. That was where Preacher was aiming for with the Hart expedition. It had been tried before, many years earlier, when a trading post and a tiny settlement called New Hope had sprung up in that area, but illness and Indian troubles had eventually wiped it out. Corliss and Jerome might have better luck now.

The terrain west of St. Louis was flat for the

most part, with only occasional stretches of gently rolling hills. For that reason, the wagons were able to move along at a fairly rapid rate. The oxen would go only so fast, though, no matter how loud the drivers yelled or how often they used their whips. Plodding was in an ox's nature, and there was nothing that could be done about that. Mules would have been faster, but if you used mule teams, you had to take along grain for them. They couldn't survive just by grazing on the grass along the way, as oxen could. It was a trade—a somewhat slower speed in return for more room to carry cargo that could be sold for a profit, instead of grain that would just be eaten by the mules.

Preacher was tireless as he walked in front of the wagons. He called a halt from time to time to let the livestock rest and graze, but mostly they kept moving.

During one of the breaks, Jake commented, "There sure ain't much to see out here, is there? Just grass and a few trees. How far is it to the mountains?"

"We won't be seein' mountains for a long time yet, and if you think there ain't much to see here, wait until we get to the real prairie," Preacher told him. "There ain't even any trees out there."

"But we *will* get to the mountains, won't we?"

Preacher chuckled. "If we keep goin' long enough, we will. They're out there, I can promise you that."

They resumed the journey, pushing on throughout the day as the sun traveled from east to west. It was lowering itself below the western horizon, turning the sky incredible shades of orange and pink and purple, when Preacher dropped back to the lead wagon, pointed to several tendrils of smoke rising ahead of them, and told Jerome and Jake, "That's where we're stoppin' tonight, the village of an old friend o' mine, Red Horse."

"Injuns?" Jake asked, his face lighting up with anticipation.

Preacher nodded and said, "Injuns."

Twelve

The Missouri were a small tribe, numbering no more than five hundred people. Approximately half of them lived in this village and were led by Chief Red Horse. Their lodges were spread out along the southern bank of the Missouri River as it swept past in its big, graceful curve. Dogs ran yapping from the village to greet the visitors, followed by a large group of curious children.

One dog in particular hung back from the pack of mongrels, padding along toward the wagons in deliberate fashion rather than running ahead. Huge, shaggy, and gray, the animal resembled a timber wolf as much as it did a dog. Preacher grinned when he saw the big wolflike cur coming toward him. He whistled, and only then did the dog break into a trot. That trot turned into an eager run after all, and by the time the massive beast reached Preacher, it was moving fast. The dog slowed down at the last minute, reared up, and rested its forepaws on Preacher's shoulders. Its tongue lolled from its mouth in a happy grin.

Preacher buried his fingers in the thick fur behind the dog's ears and wrestled playfully with the animal. As the lead wagon came up beside them, Jake called in a worried voice, "Is that wolf tryin' to eat you, Preacher?"

"He ain't a wolf," Preacher replied. "Just looks a mite like one. This here is Dog. Him and me been trail partners for a long time."

"Is that the only name he has, just Dog?"

"That's enough, ain't it?"

"Yeah, I reckon," Jake said. As Jerome Hart hauled back on the reins and brought the wagon to a halt, the boy clambered down over the tall wheel and dropped to the ground. "Can I pet him?"

Preacher took Dog's paws off his shoulders and lowered the big cur to the ground. "This is Jake," he said to Dog. "He's a friend." To Jake he added, "Stick your hand out so's he can sniff it. Don't do it too fast, though. You don't want to spook any animal, especially Dog."

Jake looked a little nervous as he extended his hand. Dog snuffled around it, then commenced to waving his bushy tail. Jake grinned.

"He likes me!"

"Appears that he does," Preacher said as Dog licked Jake's hand. "Dog's always been a good judge o' character, so I reckon it speaks well o' you that he likes you."

"Uh, Preacher," Jerome said in a worried tone from the wagon seat, "do we need to be concerned about those Indians who are approaching?"

Preacher glanced up and saw a party of warriors striding toward the wagon train, led by the tall, erect figure of their chief, Red Horse. Preacher smiled and told Jerome, "Nope, they ain't hostile. They're good friends o' mine, in fact."

He told Dog to stay by the wagon with Jake, then walked out to meet the welcoming party. With solemn expressions on their faces, he and Red Horse clasped wrists. Then hints of smiles appeared as they pounded each other on the back.

"You have returned to our village, Preacher," Red Horse said, "just as you promised you would."

"Never doubted me, did you?"

"Not hardly," the chief replied, using an expression he had picked up from the mountain man.

"I left my canoe in St. Louis," Preacher went on. "You can pick it up at Ford Fargo's place next time you go down there to trade with the white men and hang on to it for me until I come through this way again. I meant to paddle back up here when I left the settlement, but I wound up comin' with these folks instead." He jerked a thumb over his shoulder at the wagons and the white men perched on the driver's seats.

Red Horse nodded. "Ford Fargo is an honest man. That is fine."

Preacher had had a good spring with his traps, and the load of pelts he'd gathered had been too big for a packhorse. So instead of transporting them that way, he had built the canoe, loaded the furs in it, and paddled down several smaller streams that eventually merged with each other and then the Missouri River.

Dog had traveled with him in the sleek craft, sitting on the pelts, and Preacher's saddle mount, a rangy stallion known only as Horse, had kept pace with him on shore. The two animals were probably the closest friends Preacher had. When he reached the village of Red Horse's people, he had left both Dog and Horse here so that the Indians could care for them while he followed the river on to St. Louis. Even though he'd been gone less than a week, Dog had been glad to see him, and he knew that Horse would be, too.

Corliss jumped down from his wagon and walked forward, past the lead wagon, to join Preacher. The fancy clothes that the man had worn that first day Preacher met him in the cemetery had been replaced by high-topped boots, whipcord trousers, a work shirt, and a leather vest. A broad-brimmed hat was tilted back rakishly on his thick dark hair. He said to Preacher, "Are you sure it's a good idea, making camp here so close to these savages?"

Preacher saw Red Horse stiffen. So did some of the other warriors. Preacher turned to Corliss and snapped, "Most o' these so-called savages you're referrin' to speak our tongue, mister, and they're more civilized than half the folks in St. Louis."

"Civilized?" Corliss repeated. "But they live in those . . . those . . . whatever you call them." He waved a hand toward the lodges of the Missouri.

"Where you live don't have anything to do with how you treat folks. And Red Horse and the Missouri are good friends o' mine." Preacher's eyes narrowed. "You'd do well to remember that."

"All right, all right, I meant no offense," Corliss muttered. "I just don't want anything happening to our trade goods."

"They're a heap safer here than they were when the wagons were parked there on the edge of the settlement. Some Indians like to steal horses from each other, but it's more of a game than outright thievery. They're some o' the most honest folks you'll ever meet."

"Well . . . that's good." Corliss looked at Red Horse. "My apologies, Chief."

From the lead wagon, Jerome called, "Corliss, why don't you get back on your wagon? We need to get them formed in a circle before night falls. Isn't that right, Preacher?"

Preacher didn't think they would be in any real danger here at the Missouri village, but circling the wagons would be good practice, just as it had been back in St. Louis. He lifted a hand over his head, made a revolving motion with it, and called, "Yeah, circle 'em up!"

While Jerome, Corliss, and the hired teamsters were doing that, Preacher motioned Jake over and introduced him to Red Horse. The boy stared up at the chief with wide, awestruck eyes. He didn't say, "Howdy," until Preacher jogged his shoulder to remind him to be polite.

"What's the matter with you, boy?" Preacher asked him. "Ain't you never seen any Indians in St. Louis? I know they come to the settlement to trade sometimes."

"I never seen any this close before," Jake replied. "I was always a mite scared of them. Pa always said—"

Preacher squeezed Jake's shoulder this time to shut him up. He didn't want to hear what Jonathan Brant had had to say about Indians. It would be nothing but ignorant claptrap, and Red Horse and his people had already been insulted once today by Corliss Hart.

"While we're here, some of the young fellas in the village might show you how to shoot a bow and arrow and throw a tomahawk and things like that," Preacher suggested.

Jake's face lit up. "Really?"

"Yeah. Just get your chores done first."

Red Horse told Jake, "My son will come and get you. You will sleep in our lodge tonight."

Jake looked up at Preacher. "You reckon that'll be all right?"

"Sure. Now get back to the wagons and help the fellas get those teams unhitched."

Jake hurried off to tend to the chore. The other warriors returned to the village, leaving Preacher and Red Horse standing there alone. In a low voice and in the tongue of the Missouri, Red Horse said, "I did not expect you to return with people like this, Preacher. They are not like us."

Preacher was gratified that Red Horse treated him as an equal, referring to him as if he were a member of the tribe. That was a sign of high respect among the people of the plains.

"They are not like us," he agreed, "but they are not bad men. They go to the mountains to trade with the human beings who live there, and with the white travelers who will pass through on their way to the great water beyond the mountains."

Red Horse grunted. "They will all lose their hair, even the boy."

"Not if I can help it," Preacher said.

After failing to kill Preacher and steal his load of pelts on the first day the mountain man had come to

St. Louis, Schuyler Mims and Colin Fairfax had sold their horses in order to get money for food and whiskey. The broken-down nags hadn't brought much money, and it hadn't lasted long.

But now that they were flush with the funds Shad Beaumont had advanced them, they bought a couple of better mounts, and Schuyler followed the wagon train when it left that morning, hanging far enough back so that he wouldn't be spotted. Fairfax had given him the spyglass, so he was able to stop from time to time and watch the wagons rolling due west. At midday, Schuyler turned back, convinced that the wagon train wasn't going to deviate from the course that Preacher had set all morning.

When he reached the settlement again, he went straight to the boardinghouse and found Fairfax in the room on the second floor. "They're headed west," he reported.

"For God's sake, we knew that," Fairfax said. "What other direction could they go to reach the mountains?"

Schuyler frowned, crestfallen at his partner's harsh tone. "Well, yeah, sure, but they might've angled off one way or the other. If we get Beaumont's men and set off after 'em right now, we might be able to catch up before nightfall."

"We don't want to catch up to them that soon." Fairfax reached for his beaver hat. "I've been thinking about that very thing. Come on, let's go see Beaumont."

Schuyler looked confused, but he followed Fairfax out of the boardinghouse. He had always trusted Fairfax to do most of the thinking, and didn't see any reason to change that now.

A different but equally dangerous-looking body-guard admitted them to Beaumont's house. He led them to the dining room, where Beaumont was just finishing up what looked like a fine meal. The boss criminal waved them into empty chairs at the table, but didn't offer them anything to eat or drink. Schuyler tried not to lick his lips as he looked at the remains of the meal.

"The Harts' wagon train left town early this morning, just like they planned," Fairfax said. "Schuyler followed them to make sure they didn't try anything tricky, like swinging off on some different route."

"But they didn't, did they?" Beaumont guessed.

"Nope," Schuyler said. "Headed west, straight as an arrow."

Beaumont patted his lips with a napkin. "Now I suppose you need men to go with you when you follow the wagons?"

Fairfax nodded and said, "As many as you can spare. This is going to be a bit of a tough nut to crack. I'm not worried about the Harts, but some of the men working for them appear to be competent. And of course, there's Preacher."

"Yes," Beaumont said with a smile, "there's Preacher. Will twenty men be enough, do you think?"

Schuyler tried not to let the surprise he felt show on his face. With twenty of Beaumont's men, plus him and Fairfax, they would outnumber the men with the wagon train by more than three to one. Even Preacher couldn't win out against odds like that. Schuyler knew Fairfax well enough to see that his partner was impressed, too.

"That should be fine," Fairfax said. "We'll need enough supplies for a fairly lengthy journey."

"It shouldn't take you long to overtake the wagons," Beaumont pointed out. "Men on horseback can move a lot faster than those heavy vehicles, especially when they're being pulled by oxen."

"Yes, but you wanted the goods in those wagons so you could set up your own trading post, right?"

Beaumont nodded. "That's right."

"Then why not let the Harts and their men do the hard work of taking them most of the way?" Fairfax suggested.

Beaumont considered that idea, and slowly he began to nod. Something like respect was visible in his eyes as he said, "That's a good idea, Colin. You can trail them and hit them closer to the mountains. That way you won't have to take the wagons as far once you've gotten rid of the Harts and their companions."

Fairfax smiled, pleased at Beaumont's response.

"When do you want to start?" Beaumont went on.

"Tomorrow morning. It won't hurt anything for the wagons to have a lead on us. We want to stay far enough back so that no one will notice us until it's too late."

"But not so far back that you'll lose the trail."

"Don't worry about that," Fairfax said. "Schuyler here is one of the finest trackers west of the Alleghenies."

That was news to Schuyler, but he kept his face carefully impassive. He supposed he could follow a trail well enough, even if he wasn't the expert that Fairfax made him out to be. Anyway, the men with the wagons weren't trying to cover their tracks. They wouldn't know that they were being followed.

And with any luck, they wouldn't have any idea until it was too late to save their lives.

Jake had a fine time playing with Green Grass, Red Horse's son, during the evening. Meanwhile, Preacher brought Corliss and Jerome to Red Horse's lodge, and the three white men sat by the fire with the Missouri chieftain and smoked a pipe with him. Preacher had explained the tradition to the cousins from Chicago and told them that it would cement their friendship with Red Horse and the tribe he led.

"The more friends you can make out here, the better," Preacher told them.

"It's rather like having a drink in a rich man's drawing room, isn't it?" Jerome said.

Preacher nodded. "I reckon. I've never been in a rich man's drawing room, but it must be sort of the same."

"Except this is a filthy hovel you're talking about," Corliss put in.

Preacher gave him a stern look. "Don't say anything like that while we're in Red Horse's lodge," he warned.

"Of course not. Do you think I'm an idiot?"

Preacher didn't answer that question.

The evening passed without any unpleasant incidents, however. Corliss was on his best behavior, and Jerome hit it off well with Red Horse. Later, when they went back to the wagons, Preacher told the cousins, "You did fine, both of you. Next time either of you come through here, you can stop at the village and be welcomed as friends."

"Should we post guards tonight as usual?" Jerome asked.

Preacher shook his head. "No need. The dogs will raise a ruckus if anybody comes skulkin' around the village who ain't supposed to be here."

Preacher spread his bedroll under one of the wagons, as was his custom, and then checked on Horse before he turned in. He had moved the stallion inside the circle of wagons and picketed him where there was some graze. Horse had a bucket of water, too, courtesy of Jake, who had been suitably impressed by the big, gray, rangy animal. Horse was an ugly varmint, but he had plenty of speed and more stamina than any mount Preacher had ever seen. With only occasional rests, Horse could run all day without faltering.

Preacher fell asleep quickly, as he usually did when he was comfortable with his surroundings. His slumber was deep and dreamless, and when he awoke, it happened instantly, with his eyes opening and all his senses alert. He knew from that reaction that something must have happened to wake him.

Without making a sound, he sat up underneath the wagon and lifted one of his pistols from the ground. Just as he had the night before, he listened intently for any telltale sound. Hearing nothing but the normal, quiet noises of an Indian village at night, he slid out from under the wagon and stood up to look around.

The village was dark and peaceful under the vast, star-filled sky, and so was the wagon camp. Padding along noiselessly in stocking feet, Preacher went all around the wagons, searching for any sign of trouble.

He didn't find a single one.

A troubled frown creased his forehead. The night before, he had put his unease down to the fact that Gil Robinson had been sleeping on guard duty, even though he wasn't fully convinced that was what had awakened him. Tonight, he didn't have even that excuse, since no one was standing guard.

But nothing unusual was going on either. Preacher shook his head in disgust, and went back to the wagon where he had been sleeping. He didn't want to consider the idea that he might be losing his grip, that his years in the wilderness had made him a mite touched in the head, so that he heard things that weren't really there. That was a bad way to be, and Preacher wasn't convinced that was what was going on.

Instead, as he lay there trying to go back to sleep, he told himself to trust his instincts. They had never played him false in the past.

He might not know what it was, but something was wrong here. He was sure of it.

Thirteen

Nothing else happened to disturb Preacher's slumber, but he was still uneasy the next morning anyway. No one else seemed to be, though. Jake had enjoyed the hospitality of Red Horse's lodge and became good friends with Green Grass, and Corliss and Jerome were pleased that the first day of the expedition had gone so well.

But there were a lot more days to come before they reached their destination, Preacher reflected, and a lot more chances for something to go wrong.

It was a little late in the morning before the wagons rolled out. The sun was already up, but it was still an orange ball low on the horizon.

Preacher had saddled up Horse, and now he rode fifty to a hundred yards in front of the lead wagon with Dog trotting along beside him. From the way Horse pranced along, the big stallion was grateful for the chance to stretch his legs again. Preacher ran him a little bit, just to get some of the kinks out. Horse tossed his head, happy to be back on the trail.

The terrain along the river was just as easy as it had been the first day out of St. Louis. The wagons' course wasn't quite as straight as it had been the first day because now they were following the bends of the broad, muddy stream. Preacher could have led the party over some shortcuts, but he didn't see any real need to do so. Better to let the pilgrims get used to following a river. If they were able to do that, it would greatly increase their chances for survival if anything should happen to him. He wasn't indestructible, after all, and accidents happened sometimes.

During one of the times when they stopped to rest the teams and let the oxen graze, Jerome took a new flintlock rifle from one of the wagons and handed it to Jake, along with a powder horn and a shot pouch. Jake accepted the weapon with a glowing smile on his round face.

"Are you sure that's a good idea, giving the kid a gun?" Corliss asked. "He's liable to blow his own foot off, or even shoot one of us!"

"That's why he has to prove to me that he can handle a weapon safely," Jerome said. "Preacher, can you show him how to shoot it?"

Jake said, "I already know how to shoot."

"Let's see you load that rifle then," Preacher suggested.

Because he was short, Jake had a little trouble with the rifle's long barrel and equally long ramrod. But he was able to pour powder from the horn down the barrel, wrap a patch around a heavy lead ball from the shot patch, and shove the ball home with the ramrod, seating it firmly on the powder charge.

Then he pulled back the hammer and put a pinch of powder in the pan.

"All right, it's charged and primed and ready to shoot," Preacher told the youngster. "Don't point it at anybody. See that rock out yonder?" He pointed to a rock that jutted up about a foot from the earth, some twenty yards distant from the wagons. "See if you can hit it."

"I can hit it," Jake declared as he lifted the rifle to his shoulder. The weapon was heavy, and the barrel weaved from side to side as Jake placed his cheek against the smooth wood of the stock and tried to sight in on the rock that was serving as his target. He took a deep breath, and the barrel steadied.

Jake pressed the trigger.

The hammer struck the flint, and the spark set off the powder in the pan, which in turn ignited the charge in the barrel. It went off with a dull roar. The recoil kicked back hard against Jake's shoulder, staggering the boy. Black smoke poured from the muzzle. Jake caught his balance and then waved a hand in front of his face, trying to clear away some of the smoke so that he could see the rock again. He let out a whoop of triumph as he saw what Preacher had already seen.

A white streak on the rock showed where the rifle ball had glanced off it. Jake had hit the target on his first shot.

Jerome saw the evidence of Jake's accuracy, too, and nodded. "All right, I'm convinced," he said. "You can keep the rifle, Jake."

"Thanks, Mr. Hart!"

Corliss shrugged and said, "Well, maybe he won't shoot anybody else . . . if we're lucky."

Beaming with pride, Jake carried the rifle across his knees as he rode on the wagon seat next to Jerome. The wagon train pushed on, still following the Missouri, as it would until they reached the little settlement of Westport, which truly marked the edge of civilization's westward expansion. Heading southwest from there, there were no more towns until the Mexican city of Santa Fe. Heading northwest, there were no real settlements short of the ones along the Pacific coast in the Oregon country, only a few scattered British and American forts established in order to help protect the fur trade.

It was a big, wild country out there. Preacher and men like him called it home, but whether or not it would ever be settled was a question still open for debate. If it was to be settled, trading posts like the one the Hart cousins intended to establish would be the first real step in that direction.

After several days of travel, the Missouri River curved to the northwest and then took a more westerly turn. The members of the party had fallen into a routine by now. The weather had cooperated, and each day the wagons were able to cover a good stretch of ground. As the miles rolled away behind them, the nagging feeling that something was wrong continued to plague Preacher from time to time, even though he had seen no evidence of trouble.

Thinking that someone might be following them, he doubled back on their trail one day, riding more than a mile in the direction they had come from. His keen eyes searched the horizon, and narrowed in suspicion as they spotted a faint haze of dust in the air. Some more wagons, or a good number of riders, were back there several miles behind the wagon train. That didn't have to mean anything; the dust could have come from a hunting party of Indians, or some immigrant wagons, or even a troop of army dragoons on patrol.

But he was going to keep a close eye on the wagon train's back trail. If the followers came too close, he would have Jerome and Corliss and the other men circle the wagons.

Anybody who tried to raid this wagon train would get a hot-lead welcome. Preacher would see to that.

Schuyler hadn't had any trouble following the trail so far. The wagons were so loaded down with cargo that their wheels cut deep ruts in the dirt. Not only that, but it had quickly become obvious that they were following the river.

"We can get ahead of 'em any time we want," he told Fairfax one night while they were gathered with Beaumont's men around a tiny fire that had been built down in a depression so that its glow wouldn't be visible to the people they were stalking. No sense in warning Preacher that somebody was back here.

Fairfax shook his head. "We don't want to get ahead of them, not for a long time yet."

"Yeah, I know. I was just sayin', in case you'd changed your mind—"

"I haven't," Fairfax snapped. "We're sticking to my original plan."

Schuyler nodded, trying not to frown. Fairfax had been pretty sharp with him lately. He had been that way with all of them really. Shad Beaumont had made it clear to his men that Fairfax was in charge, and obviously he liked being in command. He barked orders and strutted around like some sort of military officer. He had even started treating Schuyler that way, forgetting that they had been partners ever since they'd started traveling together. Sure, Schuyler preferred to let Fairfax do most of the thinking, but that didn't mean he liked it when the other man bossed him around.

He wasn't going to say anything about it unless he had to, though. Pulling off this job successfully was more important than protecting his feelings.

Anyway, from what little Fairfax had said about his background during the months they had been partners, he'd never had much luck. Born into a well-to-do family in Philadelphia, Fairfax had clashed with his father and his older brothers, and had eventually been forced to leave the city because of some scandal. Since then he'd led a hardscrabble existence, doing whatever he had to in order to survive. Sort of like Schuyler himself, who had run away from the family farm in Ohio after killing a man during a tavern brawl. Life was just hard all the way around, but now they had a chance to make it better. All they had to do was kill seven or eight men and steal those wagons and the trade goods they were carrying.

"I want to at least be in sight of the mountains before we strike," Fairfax went on. "It might even be better to circle around the wagons and wait for them in the foothills."

"That means we'll be followin' 'em for a month or more," Schuyler said.

Fairfax nodded. "Yes, but we brought plenty of supplies with us."

Schuyler rubbed his angular jaw, frowned worriedly, and said, "That's that much more time we take a chance o' Preacher figurin' out that we're followin' the wagons."

"We'll be careful," Fairfax said in an offhand, unconcerned manner.

Schuyler nodded. Still, the idea of Preacher being ready for them when they finally attacked continued to gnaw at his guts. He was beginning to get a bad feeling about this whole deal.

But it was too late to back out now. Too late to do anything except go ahead and hope that success and a big payoff would be waiting at the end of the trail.

The wagon train reached Westport and laid over there for a day to give the livestock a chance to rest up after the haul from St. Louis. Preacher explained to Corliss and Jerome that they would make several more stops like that during the journey. It was better to spend an occasional day resting than to have the oxen start to break down.

Westport wasn't very big, but there were a couple of well-stocked stores. This was the jumping-off point for the trading caravans that headed down to Santa Fe, so a lot of wagon traffic passed through here. A few miles north, the settlement of Independence was also becoming an important departure point. Preacher knew one of the merchants in Westport, though, and was able to get a good deal for the cousins on the supplies they needed to replenish before striking out into the wilderness. If you ran out of flour or bacon halfway across the plains, you were out of luck. There was no place to buy any more.

Westport was also the last place men could stock up on whiskey and enjoy a little female companionship. The Harts' drivers all wanted to visit the local saloons and whorehouses. Preacher told them to go ahead. He would stay and watch over the wagons, along with Jake.

As for Corliss and Jerome, Preacher didn't know if they were interested in drinking and whoring. Corliss was engaged to Deborah Morrigan, of course, but that didn't stop some men from carrying on with other women while they were away from their betrothed.

Corliss climbed into his wagon to sleep, though, and Jerome joined Preacher and Jake. "This is really it, isn't it?" he said as he sat down on a wagon tongue. "The edge of civilization?"

"Yep," Preacher agreed. "From here on, it's all frontier."

Jerome stared off into the darkness to the west. "This seemed like such a good idea back in Chicago. It was going to make us rich men. Now I'm not so sure we should have come out here. There are so many dangers . . ."

"You plan on gettin' up tomorrow mornin'?" Preacher asked.

"What?" Jerome shook his head in confusion. "Of course I plan on getting up."

"Then you're already runnin' one hell of a risk, because you don't know you'll still be alive in the mornin'. You don't even know the sun'll rise, or goeth down in the evenin', like it says in the Good Book."

"In Ecclesiastes," Jerome said with a chuckle, "also known as the Book of the Preacher."

"Smart fella, ol' Ecclesiastes."

"I take your point, Preacher. We take it on faith that the earth abideth forever. So we might as well have faith that our efforts will be rewarded, too."

Jake yawned. "Grown-ups sure do like to talk a lot. I think I'm gonna turn in."

"Good night, Jake," Jerome said. When the boy was gone, he took out his pipe, packed tobacco in it, and smoked for a while as he and Preacher talked quietly about their route for the rest of the journey. Preacher had made sure that both Jerome and Corliss studied the maps they had before they ever left St. Louis, and he wanted them to keep the trail fresh in their minds. After a half hour or so, Jerome went to his wagon to sleep, too, leaving Preacher alone.

Which he didn't mind at all. He had always been a solitary sort of gent, happy when he was around other people but happy with his own company, too.

He was sitting on the ground with his back leaned against a wagon wheel when he saw someone climb stealthily out of one of the other vehicles.

Preacher drew in a deep breath, but otherwise gave no sign of what he had just seen. That wagon was the one Pete Carey drove, and Carey was off carousing in the taverns and brothels of Westport. Jake, Jerome, and Corliss were all asleep in other wagons, or at least they were supposed to be. The mysterious figure who had just emerged from Carey's wagon was too tall to be Jake anyway, and not big enough to be Corliss Hart.

That left Jerome, but Preacher had watched with

his own eyes as Jerome climbed into the lead wagon a short time earlier. He supposed Jerome could have slipped out the other side of the vehicle, snuck over to Carey's wagon, and crawled inside, but for the life of him, Preacher couldn't think of any reason Jerome would do a thing like that.

Silently, Preacher came to his feet as the shadowy figure moved away from the wagon. The starlight revealed that whoever it was wore the same sort of rough work clothes as the teamsters, as well as a dark felt hat with a large, round brim.

Without making a sound, Preacher followed the figure as it went to one of the other wagons and stopped beside a water barrel lashed to the side of the vehicle. The intruder took something that had been slung around his neck on a strap and held it to the barrel. A water skin, Preacher decided. The son of a bitch was stealing water.

That wasn't as terrible a crime where they were headed as it was in some of the more arid parts of the country. A lot of streams, some small and some large, would be crossing their trail, so they would have plenty of opportunities to refill the water barrels as they went along.

But that didn't matter to Preacher. Stealin' was stealin', and anyway, whoever this was had no right to be here, clambering in and out of wagons that belonged to the Hart cousins. Preacher wondered if the interloper had been hiding out in Carey's wagon all along. Maybe the fella only came out at night, and that was what had roused Preacher from sleep on several occasions, causing him to have those uneasy feelings. It made as much sense as any other answer.

The answer Preacher wanted now was the identity of the skulker. He moved closer, still as silent on his feet as the Indians who were his friends and sometime enemies, and by the time the intruder finished filling the water skin and turned away from the barrel, Preacher was only a couple of feet away. His hands rested on the butts of his pistols, and he drew them from behind his belt and drew back the hammers as he raised them.

"Don't move or I'll blow holes in you," he grated.

The intruder dropped the water skin and cried out in surprise at the sight of Preacher and that menacing brace of pistols, then cringed back against the wagon. With a low moan, the figure crumpled to the ground in what appeared to be a dead faint.

And Preacher was left standing there with a shocked look on his face, as he realized that the voice he had heard cry out belonged to a woman.

Fourteen

It took a lot to throw Preacher for a loop. But he was well and truly surprised as he stood there looking down at the woman who had fainted. The broad-brimmed hat had fallen off her head when she collapsed, and the thick dark hair that had been tucked up inside it had spilled out, forming an ebony pool around her face as she lay on her back.

"Son of a bitch," Preacher muttered under his breath. He realized he still had his thumbs looped over the hammers of his pistols. He uncocked them and lowered the guns with care, then tucked the weapons behind his belt again. Dropping to a knee beside the woman, he started to put a hand on her shoulder so he could try to shake her back to consciousness, but then he hesitated. It wouldn't hardly be proper to touch a woman when he didn't even know who she was.

But he had a pretty good idea, he thought, and practicality trumped chivalry. He took hold of her shoulder, gave it a good shake, and said in a low voice, "Wake up, Miss Morrigan. Best wake up now."

Deborah Morrigan moaned again and tried to lift her head. Her eyes fluttered open, and as she saw Preacher's dark shape looming over her, a short, sharp cry of fear came from her lips. He clamped his other hand over her mouth, abruptly silencing the sound.

Deborah tried to struggle against him, but his firm grip on her shoulder pinned her to the ground. Leaning closer to her, Preacher hissed, "Settle down, blast it! I ain't gonna hurt you. I just don't want you raisin' a big ruckus before I find out what in blazes is goin' on here."

Deborah's attempts to free herself subsided. Preacher went on. "If I take my hand away from your mouth, are you gonna scream or anything foolish like that?"

She shook her head.

"All right. I'm gonna take your word for it." Preacher lifted his hand from her mouth.

Deborah drew in a quick, sharp breath, and for a second Preacher thought she was about to yell. Instead, she said in a quiet voice, "Will you help me up?"

Preacher got to his feet, grasped her hands, and lifted her with ease, even though she wasn't what he would call skinny. She was a woman with a bit of heft to her, which just made her even more attractive. He was uncomfortably aware of how the tight trousers she wore molded the curves of her hips and thighs.

"I suppose you wonder what I'm doing here," she said.

"Nope," Preacher replied. "You're showin' Corliss

Hart that just because you're engaged to marry him, that don't mean he can tell you what to do, and he sure can't forbid you from doin' something you want to do."

"Well, that's not all of it, of course. I really don't want to be separated from him for a year or more."

"So you figured you'd just come along no matter what anybody said." Preacher's voice was grim. "You been hidin' in Pete Carey's wagon all along, ever since we left St. Louis, and sneakin' out at night to get some air, and maybe some food and water."

"There's food in the wagon," Deborah said. "I brought my own supplies. And I have a water skin with me and I've been making it last. But tonight I drank the last of the water and had to refill it." She sighed. "I thought everyone was asleep. I overheard you earlier telling Corliss and Jerome that it wouldn't be necessary to post any guards tonight, so I thought it would be safe to come out and stretch my legs for a while."

"What I want to know is how you managed to hide from Carey." Preacher paused as realization dawned on him. "You *didn't* hide from Carey, did you. He's known all along you were ridin' in his wagon. He must have."

Deborah nodded. "He knew. But please don't be angry with him. I begged him to help me."

And Pete Carey, like most fellas, had never learned how to say no when some good-lookin' female came to him begging for help, Preacher reckoned.

"Come on," he said, his voice gruff.

Deborah hung back. "What are you going to do?"

"Let the fella who's gonna be your husband decide what in blazes to do with you," Preacher snapped.

"No! You can't tell Corliss!"

"He had to find out sooner or later, didn't he?"

"Yes, but . . . but we're still too close to St. Louis!" A note of panic came into Deborah's voice. "He's liable to send me back!"

That sounded like a good idea to Preacher, but it wasn't his decision to make.

When Deborah still hesitated, he said, "Don't make me drag you over there, ma'am."

"You wouldn't dare!"

"I reckon it'd be better if we didn't find out what I'll dare and what I won't."

"Oh, all right." She sighed. "I suppose I might as well face up to this."

"Always best to meet trouble head-on," he told her.

They crossed to the other side of the circle, where Corliss's wagon was parked. Preacher rapped his knuckles against the sideboards and called in a low voice, "Hart! Wake up."

A moment later, muttering groggily, Corliss stuck his head out through the canvas flaps at the rear of the wagon. He leaned over the tailgate and said, "Preacher? What the hell's going on? Is there trouble?" His sleep-blurred gaze landed on Deborah. "Who's that with you? It looks like— *My God! Deborah!*"

Corliss's startled shout did away with any chance of settling this problem without rousing the whole camp. He scrambled over the tailgate and dropped to the ground. Grabbing Deborah by the shoulders, he demanded, "What in heaven's name are you *doing* here? Why are you dressed like that?"

"Please, Corliss," she said in a strained voice. "You're hurting me."

Corliss let go of her and took a step back. Even in the faint light from the stars and the low-rising moon, Preacher could see that his eyes were wide with shock.

"What's going on out there?" Jerome called from the next wagon. "Corliss? Preacher? What's wrong?"

"You'd better get out here, Jerome," Corliss replied. "We've got a problem."

Jake had been sleeping under Jerome's wagon, but the commotion had awakened him, too. He crawled out as Jerome climbed down, and together they came over to the little group beside Corliss's wagon.

"Miss Morrigan?" Jerome exclaimed when he saw Deborah. Jake just let out a whistle of surprise.

"My goodness," Deborah said. "You all act like you've never seen a woman before."

"I certainly didn't expect to see *you* here, Miss Morrigan," Jerome said. "How in the world did you get here?"

"She's been travelin' with us all along, ever since we left St. Louis," Preacher explained. "Hidin' out in Pete Carey's wagon."

"Carey!" Corliss said. "I'll thrash him!"

"You'll do nothing of the sort," Deborah said as her chin tilted in defiance. "He's been very helpful to me, and he's conducted himself like a perfect gentleman. You have no reason to be angry with him."

Jerome said, "Other than the fact that he knew you weren't supposed to be here, and yet he brought you along anyway and helped you hide from the rest of us."

Deborah shrugged.

"Don't worry about Carey right now," Preacher suggested. "What're you gonna do about the lady here?"

"Send her back to St. Louis, of course," Corliss snapped. "The frontier is no place for a woman. You said so yourself, Preacher."

So he had, but Preacher had been thinking the situation over, and he realized now that the problem was even worse than his first impression of it had been. The solution wasn't as simple as Corliss made it sound.

"Just how do we go about doin' that?" he asked.

"Doing what?"

"Sendin' Miss Morrigan back to St. Louis."

"Well, we just—" Corliss stopped short and frowned. "I suppose we could . . . surely there must be some way . . ."

"Wait just a moment," Jerome said. Obviously, he had been thinking about the problem, too. "We don't have any extra men. Everyone except Preacher is needed to drive the wagons, and we have to rely on Preacher to scout out our route and guide us."

Preacher nodded. "That's right. You can't spare a man to go back with Miss Morrigan, and you sure can't make her start out across Missouri on her own."

Corliss was thinking hard, trying to come up with an answer. "Maybe we can hire somebody here in Westport to accompany her," he suggested.

"You'd trust one of these frontiersmen to escort your fiancée all the way back to St. Louis?" Jerome protested.

"I won't go," Deborah said.

The men ignored her. Corliss said to his cousin, "No, I suppose that wouldn't be a very good idea. Maybe she could stay here in Westport instead of waiting for me in St. Louis."

It was Preacher's turn to shake his head. "Westport may be a settlement, but it's still a mighty rough place. No place for a gal by herself unless she's plannin' on goin' to work in one of the houses."

"I beg your pardon!" Deborah burst out. "How dare you make such an insinuation!"

"I ain't insinuatin' nothin'," Preacher said. "I'm just sayin' it wouldn't be a good idea to leave you here by yourself for the next year or so."

Jerome shook his head. "We have no choice. We'll all just have to turn around and take the wagon train back to St. Louis. Then we can start west again."

"But that means we will have wasted two weeks!" Corliss said.

"Do you have a better idea?" his cousin shot back.

Corliss didn't say anything, but Preacher did. He could hardly believe the words were coming out of his mouth as he said, "Take her with us."

Corliss, Jerome, and Jake all turned to stare at him. So did Deborah, for that matter. They all seemed to be struck speechless.

Finally, Corliss said, "Take her with us? Preacher, have you gone mad? We all agreed back in St. Louis that the frontier was no place for a woman, especially not for one as pampered and helpless as Deborah!"

"I can take of myself!" she said. "Haven't I proven it by making it this far without being discovered?"

"You've been discovered now," Jerome said. "That changes everything."

Preacher scratched at his bearded jaw and said, "I ain't so sure about that."

They all stared at him again. He went on. "Think about it for a spell. Miss Morrigan spent nearly a week ridin' in that wagon, hidin' out so that we didn't find out about her, and that couldn't have been easy."

Deborah sniffed. "I should say it wasn't easy. I made myself a hiding place in the middle of the cargo, stacking the crates around me so that no one could see me. It was cramped and hot and . . . and miserable. Delicacy forbids me from telling you just *how* miserable it was at times. But I persevered."

"Just because you're stubborn doesn't mean it's all right for you to go to the mountains with us," Corliss said.

Preacher said, "Sometimes pure mule-headedness is the only thing that keeps folks alive out on the frontier."

Jerome shook his head. "I don't understand you, Preacher. You were dead set against Miss Morrigan coming along with us, and now you seem to think it's a good idea."

"Don't get me wrong," Preacher said, giving Deborah a hard stare. "It'd be a whole heap better if the lady was back yonder in St. Louis where she's supposed to be. But if we can't leave her here and we can't send her back, maybe lettin' her come would be a better idea than turnin' the whole wagon train around."

"That's our decision to make, not yours," Jerome snapped. "I don't want to put her life in danger."

"Why, Jerome," Deborah said. "How sweet of you."

"He's not sweet," Corliss said. "He's a fool. Every week we delay gives someone else a chance to get to the mountains before us and establish a trading post in the same location we want."

Jerome stared at him. "You'd put business over your own fiancée's life?"

"I didn't say that." Corliss made a growling noise in his throat, shook his head, and threw up his hands. "You've all got me half-crazy here! I don't know what to do!"

"Let me come with you," Deborah suggested calmly.

"Well . . . it might work out," Jerome said with grudging reluctance. "If Preacher thinks that might be best . . ."

"I suppose we could give it a try," Corliss allowed.

Preacher shook his head. "There won't be any givin' it a try. Miss Morrigan either comes along, or she stays here and takes her chances. Once we get farther west, there sure won't be any turnin' back."

"I still have reservations," Jerome said. "But if you think that's what we should do, Preacher, and if Corliss agrees . . . then I say we let Miss Morrigan accompany us."

"All right, fine," Corliss said. "She can come."

Deborah's eyes sparked with anger. "You could at least act like you're happy to see me."

"I could," Corliss said with a nod, "but I'd really rather you were back in St. Louis."

Deborah lifted her chin again and turned away from him, sniffing, clearly put out by his reaction.

"You can continue sleeping in Carey's wagon," Jerome said, "but we'll rearrange the cargo and make a better place for you, since you don't have to hide anymore."

"Thank you, Jerome," she said. "I know you don't really want me here either, but at least you're considerate."

Deborah and the cousins walked off toward Pete Carey's wagon. Preacher and Jake watched them go, and after a moment the youngster said, "This is just the start o' more trouble, ain't it?"

"More'n likely," Preacher said with a nod. "More . . . than . . . likely."

Fifteen

When Pete Carey came dragging in from his night of carousing in Westport and found out that his part in Deborah's deception had been discovered, he apologized to Corliss and Jerome up one way and down the other.

"Just be glad we need you to drive one of the wagons," Corliss told him in a cold, angry voice. "Otherwise, you'd be looking for a job right about now, Carey."

The chunky, sandy-haired teamster shook his head ruefully and said, "I knew better, I really did. But when Miss Morrigan looked at me like that, and her bottom lip started to tremble just a mite when she said she really needed my help, I . . . I just couldn't stop myself from goin' along with what she wanted."

Now that Deborah's presence was no longer a secret, she rode openly on the seat of the second wagon the next day, next to Corliss. The Missouri River took a sharp northwestward turn here, but as the wagon train rolled out of Westport, Preacher led them almost due west again, along the southern bank of a stream he told the others was known as the Kansas River. The Kansas, which flowed into the Missouri, was smaller than the Big Muddy.

"We'll follow this one a ways, then cross it at a good ford I know and head north to the Platte," Preacher explained. "That'll lead us the rest of the way to South Pass."

"And that's where we'll set up our trading post?" Jerome asked.

Preacher nodded. "That's up to you, o' course. I'm no storekeeper, so it don't matter none to me. But it's a good place. If the immigrant wagons really do start rollin' to the Oregon country like folks say they will before long, they'll have to travel right through there. Time they get that far, they'll need to stock up on supplies, too. There's a tradin' post at Fort Laramie, but it's a mighty long haul from there over the mountains to Fort Hall. Your place will be right about in the middle o' that stretch."

"Sounds good to me," Jerome said, and Corliss nodded his agreement. Corliss had been unusually quiet since Deborah's discovery the night before, as if he were holding in his opinions because he didn't want to start another argument. And he was probably feeling a mite humiliated that his fiancée had gone directly against his wishes—and gotten away with it.

That night, Deborah joined the men around the fire. As Preacher hunkered on his heels and ate salt pork and beans, washed down with coffee, he didn't look directly into the flames because that was the fastest way to ruin a man's night vision. Instead, he glanced at the faces of the other men, and saw the way Gil Robinson and Lars Neilson watched Deborah without appearing to do so.

She was a pretty woman, so naturally the men were interested in her. One might have thought that Robinson and Neilson might have gotten their fill of whores back in Westport, but when it came to women, most men could never get enough.

Even though the two teamsters were trying to be careful, Corliss noticed the way they were looking at Deborah. The frank admiration in their eyes bordered on outright lust. Corliss put his coffee cup down, frowned, and said, "All right, Deborah, go get in the wagon."

"What?" She looked and sounded genuinely surprised. "Why should I do that, Corliss?"

"Because I don't like the way these two are staring at you," he snapped as he nodded toward Robinson and the big Swede.

"We're not looking at anybody," Robinson said, a defensive tone in his voice. "And we didn't mean any offense."

"Well, you've offended Miss Morrigan," Corliss said.

Deborah shook her head. "No, they haven't, Corliss. I'm fine."

"Don't argue with me. You didn't see the way they were staring."

Robinson got to his feet. "Keep your seat, ma'am," he said to Deborah. "Lars and I will go on over to the other side of the wagons. Come on, Lars."

Neilson stood up, too, but Corliss wouldn't let them walk off. "You're not going anywhere until you've apologized to Miss Morrigan."

Deborah caught at his sleeve. "Really, Corliss,

that's not necessary. Even if Mr. Robinson and Mr. Neilson *were* looking at me, I'm not insulted or offended. There's no need for an apology—"

He pulled away from her. "And I say there is."

Robinson's jaw was tight with anger, but he swallowed and said, "Sorry." The single word came out brusque and hard and not the least bit sincere.

Corliss shook his head. "Not good enough. You didn't mean it."

"I said I was sorry. That's all I'm sayin'."

"If you care about your job—" Corliss began.

Jerome stopped him. "That's enough, Corliss," he told his cousin. "Gil apologized, and Deborah's not upset. Now stop aggravating the situation."

Corliss swung toward Jerome. "Oh, it's Deborah now, is it? Are *you* going to get too familiar with her, too, Jerome?"

"Oh, stop being so blasted touchy. There's no need for this."

On the other side of the fire, Jake glanced up at Preacher and asked in a low voice, "Is there gonna be a fight?"

"Don't know," Preacher said with a shake of his head. "As long as they don't kill each other and can still handle those oxen in the mornin', it ain't any o' my business."

That was really the way he felt, too. Deborah's presence with the wagon train had practically insured that there would be trouble sooner or later. One woman and six or seven men was a recipe for disaster, especially when she was spoken for by one of the men. But they would have to sort that out on their own, Preacher thought, because he wasn't getting involved.

Robinson said again, "Come on, Lars. I ain't hungry no more."

Corliss took a quick step toward him and reached out to grab his shoulder. "Damn it, I'm not through with you!"

Preacher could have told Corliss that wasn't a good idea. He didn't have a very high opinion of Gil Robinson—the man had fallen asleep on guard duty, after all, and was slow to do any more than he absolutely had to when it came to work—but just about anybody would react badly to being manhandled like that. Robinson was no exception.

He whirled around, moving fast enough so that Corliss was taken by surprise. Robinson's bony fist lashed out and cracked against Corliss's jaw. That knocked Corliss's grip loose and sent him stumbling backward. He looked like he was about to trip and fall over into the fire when Jerome leaped up and caught him.

"For God's sake, Corliss!" Jerome said as he steadied his cousin. "What do you think you're doing?"

"Fighting for the honor of the woman I love!" Corliss rasped as he pulled free from Jerome. With an angry shout, he launched himself at Robinson, tackling the teamster around the waist.

They both went down. Corliss began slugging at Robinson as they sprawled on the ground. Robinson tried to cover up, but Corliss pounded a couple of blows into his face. City-bred or not, Corliss Hart was no weakling, and clearly he knew something about fighting.

But before he could continue the battle with Robinson, he was grabbed from behind by Neilson.

The big Swede lifted Corliss into the air. Corliss yelled and flailed, but to no avail. Neilson got his brawny arms around him in a bear hug and called to Robinson, "I ban got him, Gil!"

"Hang on to him," Robinson rasped as he pushed himself to his feet and closed in on Corliss, who was held helpless in Neilson's arms. Robinson's fists clenched. From the savage look on his face, he intended to give Corliss a beating while Neilson held him.

Jerome threw a wild-eyed look at Preacher and asked, "Aren't you going to *do* something?"

"This ain't my fight," Preacher said with a shake of his head.

Deborah didn't wait for anyone to do anything. She took matters into her own hands by running up behind Neilson and pounding her small fists against his back. "Let go of him, you brute!" she shouted.

Neilson ignored her, as if he didn't even feel her blows against his broad, muscular back. Maybe he didn't, Preacher thought.

"Hold him still," Robinson snarled at the Swede as he closed in on Corliss, who continued his futile writhing in Neilson's grasp. Suddenly, Robinson slammed a punch into Corliss's belly. Corliss gasped in pain and stopped struggling as he turned gray in the firelight.

"By God, that's enough!" Jerome said. "Deborah, get out of the way!"

Then with a yell, he charged across the intervening ground, leaped into the air, and landed on Neilson's back. He wrapped his legs around the Swede's waist and one arm around his neck. With his other hand he started hammering punches against the side of Neilson's head.

"This is the best fight I ever seen," Jake said as he stared raptly at the knot of struggling men.

It looked pretty damned ridiculous to Preacher, but he supposed it was possible one of the men might accidentally hurt himself or somebody else. He started giving some thought to putting a stop to the fracas, but he wasn't going to get in any hurry about it. They would still be out here on the prairie for a long time, and it would be better to go ahead and clear the air now. Otherwise, Deborah's presence would be like a festering sore all the way to the mountains. If Corliss was going to stake his claim to her and make it stick, he needed to do it now. That was the only way the other men would respect him—and her.

Corliss's arms were pinned to his sides by Neilson's bear hug, but his legs were still free. He jerked one booted foot up and drove it forward in a kick that sank into Robinson's midsection. Robinson doubled over and staggered back.

Meanwhile, Jerome stopped punching Neilson in the head, which was having about as much effect as hitting a block of wood, and grabbed one of the Swede's ears instead. He hung on tight and twisted it as hard as he could.

Neilson bellowed in pain, and let go of Corliss to reach up and swat and claw at Jerome, who was still viciously twisting his ear. Neilson got hold of the smaller man's shirt. The muscles in his arms and shoulders bunched as he hauled upward and bent forward. Jerome let out a startled shout as he found himself flying over Neilson's head and somersaulting toward the ground.

Corliss rushed Robinson while the man was off balance. His arms pistoned forward as he threw a flurry of punches. Several of the blows landed cleanly, jerking Robinson's head from side to side and rocking him back even more. Corliss swung a long, looping right that caught Robinson on the chin and sent him flying through the air.

Corliss didn't have time to feel any triumph, because now that Neilson was free of the annoyance that was Jerome, he rushed at Corliss's back, sledgehammer fists raised. However, he had to charge right past Jerome, who had crashed to the ground on his back so hard that all the breath was knocked out of his slender body.

Despite being half-stunned, Jerome had enough of his wits about him to realize that Neilson was going after Corliss again. He reached out, grabbed hold of one of the Swede's legs, and hung on tight, forcing Neilson to curse in Swedish and drag him along. Neilson tried to kick himself free of Jerome's grip.

The distraction provided by Jerome gave Corliss enough time to reach into the back of one of the wagons and grab an ax handle from a stack of them bound for the trading post. He swung the makeshift club at Neilson's head and bounced it off the Swede's skull. Neilson was tough enough to take a lot of punishment, but being clouted by an ax handle like that fazed even him. His fists dropped and he stood there for a few seconds, shaking his head groggily, before Jerome finally succeeded in jerking his feet out from under him. Neilson crashed to the ground like a falling redwood. Jerome clambered upright.

"Holy cow!" Jake said. "Mr. Hart and Mr. Hart *won!*"

It was true. Corliss and Jerome were both still on their feet, while Robinson and Neilson lay stunned on the ground with all the fight knocked out of them. Preacher hadn't really been expecting that outcome either, but he was glad to see that things had worked out that way.

He looked over at Pete Carey and Blackie, saying, "You boys got any stake in this fight?"

Both men shook their head. "No, sir," Blackie said. "That was all their lookout."

"Yeah," Carey agreed. "Gil and Lars ain't bad fellas, but they was out of line, I reckon. Of course, so was Mr. Hart. Seems like everything's pretty much square to me."

Deborah hurried over to Corliss, who stood there bruised and disheveled, with his chest heaving as he tried to catch his breath. "Oh, my God!" she said as she clutched at his arms. "Are you all right, Corliss?"

"I'm . . . fine," he managed to say. He looked over at Jerome, who was also some the worse for wear. "Thanks for . . . giving me a hand."

"I couldn't let them . . . gang up on you like that," Jerome responded. "It wasn't . . . fair."

"Yeah, but you're no fighter. You're lucky they didn't kill you."

Jerome summoned up a grin. "I guess I'm . . . tougher than you thought I was."

Preacher stood up and leaned on his long-barreled flintlock rifle. "Before you boys go to congratulatin' yourselves too much," he said, "you best remember that you still need Robinson and Neilson to drive a couple o' those wagons."

Jerome nodded as if he understood what Preacher was talking about. "Yes, you're right," he said. "We need to mend some fences now."

He stepped over to Neilson, who was starting to get his wits back about him, even after that wallop from the ax handle. As the Swede sat up and shook his head, Jerome extended a hand to him and said, "That was a good fight, Lars. Let me help you up."

Neilson blinked and stared at Jerome's hand for a second before a grin appeared on his face. "Yah, good fight," he agreed. He took Jerome's hand, his massive paw practically swallowing up the smaller man's fingers. The scene reminded Preacher of a bear being helped to its feet by a badger.

Corliss didn't look happy about it, but he went over to Robinson and hauled the man upright. As Robinson tried to shake the cobwebs out of his head, Corliss said, "No hard feelings, Gil?"

"No . . . No, I reckon not," Robinson said.

Sternly, Corliss added, "But you'll have to treat Miss Morrigan with respect from now on. Keep a civil tongue in your head, and don't stare at her."

"Sure," Robinson muttered with a nod. Eyes downcast, he faced Deborah and went on. "I'm mighty sorry, ma'am."

"That's all right," she told him. "I accept your apology. Now, why don't we all sit down and continue our supper?"

That sounded like a good idea to Preacher. Everyone took their seats around the fire, and while there was still a bit of tension in the air, it wasn't like before. Robinson and the big Swede wouldn't cause any more trouble. In some cases, nothing cemented the bond between men like a good knock-down, drag-out brawl, and Preacher hoped that was what had happened here.

He told Carey and Neilson to stand the first watch. Everyone else turned in, except for Preacher himself. He prowled out onto the prairie near the wagons and stood there for several minutes, watching and listening. No suspicious sounds came to him on the warm night breeze. For a long time he looked back in the direction they had come from, searching for a tiny pinpoint of light that would mean someone was behind them. He saw nothing but darkness.

But that didn't mean no one was following them. Anyone dogging their trail might be smart enough to have a cold camp, or at least keep the fire small and hidden somehow. Preacher's nerves were still on edge, and he couldn't blame that feeling on Deborah Morrigan anymore, even though he wasn't sure that her presence wouldn't cause more trouble before the journey was over.

With the night so quiet and peaceful, though, there was nothing he could do except return to camp and try to get a little shut-eye himself.

Tomorrow would be another long day, and there was no telling what challenges and dangers it would hold.

Sixteen

As it turned out, the next day went quite well. The wagons forded the Kansas River without a hitch and angled northwestward, soon picking up an even smaller stream that was a tributary of the Kansas. They would follow it almost all the way to the Platte, Preacher told the others.

One day turned into the next, and the miles continued to unspool beneath the wagon wheels. Gil Robinson and Lars Neilson were a little sullen for a few days, but they got over it. The Swede was soon his usual smiling self again. And as for Robinson, he had never been that friendly, even before the fight with Corliss. But he handled his team well enough and pitched in around the camps as much as he ever had.

One day while the wagon train was stopped at noon, Deborah decided that she wanted to learn how to shoot a rifle. Corliss laughed at the idea, but Deborah frowned and said, "No, I mean it. I think I ought to learn how to do that."

"That ain't a bad idea," Preacher put in. "We're

already a long way from civilization and gettin' farther away every day. Might come a time when Miss Morrigan knowin' how to handle a rifle would come in mighty handy."

"Well, all right, if both of you insist," Corliss said. He got his flintlock from the wagon and brought it over to Deborah. He thrust the weapon at her, and she took it.

"Oh, my," she said as she felt how heavy it was. Her arms sagged a little before she was able to tighten her muscles. "Do I really have to lift it all the way to my shoulder?"

"You do if you want to shoot it," Preacher told her. "That's the only way to aim. A few fellas can shoot a rifle from the hip, but I don't advise it, especially for you, ma'am. Might break a wrist that way."

"All right." Deborah struggled to raise the rifle. When she had it in place, with the butt firmly socketed against her shoulder and the barrel weaving even worse than when Jake was trying to shoot one of the long rifles, she said in a strained voice, "Now what do I do?"

Preacher looked at Corliss. "Loaded and primed?"

"Of course."

"All right," Preacher told Deborah, "point the barrel at that little clump o' sagebrush out there."

"What sagebrush?"

"Yonder." Preacher leveled a finger at the plants he was talking about.

"Oh, I see it now." Deborah managed to aim the rifle in the general direction of the sagebrush. The barrel was weaving around so much, she probably wouldn't be able to hit what she was aiming at. It would be blind luck if she did. But at least she was pointing the rifle away from the wagons.

"Reach up with the thumb o' your right hand," Preacher went on, "and use it to pull the hammer back."

"The hammer?"

"That part right there."

Biting her bottom lip in concentration as the men gathered to watch this display of her shooting ability, Deborah got her thumb on the hammer and eared it back.

"Keep pullin' until you hear it click," Preacher said. "That's the way you know it's cocked."

Deborah did so, a look of excitement and satisfaction appearing on her face when she heard the hammer lock into place.

"Is it ready to shoot?" she asked.

"It's ready," Preacher assured her. "You got the sights on that sagebrush?"

"I'm trying . . . but this gun is awfully heavy. Do I pull the trigger now?"

"Take a deep breath," Preacher advised her. "Steady yourself. Then squeeze the trigger. Don't jerk it. That'll just throw your aim off."

Deborah drew in a breath. It didn't steady her all that much, but the rifle barrel stopped weaving quite so much. She squeezed the trigger.

The roar of exploding powder mingled with her cry of shock and pain as the rifle kicked so hard against her shoulder that it drove her backward. She fell, landing hard on her rump, and the rifle thudded to the ground in front of her.

"Good Lord!" Corliss exclaimed as he leaped forward to snatch up the rifle. "I hope you didn't hurt it!"

"It!" Deborah said. "What about *me*?"

Jerome took her arm and helped her up while Corliss examined the rifle to make sure it was undamaged. Deborah looked like she couldn't decide whether to rub her shoulder or her rump. Both would be bruised from this incident. Finally, in the interests of decorum, no doubt, she settled for rubbing her shoulder.

"You didn't hold the rifle tight enough against your shoulder," Preacher told her. "That's why it kicked so hard. That powder's got a heavy recoil to start with, but you made it worse."

"Why didn't you warn me?" she demanded in an aggrieved tone.

"You'll remember what to do next time, won't you?"

She pouted. "I suppose so. Still, I think it was a mean trick."

"You'll get used to shootin'," Jake told her. "I did."

As a matter of fact, over the past few days the youngster had become a pretty good shot, Preacher thought. Jake had knocked over several rabbits and prairie hens that had been good eatin' when they were roasted over the fire at night.

Corliss showed Deborah how to reload the rifle, and she tried another shot. This time she came closer to the sagebrush, which she hadn't hit at all with her first shot. This ball kicked up dirt about ten feet in front of the brush. Preacher thought that wasn't too bad. Also, Deborah kept the rifle butt tight enough against her shoulder so that the recoil didn't knock her down, although it did make her stagger back a couple of steps.

"That's enough," she said. "My shoulder is going to be so bruised tomorrow!"

"It'll heal," Preacher told her. He wished Deborah had stayed back in St. Louis like she was supposed to, but he had to admit that she hadn't complained a lot. She seemed to be made of fairly tough stuff, which was good considering where they were going.

Deborah and Jake both continued to practice with the rifles over the next few days, while the wagon train was stopped to allow the oxen to rest.

They had reached the Platte River by now. It was a broad, shallow stream, sometimes not more than a foot deep, that had a tendency to split up into numerous channels. It was also extremely muddy in places, prompting Preacher to explain to his companions that frontiersmen sometimes referred to the water in the Platte as "too thick to drink, too thin to plow."

"We won't try to cross it yet," Preacher told the others. "There are too many places along here where the wagons might bog down, and if that ain't bad enough, there's quicksand out there, too. That stuff can suck an ox right under, or a man if he's damn fool enough to get stuck in it."

One morning after they had been following the south bank of the Platte for several days, Preacher didn't like the looks of the sky up ahead. It was a flat, silvery color, and the air had an ominous heaviness to it as it lay hot and still over the prairie. Even greenhorns like Corliss and Jerome sensed that something was wrong.

"What is it, Preacher?" Jerome asked as the mountain man stood next to Horse and peered at the sky. Beside him, Dog sat and whimpered a little. The stallion's ears pricked forward, and his tail swished back and forth as something disturbed him, too.

"Storm comin'," Preacher said, his tone as flat and heavy as the air.

"So it rains a little," Corliss said. "I think we can handle that."

Preacher turned to look at him. "Some mighty bad storms boil up sometimes out here on the plains. Rain so hard you can't see your hand in front of your face, lightnin' that seems to set the air on fire around you, and twisters that can pick up a wagon and fling it a mile through the air."

"Surely you're exaggerating."

Sitting on the wagon seat beside Corliss, Deborah said, "I don't think he is."

"Should we try to take shelter somewhere?" Jerome asked.

A wave of Preacher's hand took in the grassy plains that stretched for miles and miles around them. "If a storm comes along, there ain't no place to hide," he said. "We'll just have to ride it out as best we can."

"So you think we should push on?"

"No point in sittin' and waitin'," Preacher replied with a shrug. "Might as well get movin'. Could be the storm will go around us."

"Or maybe you're wrong about it," Corliss said.

Preacher swung up into the saddle without saying anything else. He wasn't going to waste time arguing with Corliss.

But he was beginning to wonder just what Deborah saw in him. Corliss was arrogant, stubborn, and downright unpleasant at times.

Preacher had long since given up trying to figure out how the female brain worked, or why they liked some fellas and not others. He suspected that a man could study on it for years and never make sense of it. That would be just a plumb waste of time.

The oppressiveness in the air grew worse as the morning wore on. The temperature climbed. It was a sultry heat that stole a man's breath away, and made him long for shade and a cool breeze, neither of which he was liable to find out here on the prairie.

But the storm didn't break. It just continued to threaten during the afternoon. Preacher had begun to hope that luck might be with them and that they would avoid the worst of it, when he noticed that the sky was finally beginning to darken. A sudden wind gusted in their faces.

Horse tossed his head and let out a whicker. Padding alongside, Dog growled as if he had just scented a predator. "Yeah, I know," Preacher told his four-legged trail partners. "It's comin', all right."

He turned around and rode back to the wagons from his position up ahead. "Circle 'em up!" he called as he made the revolving motion over his head. "Circle 'em up tight!"

"It's too early to make camp," Corliss protested as Preacher reined to a stop. "We're wasting time."

"Feel the chill in that wind?" Preacher asked. "That means it's just gonna get harder and harder. And you can smell the rain headin' this way, too."

"Is that what that smell is?" Jerome asked. "It's refreshing in a way."

"You won't think so in a little while when the skies open up," Preacher said. "Get the wagons in a circle and the teams unhitched! Otherwise them oxen are liable to be scattered hell-west and cross-wise by the time the storm's over."

The urgency in Preacher's voice must have convinced Corliss, Jerome, and the other men, because they began working swiftly to follow his orders. Jake and even Deborah helped out in the hasty preparations.

By the time the wagons were drawn into a tight circle, the teams unhitched, and the oxen corralled in the middle of the circle, the silver of the sky had turned to a dark blue. The wind blew hard now, and occasional drops of rain spat down. Thunder rumbled in the distance, and twisting, brilliant fingers of lightning clawed at the clouds. The storm appeared to have the wagon train right in its sights. It was going to be as bad as Preacher had worried it might be.

"Everybody inside the wagons!" he called. "Make sure anything that might blow away is tied down! And once the storm hits, keep your head down!"

He hoped the arching canvas covers over the wagon beds were secured nice and tight; otherwise, once the wind really got up, it would whip them right off the vehicles, leaving everything— and everyone—exposed. He left Horse loose in the center of the circle, knowing that the stallion wouldn't spook and run off no matter how bad the storm got. Then he and Dog crawled under the wagon where Jerome and Jake hunkered inside.

Preacher stretched out on the ground, while the big cur huddled against his side. Preacher put an arm around Dog's neck and dug his fingers into the thick coat.

"Hang on, fella," he said, and a sudden lightning strike punctuated his words. Electricity fanged down from the sky and smashed into the earth no more than a hundred yards from the wagons. The ground shook from the instantaneous boom of thunder.

That was just the beginning of a terrific lightning storm that went on for a seeming eternity, crashing and booming all around the wagon train. The bolts seared down out of the sky in a dazzling, near-constant glare that Preacher could still see even after he squeezed his eyelids tightly shut.

While the lightning was still going on, the rain hit in earnest, and as Preacher had warned, it was like the skies had opened up to dump all the water they held on this one place. At first, the rain came almost straight down, closing in around the wagons like a thick gray curtain. Then, as the wind blew harder, it began to slant, until the drops seemed to be moving almost horizontally. It was like being trapped inside a river, Preacher thought as the rain blew under the wagon and lashed at him and Dog. The moisture had to be penetrating inside the wagons, too, even though the canvas flaps at the front and back of the wagon beds were drawn closed and tied tightly. Nothing could completely keep out such a deluge.

The only good thing about a storm like this was that it usually didn't last very long. This one moved quickly, and after a half hour or so that seemed much longer, the rain began to let up, the lightning strikes were fewer and farther apart, and the terrible wind slowed somewhat.

Preacher was just beginning to feel optimistic that they were going to be able to ride it out when he heard a distinctive rumbling. "Oh, hell," he spat out as he crawled closer to the edge of the area shielded by the wagon above him. As he peered through the spokes of one of the wheels, the rain thinned out enough for him to be able to see the writhing black funnel of a tornado as it danced across the prairie a few hundred yards away, darting this way and that but always traveling in the general direction of the circled wagons.

Preacher hated being helpless, but that was exactly the way he felt in the face of this terrible threat from nature. He couldn't do a damned thing to stop the tornado or alter its capricious course. It was going to go wherever it wanted to and destroy anything that fate placed in its path.

And there was no point in trying to warn the others, because they would be just as powerless as Preacher was.

He slid back to where Dog lay with his head on his paws and wrapped his arms around the big cur again. By lifting his head, Preacher could still see the base of the tornado as it capered toward them. A hundred yards away now . . . fifty . . . a sudden swerve to the side, as if the super-destructive black column of air was going to miss them . . . then another swerve so that it was bearing down on them again, twenty yards away, the roaring so loud now that it slammed against Preacher's ears like physical blows as the ground shook and the world seemed to moan in agony—

Then the tornado lifted into the sky, passing a short distance above the wagons. The very capriciousness that had threatened Preacher and his companions had now saved them.

"Lord," Preacher breathed. "Lord, that was a close one!"

Once the twister was gone, the rest of the storm followed hurriedly after it. The rain subsided to a drizzle, the wind died away to almost nothing, and the lightning moved off to the east, trailing grumbles of thunder behind it.

Preacher crawled out from under the wagon and looked around to see how bad the damage was.

Amazingly, the wagons all seemed to be intact. The canvas covers hadn't been ripped off any of them. The oxen were soaked and miserable and a little walleyed, but they seemed to be all right, too, as was Horse.

"Everybody all right?" Preacher called as he strode around the circle. "You can come out now! Storm's just about over."

One by one, the people inside the wagons poked their heads out to look around. Seeing that the danger was over, they climbed out of the vehicles, dropping down to the muddy morass that the downpour had made out of the prairie.

"Is anyone hurt?" Jerome asked. "Corliss? Deborah?"

Both of them were pale but unharmed. "We're just shaken up a little," Corliss said. "I never saw such a storm in all my life. You were right, Preacher."

"I'd just as soon I hadn't been," Preacher said, "but we seem to have come through it with no harm done."

"What was that horrible noise there at the end?" Deborah asked. "I've never heard anything quite like that before." A shudder ran through her. "And it would be all right with me if I never heard it again!"

"That was a twister," Preacher said. "A tornado or a cyclone, some folks call 'em. I've seen a few in my time. They can flatten even a sturdy buildin' if they hit it straight on."

"Do they happen a lot out here?"

"Pretty often, durin' the spring and summer."

The mud pulled at Jerome's boots as he walked around, and he said, "I don't think we can travel as long as the ground's like this. The wagons would get stuck."

Preacher nodded. "More'n likely. But it's late enough in the day we can just go ahead and make camp here for the night. It'll have to be a cold camp, though. I don't reckon we'll find any buffalo chips dry enough to burn right now."

"You mean we're going to be stuck here until the ground dries out?" Corliss asked.

"Yeah, but that won't take too long. It might even be dry enough come mornin'. If it ain't, then it should be by day after tomorrow, for sure."

"I hope you're right. I hate to be delayed."

"Might as well take it easy and not worry about it," Preacher advised. "Gettin' a burr under your saddle over somethin' you can't do a blamed thing about will just angrify your blood."

"I'll certainly pay heed to that bit of homespun wisdom," Corliss said.

Preacher's eyes narrowed, but he didn't say anything else. He was getting used to Corliss acting like a jackass more often than not.

They ate an early supper of cold beans left over from the midday meal; then everyone turned in except for Preacher, who planned to stand the first turn on guard by himself. After the storm moved on, the clouds had broken up, allowing the sun to shine for a few minutes before it set. A faint red glow remained in the western sky as the camp grew quiet. With Dog sitting beside him, Preacher watched until it faded completely to black.

The thoroughbraces on one of the wagons creaked a little as the weight on them shifted. The noise was so slight that anyone with ears less keen than Preacher's might not have noticed it. But he heard it and turned his head to look as a figure climbed out of one of the wagons and dropped silently to the ground.

That was the wagon shared by Jake and Jerome. The fella who had just climbed out was too big to be the boy, so that left Jerome. Probably answering the call of nature, Preacher thought, but since he couldn't be sure about that, he cat-footed along behind the figure as Jerome walked out onto the prairie, away from the wagons. He was sure going out a long way, Preacher thought, if all he wanted to do was dig a hole or some such.

Preacher suddenly veered off to the side as he heard somebody coming up behind him. Whoever it was didn't move as quietly as Jerome did. Preacher dropped to a knee, and then flattened out on the ground as he waited to see what the hell was going on here. The moon hadn't risen yet, but the starlight was enough for him to see the second person from the wagon train come up and join

Jerome, who had stopped about a hundred yards away from the vehicles.

Preacher's jaw tightened as he watched the two of them embrace. He heard Jerome say, "Thank God you weren't hurt during that storm this afternoon, darling. I don't think I could stand it if anything happened to you."

"And I feel the same way, Jerome," Deborah Morrigan said. She moved closer to him, and Preacher knew from the way their heads came together that they were kissing.

Well, hell, the mountain man thought.

Seventeen

The Indians showed up the next morning. They sat on their ponies, a dozen strong, about two hundred yards away on the bank of the Platte River. Preacher was the first one awake, as usual. He spotted the Indians as the sky began to turn gray, but since they were just sitting there, he didn't do anything about it.

Best to wait and see what they had in mind. Could be they were friendly.

Or could be they were just trying to make up their minds whether they wanted to kill these white interlopers in a land they considered their own.

Preacher hadn't said or done anything about the encounter he had witnessed the night before either. Jerome and Deborah had hugged and sparked and talked quietly for a while, then slipped back to the wagon train separately. Preacher stayed where he was until they were safely in their wagons, then returned to the circle of covered vehicles himself.

The fact that Jerome was romantically involved

with his cousin's fiancée was bothersome because it held the potential for causing trouble, but other than that, Preacher didn't see that it was any of his business. He planned to keep his mouth shut about what he had seen, although he reserved the right to make a discreet suggestion to Jerome that he and Deborah ought to be careful.

The whole thing might not amount to a hill o' beans, though, Preacher thought as he watched the Indians sitting there on their ponies—because it was possible that none of them would survive the rising of the sun long enough to worry about such problems as romance.

He found some buffalo chips that had dried out enough overnight to burn, built a fire, and put the coffee on to boil. The Indians would smell it and take it for a sign that he wasn't worried about their presence. That might help determine what they did. Like animals, they would be quicker to attack if they sensed fear or weakness.

Preacher walked over to where Blackie slept under one of the wagons and nudged the man's foot with the toe of his moccasin. After having been on the trail with all these folks for a while, Preacher had determined that the soft-spoken Blackie was the toughest and most experienced of the lot. Blackie proved that by the way he woke up at Preacher's prodding, instantly alert but calm and clear-headed.

"We got company," Preacher said in a quiet voice.

Blackie slid out from under the wagon, bringing his rifle with him, and stood up. "Cheyenne or Arapaho?" he asked, equally softly.

"Not sure. They ain't close enough yet to tell. But it don't make much difference."

"No, I reckon it don't," Blackie agreed.

The two tribes were close allies and had fought on the same side many times, most notably against their hated enemies the Kiowa. Both the Cheyenne and the Arapaho sometimes got along with white men and sometimes didn't.

"Wake up the other drivers," Preacher said. "I'll let Jerome and Corliss know. We go on about our business like the Indians aren't there, except for makin' sure that there are rifles close at hand. Make sure everybody understands that. If anybody starts the ball, I don't want it to be one of us."

Blackie nodded. "Got it." He moved off to follow Preacher's orders.

Preacher went to the wagon shared by Jerome and Jake and stuck his head in the entrance flap at the rear of the vehicle. It was too dark inside to see much, but he heard Jake snoring, and then made out Jerome lying wrapped in blankets on top of some crates. He reached into the wagon to grasp Jerome's foot and give it a shake. Jerome stirred, lifting his head and smacking his lips.

"Rise and shine," Preacher said. "Injuns have come to call."

That news made Jerome sit bolt upright. "Indians!" he yelped.

That woke Jake, which was all right; the boy had to know what was going on sometime. He sat up, knuckling his eyes, and said, "Injuns? Did you say Injuns, Preacher?"

"Yeah, 'bout a dozen of 'em sittin' a couple of hundred yards away, watchin' us."

Jerome reached for his rifle. "Are they going to attack?"

"Too soon to tell. Right now they're just watchin'. Come on out of the wagon, but don't panic. They might just want to parley and then ride on. If they do, we'll have to give them some gifts. I reckon it'll be all right to break into the trade goods?"

"Yes, of course," Jerome answered without hesitation. "Take whatever you need to placate them. The last thing we want to do is fight Indians."

Fighting Indians wasn't so bad, Preacher thought. He had done that many times before. What they wanted to do was avoid getting *killed* by Indians.

He backed away from the wagon and turned toward the one where Deborah slept, which was next in the circle. Corliss was already climbing out from under it, having been awakened by the men moving around. He yawned and stretched, clearly unconcerned, until he saw the grim look on Preacher's face and asked, "What's wrong?"

Preacher didn't say anything. He just raised his arm and pointed outside the circle of wagons toward the Indians. Corliss's eyes widened in alarm as he saw the mounted figures, and he exclaimed, "Oh, my God! Savages!"

"You had to figure we'd run into 'em sooner or later," Preacher pointed out. "They consider this their country, you know."

"Yes, of course." Corliss bent down and reached under the wagon for the rifle he had left there. As he straightened with the weapon in his hands, he went on. "Are they going to attack?"

"Good question. I reckon we'll find out after a while."

"Damn it, how can you be so calm in a situation like this?"

"Won't do any good to run around like a chicken with its head cut off," Preacher said. "We might as well go on with our breakfast."

"How can you even *think* about eating at a time like this?"

"Because I ain't et since supper last night, and my belly's empty, that's how." Preacher turned toward the fire, adding over his shoulder, "Better wake Miss Morrigan, but tell her to keep her wits about her. The steadier we all are, the better our chances o' comin' through this alive."

Corliss looked like he doubted that. In fact, he looked like he wanted to start taking potshots at the Indians, which was downright worrisome. The possibility bothered Preacher enough so that he stopped and said, "Nobody fires a shot unless I give the word. You understand that, Corliss?"

"Yes, I suppose so," Corliss said with a nod. "You must know what you're doing. But that doesn't mean I have to like it."

"Not much about this situation that *I* like," Preacher said.

By now Jerome and Jake had climbed out of their wagon and the other drivers were up and moving around. Everybody was awake and alert except for Deborah. Preacher wished she was a better hand when it came to loading a rifle. They had plenty of rifles and ammunition if it came to a fight, but it would be better if a couple of people could spend their time reloading. From what Preacher had seen, Jerome was the worst shot among the men. If Preacher needed to, he would assign the chore of reloading to Jerome and Deborah. Even though Jake was a boy, he was a decent shot, so he would need to handle one of the rifles. Preacher hated the thought of telling a youngster to do his best to kill as many of the enemy as he could, but sometimes such things couldn't be avoided.

But there was still a chance that violence could be avoided, so Preacher was going to hang on to that hope as long as possible.

He cooked breakfast, and still the Indians sat out there. Everyone ate, but they did so with one eye on the mounted figures, who had remained motionless ever since Preacher had first seen them. They might have almost been statues, if it weren't for the wind ruffling the long manes of the ponies and tugging at the feathers tied to strips of buckskin that were attached to the lances they carried. If their goal was to make the whites nervous, they had sure as hell succeeded.

Deborah had emerged from the wagon looking pale and drawn. Corliss stayed close to her and from time to time put an arm around her shoulders in a reassuring gesture. Preacher saw the glances Deborah threw toward Jerome, though, and figured that she wished it was him comforting her and not his cousin. He noted Jerome's reaction to those glances as well. Clearly, Jerome was more concerned with Deborah's safety than with his own.

Preacher was hunkered next to the fire, sipping the last of his coffee, when Blackie said his name in a quiet voice. Looking up, Preacher saw that the one-eyed man was gazing toward the Indians. Preacher turned his head and looked and saw the same thing Blackie had noticed.

One of the Indians was riding slowly toward the wagons.

Preacher straightened to his feet. The others noticed what was going on, and Corliss asked, "What does that mean, that only one of them is coming in?"

"It's a good thing," Preacher said. "They want to talk."

"Is that their chief?" Jake asked.

"Probably a subchief in charge of that huntin' party," Preacher explained. "The big chief'll be back at their village, wherever that is."

Jerome said, "How do you know it's not a war party?"

"Because now that that fella's closer, I can see he ain't painted for war. He's Arapaho. I suspected as much from their lances, and now that I'm gettin' a better look at the beadwork on his shirt, I'm sure. Every tribe does things like that a mite different."

"Are these . . . Arapahos . . . hostile?" Deborah wanted to know.

Preacher gave her an honest answer. "They can be. But I figure this bunch was just out huntin' and came across us. They ain't lookin' for trouble. As long as we keep our wits about us, there's a good chance they'll go on about their business." He leaned his rifle against a wagon wheel as the Arapaho warrior brought his pony to a halt about fifty yards away. "I'll go talk to him."

"Is that safe?" Jerome asked, clutching his own rifle.

Preacher nodded. "Safe enough. His honor won't let him try anything tricky. He'd be shamed if he did."

Preacher stepped over a wagon tongue and walked toward the Indian. His stride was calm and unhurried. When he was about a dozen feet from the mounted man, he stopped and moved his head in a curt nod.

The Arapaho tapped his chest with a clenched fist and said in his native tongue, "I am Antelope Fleet as the Wind."

Preacher nodded again. "I have heard of you. It is said that you are a brave and honorable warrior." That was stretching the truth. Outright lying actually, since he'd never heard of this fella before. But he knew what Antelope Fleet as the Wind wanted to hear. He tapped his own chest and went on. "I am called Preacher."

The look of recognition on the Arapaho's face was genuine, or Preacher missed his guess. "The slayer who comes in the night? The confounder of the Blackfeet? Brother to the wolf?"

"I've been called all those things," Preacher admitted.

"Why do you travel through the land of the Arapaho? Who are those white men with you?"

"They are my friends," Preacher said, stretching the truth again. "We go to the Shining Mountains, to trade with the human beings who live there and with other whites who will come as well in wagons like those."

Antelope Fleet as the Wind made a face. "There are no human beings in the Shining Mountains. Human beings live on the plains. And if more white men come in wagons like those, we will stop them and burn them, so the white men will know this is the land of the Arapaho and will not come back."

"We are not the enemy of the Arapaho," Preacher insisted. "We will not trouble you or interfere with your hunting. We wish only to travel on to our destination in peace."

Antelope Fleet as the Wind thought about it for a long time and then finally nodded. "The Arapaho are a fierce, warlike people, much to be feared," he declared.

Preacher nodded. "This I know."

"But we do not fight those who do not seek to fight us. You and the other white men may go in peace, Preacher, if you will tell those you encounter about the honor and courage of the Arapaho."

"Of course," Preacher agreed.

"And if you give us each a rifle and powder and shot for them."

That was what ol' Antelope had been angling for all along, Preacher knew. Everything else had been just a prelude. Now that the proposed deal was out in the open, Preacher shook his head.

"We will give you two rifles, one horn of powder, and a pouch of shot," he counter offered.

"Ten rifles," Antelope Fleet as the Wind snapped.

"Four," Preacher said.

"Eight."

"Six."

A shrewd look appeared on the face of the Arapaho subchief. He was ready to split the difference.

But before he could suggest that, Preacher said again, in a firm voice that showed he wasn't going to budge, "Six."

"I have twelve men," Antelope said, obviously angry.

"And half of them will have rifles," Preacher countered. "You can arm the other half some other time."

"Six horns of powder."

"Three."

They settled on four, along with a commensurate amount of ammunition. That ended that part of the negotiation. Now they just had to agree on the details of delivery.

"We will leave the rifles, powder, and shot here where we are camped," Preacher said. "You and your men can get them after we leave."

Antelope Fleet as the Wind looked like he wanted to haggle some more, but at this point there was no real reason to do so. He nodded and said, "This is good."

"And each of us will go on our way in peace."

"There will be no fight today," the Arapaho promised.

Preacher's jaw tightened. Antelope Fleet as the Wind would keep his word. The hunting party would not attack the wagon train—*today*.

But he wasn't promising anything about tomorrow or any other day. He was a sly devil, but it wasn't really anything Preacher hadn't been expecting. He nodded his agreement. A lot of things could happen to divert the Arapaho from attacking them later. It was a chance Preacher had to take in order to get the wagons safely on their way today.

Antelope Fleet as the Wind turned his pony and rode back toward the other warriors. Preacher swung around and strode toward the wagons. Neither man worried about any trickery on the part of the other.

Corliss, Jerome, and Jake all wore anxious expressions when they met Preacher as he got back to the wagons. "What did he say?" Corliss asked. "Are they going to attack us?"

"Not today," Preacher replied.

"Not today?" Jerome repeated. "What does that mean?"

"Just what I said. They're gonna go on their way, and we're gonna go on ours. All we have to do is leave behind six rifles and some powder and shot for 'em."

"Six rifles!" Corliss looked astounded and angry. "You're *arming* those savages?"

"In case you ain't noticed," Preacher said, "they're already armed. They've got lances and bows and arrows. If they just wanted to kill us they could probably manage to get it done with that they got. And there's a good chance none of 'em can shoot a rifle worth a damn. They ain't had enough practice."

"Then why do they want the guns?" Jerome asked.

"For the buffalo. So they can hunt without havin' to get right amongst the shaggy critters and risk gettin' trampled or gored. There's a lot of ritual involved in the way they hunt buffalo, so they won't give it up entirely, but they're practical folks, too." Preacher chuckled. "Like I said, they ain't had much practice with firearms. So they'll use 'em on the buffalo first and get good with them . . . then they'll come after traders and immigrants and settlers."

"Well, I hope you're proud of yourself," Corliss

snapped. "You've put the means of killing white people in the hands of those red savages."

Preacher's voice hardened. "What I've done is saved our hair right here and now. I'll be satisfied with that for the time bein'." He turned away from the cousins and called out to the drivers, "Let's get them teams hitched up. The ground's dry enough for the wagons to roll this mornin', so roll they will!"

Eighteen

The party led by Colin Fairfax and Schuyler Mims had stayed a good five to ten miles behind the other group ever since leaving St. Louis. Fairfax was careful to the point of obsession. He didn't want Preacher to know they were behind him.

Following the trail continued to be easy, since the members of the Hart expedition took no pains whatsoever to conceal their tracks. Not only that, but even though Schuyler and Fairfax had never traveled this route before, they knew in general where it ran. Once they reached the Platte River, it was obvious the wagons were going to follow that stream all the way to the mountains.

From time to time, Schuyler rode ahead just to check on the wagons, one lone man drawing close enough so that he could see the lumbering vehicles through Fairfax's spyglass. He was always careful. The plains weren't as flat as they appeared at first glance. There were little depressions, gentle ridges, gullies, and dry washes that could be followed by someone who didn't want to be seen.

Schuyler took special care not to show himself on the occasional higher ground, and he shielded the lens of the spyglass with one hand whenever he held it to his eye, so that the sunlight wouldn't reflect off it and possibly warn Preacher that the wagons were being followed.

The same storm that swept over the wagon train also barreled down on the men following it. The difference was that the riders, their mounts, and the packhorses that carried their supplies had no place to take shelter. As the lightning bolts began to smash into the earth around them, Fairfax hurriedly dismounted and screamed at the other men to get down and to pull their horses down, too. Out here on this flat ground, a man on horseback was more likely to be struck by lightning, which usually sought out the highest point around.

The roaring thunder and the shaking earth spooked some of the horses, and the men had a hard time wrestling them to the ground. One of the pack animals tore away from the man holding its reins and galloped across the prairie. The man started after the horse, but Fairfax bellowed over the uproar of the storm, "Let him go! Get down on the ground!"

The man did as he was ordered. A moment later, when the runaway packhorse had galloped perhaps a hundred yards, a jagged, eye-searing bolt of lightning sizzled down from the heavens and struck it. Schuyler saw it happen. He winced and had to look away as the horse fell as if it had been poleaxed.

When the rain started, the heavy drops pounded into the men like millions of tiny fists, pummeling them into a state of soaked misery. They struggled to keep the horses lying down, and choked as rainwater sluiced into their mouths and noses. Sheer terror coursed through them with each bolt of lightning that struck nearby. It was a hellish ordeal, and it seemed to last forever.

As Schuyler huddled there in the mud, a distant roaring came to his ears. As it happened, he had once seen a tornado back in Ohio, and he had never forgotten the funnel cloud's ominous, deep-throated roar. He knew a twister was nearby now, and the knowledge turned his blood to ice in his veins.

But then the rumbling faded, and Schuyler's fear subsided a little. The rain was easing up, as were the lightning strikes. That meant the storm was moving on.

When the rain had let up until it was just a drizzle, the men stood and allowed the horses to get back on their feet as well. Man and animal alike were soaked. Even though the clouds had begun to thin, it was late enough in the day so that darkness was about to descend.

"We'll make camp here," Fairfax decided. "Schuyler, take a couple of men and get the supplies off that horse that was struck by lightning. We'll redistribute them among the other pack animals."

Schuyler nodded and picked two men to go with him. As they neared the dead horse, his nose wrinkled. He had smelled horse meat cooking before and never cared for the smell. But that was what hung in the air now around the unfortunate beast. A large black spot on the horse's head showed where the lightning had struck it. A similar spot on one of the rear legs marked the location where the terrible force had leaped out of the horse's body to the ground. Everything in between had been blasted and seared by the lightning.

Working as quickly as they could, the men loosened the packs, removed them from the horse, and hauled them back to the spot where the others were making camp. A fire, even a concealed one, was out of the question because everything was too wet. Nor was there any place dry to sleep. It was going to be a long, uncomfortable night, but there was nothing they could do about that except endure it.

Schuyler ate a soggy biscuit and called it supper, then wrapped himself in a wet blanket and lay down on the ground. Even though it was summer, the dampness made a chill go through him. His teeth chattered and he twisted around, trying to find some comfortable position in which to lie. He never accomplished that, but he did finally doze off.

He woke up numerous times during the night, and began to think it would never be morning again. Finally, it was. Not getting in any hurry, the men welcomed the rising sun. They spread their blankets to let the growing warmth dry them out. Some of the men took off their clothes and spread them on the ground as well.

Fairfax came over to Schuyler and said, "It may still be too muddy for those wagons to travel. We can't start after them until we know for sure one way or the other."

"Because we don't want to accidentally ride right up on them," Schuyler said.

"Exactly."

Schuyler stretched his back, which was stiff and

achy this morning, and said, "So I reckon you want me to scout up ahead and see whether they're movin' again or not."

Fairfax nodded. "That's right. Are you up to it?"

"Sure. I reckon. I have to be up to it, don't I?"

"It's important," Fairfax agreed.

"Lemme get some coffee, and then I'll get started."

Fairfax shook his head and said, "No coffee. There's no place to build a fire where Preacher might not see the smoke."

Schuyler grimaced. "Are you sure, Colin?"

"Sorry."

Schuyler sighed and nodded. He went over to his horse, which he had picketed nearby the night before, and threw his saddle on the animal. He took the time to clean and reload his rifle and pistols, then mounted up and rode out, heading west by northwest with the Platte about a hundred yards off to his right. The river was so broad and sluggish that the downpour of the night before hadn't had any noticeable effect on it.

Even though the sun was warm as it rose, the air didn't have the sultry, oppressive heaviness of the day before. Schuyler wished that he'd been able to get some coffee and maybe something to eat before starting out on this scouting mission, but despite that, he began to feel pretty good. The air was clean and crisp, and he could see for a long way.

Not that there was much of anything to see. Even if the wagons were able to travel, the ground was still wet enough so that the vehicles' wheels and the hooves of the oxen wouldn't raise any dust. Schuyler would have to actually come within sight of the expedition to find out if it was on the move again.

That made him a little nervous. If he could see the wagons, that meant the people with the wagons could see him. And Preacher struck Schuyler as the sort of fella who would keep a close eye on his back trail.

Schuyler pushed on as the sun climbed higher in the sky, and after a while, he spotted some dark shapes on the horizon. Not the wagons, he knew. The light-colored canvas covers over the backs of the wagons were easy to distinguish, even at a distance. This was probably a small herd of buffalo, he decided. During the journey from St. Louis, they had seen quite a few of the great, shaggy beasts.

No, not buffalo, he realized a moment later. What he was looking at were riders, a good-sized group of them, and they were coming toward him. Instantly, he reined in and dismounted. He took the spyglass from his pocket and pulled it out to its full extension, then lifted it to his eye and squinted through the lens.

What he saw made his blood turn cold.

A dozen or more Indians were riding straight toward him.

They were at least half a mile away, and he didn't know if they had seen him or not. He was just one man, which made him more difficult to spot than a group of riders. For a second, he thought about trying to find someplace to hide while the savages rode past, but a swift glance around told him there was no place on this trackless prairie that would offer enough concealment.

The Indians were coming on faster now, too,

urging their ponies to a gallop. Schuyler let out a terrified curse as he realized they must have seen him. He didn't have much experience with Indians, but he knew from stories he'd heard that they couldn't resist the temptation to attack when they came across a lone white man.

Schuyler leaped into the saddle without even taking the time to put away the spyglass. He stuck it inside his shirt while he was using his other hand to haul his mount around in a sharp turn. Then he dug the heels of his boots into the animal's flanks and sent it leaping into a run, back in the direction he had come from.

Back toward Fairfax and the rest of the men. Schuyler knew his only chance was to reach them before the savages caught up to him.

He leaned forward and banged his feet against the horse's sides, urging it on to greater and greater speed. The animal responded, stretching out into a hard run, its legs moving so fast that they would have been a blur to anyone watching.

As swift as Schuyler's horse was, though, the Indian ponies were faster. On and on they came, and every time he looked back over his shoulder, wide-eyed with terror, they seemed to be closer. It wasn't just his imagination, he decided. They really *were* gaining on him.

He couldn't hear anything over the pounding hoofbeats of his mount and the frantic hammering of his own pulse, but once when he glanced back he saw several spurts of smoke from the pursuers. The savages were *shooting* at him! It was bad enough that these plains were populated by such fearsome creatures. The idea that they possessed firearms was even worse.

The range was still too great for rifles, and Schuyler doubted if the Indians could hit him anyway, firing from the backs of galloping ponies like that. But there was such a thing as sheer bad luck, as he knew all too well. One of those shots *might* find its target in his back. He hunched even lower in the saddle.

It seemed to him that he should have gotten back to Fairfax and the others by now. His blood turned icy again as he wondered if he had somehow veered off of his original path enough so that he was going to miss the rest of his party and have to deal with the Indians by himself. He would put up a fight, of course, but it wouldn't last long, outnumbered as he was by at least twelve to one.

Then he realized that it wasn't possible he had gone astray. The broad, muddy expanse of the Platte River was still over there on his left now, shining in the sun about a hundred yards away. As long as he could stay ahead of the Indians, he had to run into Fairfax and the others sooner or later.

But the pursuers were less than a quarter of a mile behind him, he saw as he looked back again. They had cut his lead by more than half. And his mount was beginning to falter a little. The horse couldn't keep up the breakneck pace for much longer.

Suddenly, Schuyler spotted riders ahead of him. His heart leaped; then he gulped as an even more frightening possibility occurred to him. What if more Indians had gotten ahead of him somehow, cutting him off from the rest of his group? If that was the case, he was well and truly doomed.

But within minutes, he could tell that the other riders were Fairfax and the rest of Shad Beaumont's men. He recognized the buckskins, the coonskin caps, the rough work clothes, the broad-brimmed frontiersmen's hats. Even though they probably couldn't hear him yet, he shouted, "Indians! Indians!" as he waved his rifle over his head to signal alarm.

Fairfax and the others either saw the Indians or figured out from Schuyler's actions that something was wrong, because they started spreading out in preparation to do battle. They galloped forward, helping to cut down the distance between them and Schuyler. As he clung to the back of his racing horse, he almost wept with relief at the sight of his companions.

Moments later, Schuyler reined in as Fairfax and the other men rode past him, firing at the Indians. Schuyler wheeled his horse to watch. The white men were better shots. A couple of the savages were hit and tumbled off their ponies. The others must have realized they had gotten themselves into a lot more trouble than they had expected when they started chasing Schuyler. The group of riders broke apart as the Indians turned to flee.

Fairfax shouted for his men to halt, dismount, and fire. Within moments, a ragged volley of shots rang out, and several more Indians pitched off their mounts. A couple of the ponies stumbled, obviously hit, and threw their riders. Some of Beaumont's men leaped back into their saddles and dashed forward. They rode down the Indians on foot and blasted them into oblivion with pistols.

Two, maybe three, of the savages got away, Schuyler estimated. They would think twice before they attacked another white man they found riding alone, he thought with a grin of satisfaction.

Fairfax mounted up and rode around to check on the fallen Indians. One of them must have still been alive, even though from a distance Schuyler couldn't see him moving. Fairfax got down off his horse, pulled out a pistol, and shot the Indian through the head. The savage's body jerked then. In a calm, unhurried manner, Fairfax reloaded his pistol and then put it away.

When Fairfax rode back to join him, Schuyler said, "Thanks, Colin. I'm lucky I didn't get farther away from you fellas before those damned redskins jumped me."

"You led them right back to us," Fairfax snapped. "What if there had been more of them?"

Schuyler gaped at him in surprise, unsure why Fairfax was angry with him. "What was I supposed to do?" he asked. "I couldn't fight all of them!"

"So you'd have gotten us killed to save your own hide?"

Now Schuyler was getting a little mad at his attitude. "I could see there were only a dozen or so of them. I knew you and the rest of the boys wouldn't have any trouble handling them."

"We heard shots. That's why we started in this direction. I was afraid you might have run into trouble."

Schuyler nodded. "Yeah, a few of 'em had rifles. But they didn't seem to be very good shots."

"Some of us could have gotten killed, even if it was by accident."

"Well, damn it, if I hadn't lit a shuck out of there, *I* would've gotten killed! It's startin' to sound like you'd rather that's what I done!"

Fairfax shook his head and lifted a hand. "No, no," he said. "You misunderstand, Schuyler. Of course you did the right thing by saving your own life. I just don't want anything to interfere with this mission we're on for Beaumont. I lost my head for a second, that's all."

"That's fine, I reckon," Schuyler grumbled, not completely mollified by his partner's words. "I don't want to let Beaumont down neither. If we do a good job for him on this, he'll keep on workin' with us. We'll never be poor again, Colin."

"We're still a long way from rich," Fairfax pointed out. "Did you see whether or not that wagon train had started out before you encountered the savages?"

Schuyler grimaced. "Hell! I never saw the wagons before those Injuns started chasin' me. I don't know any more about that than I did when I left. Sorry."

Again, Fairfax shook his head. "There was nothing else you could do. And now, if the wagons *didn't* push on this morning, they're probably close enough so that Preacher and the others heard the shooting."

Schuyler tried not to groan in dismay. "That's liable to make them more watchful than ever, knowin' somebody's behind them."

"Well, there's nothing we can do about it now. Are you ready to go see how far ahead they are?"

"You mean you still want me to do that?"

"Someone has to," Fairfax said. "You've had more experience on the frontier than any of the rest of us."

"A farm in Ohio ain't really the frontier," Schuyler muttered. But then he nodded and went on. "Yeah, I'll give it another try. Sure hope I don't run into any more redskins, though."

"That goes without saying."

"I better swap horses with one of the other men. I had to run this one pretty hard to get away from them Injuns. If I come across any more trouble, I'll need a fresher horse."

Fairfax nodded in agreement and called one of the men over. The fellow wasn't too fond of the idea of swapping his mount for Schuyler's played-out one, but Fairfax didn't give him any choice in the matter. A few minutes later, Schuyler was on his way again, riding west on the trail of the wagon train.

An idle thought crossed his mind. It probably would have been better in the long run if they had managed to kill *all* of the Indians . . .

Nineteen

The wagons had gone about a mile when Preacher suddenly reined in at his position in front and turned his head toward the rear. If he'd had ears like Dog or Horse, they would have pricked forward quizzically at that moment, as he tried to decide whether or not he had just heard shots coming from somewhere behind them.

The sounds had been faint, and a breeze had sprung up, making it even more difficult to hear. If those *were* gunshots, they were several miles away, back to the east.

Preacher had never quite shaken the feeling that someone was following them. Of course, the possibility that somebody was shooting back there didn't have to have anything to do with the Harts' wagon train. Maybe those Arapaho led by Antelope Fleet as the Wind were taking some target practice with the rifles Preacher and his companions had left behind, as agreed. Or there could have been some other Indian hunting party armed with rifles, or some white trappers, or, hell, almost anybody.

The prairie was a big place. There was plenty of room for a lot of different people. Preacher's brain knew that.

His gut told him that trouble was dogging their trail.

He waved the wagons forward and rode out to the side, turning Horse so that he could stare back at where they had been. His keen eyes searched the mostly flat landscape for a long time without seeing anything unusual. Nor did he hear any more shots after that brief flurry. Finally, he rode after the wagons, drawing rein and bringing Horse to a walk as he came alongside the wagon driven by Jerome Hart.

"What's wrong, Preacher?" Jerome asked. "You must have been looking behind us for a reason."

"Thought I heard some shots from back yonder somewheres," Preacher replied. "Didn't see nothin' suspicious, though."

"Do you think we're being followed?"

"It was no secret, back in St. Louis, that you were comin' out here with six wagons full o' trade goods. Some men who ain't no better'n they have to be would take that as a mighty temptin' target."

"Yes, I can see where they would. But wouldn't they have attempted to steal our goods before now?"

"Maybe, maybe not. Depends on what they planned on doin' with 'em. As long as you're haulin' the stuff to the mountains, they might figure to let you go ahead, thinkin' they could ambush the wagons when you get there."

A worried frown creased Jerome's forehead. "Do you think that's possible?"

"There's a good reason I keep my eyes peeled for trouble," Preacher said by way of answer. "For now, though, nobody's chasin' us, leastways not that I can see, so we might as well keep on pushin' west."

Jerome nodded. "All right, but I think I understand now why it's so important that we stand guard at night."

Preacher didn't say anything to that. He thought Jerome should have figured it out long before now.

Nor did he mention what he planned to do once night fell again. After the wagons were circled and everyone had settled down for the night except the men standing watch, Preacher intended to go on a little scouting mission. He had learned the Indian trick of being able to trot along for miles without stopping, tireless in his ground-eating stride. He would leave Horse here but take Dog with him, so that he could double back on their trail and find out once and for all if anybody was following them. If he was able to determine that somebody really *was* back there and meant harm to the Harts' party, then Preacher would pay their camp a visit. Like a wraith, he would slip in, unseen in the darkness, and slit a few throats. That might convince the sons o' bitches to turn back, when they woke up in the morning and found some of their number dead.

But that was still a ways off, Preacher reminded himself. He couldn't go skulking around in broad daylight. So he lifted a hand in farewell to Jerome and Jake and heeled Horse into a trot, taking his accustomed position again a short distance in front of the wagons.

Schuyler didn't run into any more Indians or any other sort of trouble. He found the spot where the wagon train had been camped the night before. Easy to tell that was what it was because of the concentration of droppings from the oxen. Also, the wheel ruts leading west were deeper than the ones coming in because the ground was softer this morning, after the storm of the day before.

Schuyler turned and rode back to rejoin Fairfax and the rest of the group, arriving at the place where they waited around midday. "It's safe to go on," Schuyler reported. "They're headin' west again, still followin' the river."

Fairfax nodded in satisfaction. "All right. We'll hang back the way we've been doing. Another week or so and they'll reach the mountains. That's when we'll jump them, there in the foothills."

Schuyler thought his partner sounded awfully confident about how long it was going to take the wagon train to reach the mountains, especially since Fairfax had never been out here before and was sort of guessing, based on what he had seen of the maps Shad Beaumont had. But Fairfax usually turned out to be right, Schuyler reminded himself, at least enough of the time that they'd been able to get by so far, even if they hadn't gotten rich.

Getting rich required more than being smart and ruthless. It took luck, too, and that commodity was something that had always been in short supply in Schuyler's life. That had changed now, though. Being hired by Shad Beaumont was just the break that he and Fairfax had always needed. Things were going their way now.

Schuyler told himself that he ought to think about that more often. A lot of times, a man made his own breaks . . . and that started with believing in himself.

Schuyler believed that he and Fairfax could do this. They could take over that wagon train, kill everybody with it, and take the goods for themselves. Well, for Shad Beaumont actually, but they would get a healthy share of the profits.

It was worth killing for, being a success at last, he thought.

Even though the wagons didn't bog down, the softer ground meant that their pace was somewhat slower that day. Preacher estimated that they covered only about five miles before he called a halt late that afternoon. The ground would be slow in drying out, so it might continue to delay their progress for several days. But they would push on anyway and make what headway they could.

They were able to find enough buffalo chips that would burn in order to make a small fire. Preacher tended to Horse as he normally would while Jerome and Deborah prepared supper. He hadn't told anyone about the nocturnal scouting trip he planned, and he didn't intend to let anyone in on it except Blackie, who was the only one of the bunch Preacher fully trusted.

Nor had he told anyone about what he had witnessed going on between Jerome and Deborah. He watched them together now, as they cooked supper, and everything seemed as proper as it could be. They were friendly with each other, but nothing more. There were no furtive touches on the arm or shoulder, no shared private laughter between them.

Jerome was treating her just the way he ought to be treating the betrothed of his cousin and business partner, with courtesy and respect.

When Jerome announced that the food was ready, everyone gathered around the fire to eat. Corliss said, "What was going on this morning, Preacher? You looked like something was wrong."

"Just thought I heard some gunshots off in the distance," Preacher replied.

Corliss frowned. "That's not good, is it?"

"Don't necessarily mean a blamed thing. I know when you look around, it seems like we're the only folks in a hundred miles or more, because the prairie's so big and open and empty. But that ain't the way it is. There are Indian huntin' parties, like the one we saw this mornin', and fur trappers comin' and goin' to the mountains, and even some surveyin' expeditions every now and then, with an army escort." Preacher waved a hand to take in the plains around them. "I've heard some folks who don't know no better call this the Great American Desert. Well, it ain't a desert, which same you can see for yourself just by lookin' around, and it ain't deserted neither."

"So you're saying that we don't have to worry about the shots?" Corliss persisted.

Preacher frowned. "No, I ain't sayin' that at all. Out here, it pays to worry about anything that's even a mite unusual. O' course, nine times outta ten, it don't amount to anything . . . but that tenth time, you'd danged well better be ready for all hell to break loose." He nodded to Deborah. "Beggin' your pardon, ma'am."

"That's all right, Preacher," she told him with a

smile. "I'm familiar with the concept of hell breaking loose, even though I suppose I've never really
experienced it."

Corliss grunted. "If you were back in St. Louis,
where you're supposed to be, you wouldn't have to
worry about such things."

"I'm not worried," Deborah said. "In fact, I'm
having a wonderful time."

She seemed to be telling the truth about that,
too, Preacher thought. She hadn't complained
about any of the hardships, and she had pitched in
willingly to do her share of the work. Even though
she wore a hat most of the time, her face had gotten
enough sun to give it a nice, healthy tan, which just
made her prettier than she had been to start with.

Corliss turned away from the fire, muttering.
Deborah's lips tightened. Jerome looked at Deborah and shrugged as if sympathizing with her. That
was the only indication Preacher saw of any sort of
connection between the two of them, and it was
very fleeting.

After everyone had eaten, Preacher told Blackie
and Neilson to take the first watch. The men nodded
in agreement and picked up their rifles. They headed
for opposite sides of the circle of wagons. Everyone
else began getting ready to turn in, including
Preacher, who planned to make it look like he had
gone to sleep before he left on his scouting mission.
Once the camp was settled down, he would slip over
to Blackie and inform the one-eyed man of his plans.

To make things look normal, Preacher stretched
out on his blankets underneath one of the wagons
and listened. It wasn't long before he heard snoring from some of the vehicles. He waited a while

longer, then was about to crawl out and get started, when he looked out and saw a dark shape flitting across the camp.

Preacher frowned and his jaw clenched. Somebody else was skulking around tonight, and he didn't like it. This was going to interfere with his plans. He watched as the shadowy figure left the camp. Figuring that he knew what was going on, he wasn't surprised when a few minutes later someone else slipped away from the circle of wagons, being careful to avoid the places where Blackie and Neilson stood guard.

Muttering a curse under his breath, Preacher told himself he'd just have to wait until Jerome Hart and Deborah Morrigan were finished with their clandestine courting. He was sure they were the ones he had seen sneaking out of the camp. They were taking chances, not only with their affair, but also by venturing out onto the plains like that after dark. If they ran into any trouble out there, the odds were they wouldn't be able to handle it themselves. If a Cheyenne or Arapaho or Pawnee war party came across them, they would lose their hair for sure.

Preacher debated whether to go after them and keep an eye on them or just hope for the best, when that decision was taken out of his hands. He saw someone *else* cat-footing across the camp, then stepping over a wagon tongue and vanishing into the darkness. Now what the hell—!

Preacher slipped out from under the wagon. Looked like there was gonna be a damned caravan of skulkers tonight.

He was on his way past the wagon shared by

Jerome and Jake when the youngster's head poked out through the flap. "Preacher? Is that you?" Jake asked in a fairly loud voice.

Preacher shushed him. "Keep it down, boy. Sound carries out here at night."

Jake dropped his voice to a whisper. "What's goin' on? Is there trouble? I woke up and Mr. Hart was gone. Have you seen him?"

"Yeah, I know where he is," Preacher said. "No need for you to worry about him."

"I thought maybe the Injuns had come back and there was gonna be a fight. I didn't want to sleep through it."

"No, no Indians," Preacher told him. "Go on back to bed now."

"All right. I guess Mr. Hart just went to answer the call o' nature."

Yeah, it was a call of nature that Jerome was answering, all right, Preacher thought, but not the same sort of call that Jake was talking about.

He waited until the boy had ducked back into the tent, then turned toward the spot where he had seen the three surreptitious figures disappear into the darkness.

But he was too late, Preacher realized a second later when he heard Corliss Hart shout, "Deborah! Jerome! Oh, my God!"

Deborah was about to get that first-hand experience with all hell breaking loose that she'd been talking about earlier.

Twenty

Deborah screamed, although the cry sounded more like it was prompted by surprise rather than fear. Preacher bit back a curse and loped toward the commotion. The voices of Corliss and Jerome were both raised in anger as they shouted at each other.

"How dare you?" Corliss said. "My own cousin!"

"This has nothing to do with you, damn it—" Jerome began.

"Nothing to do with me! For God's sake, it has *everything* to do with me! That's the woman I intend to marry, and I find you with your hands all over her!"

"Deborah will never marry you! She's a fine woman, and she deserves a lot better than a man who treats her so badly like you, Corliss!"

"You're insane! I've never done anything to harm her!"

"No, nothing but scold and belittle her in front of everyone! Good Lord, Corliss, can't you even see how obnoxious you've been to her?"

"She shouldn't have come along!" Corliss insisted. "I knew something bad would happen!"

"The only bad thing that's happened is that this poor woman made the mistake of accepting your marriage proposal!"

Deborah screamed again, but this time it was in words rather than an incoherent outcry. "Stop it, both of you! Just stop it!"

Preacher heard shouts of confusion and alarm from the wagon camp behind him as the uproar roused everybody else. Not only that, but if there was anybody who meant them harm within hearing distance, then they knew what was going on, too, and might choose this moment as an opportune one to strike.

"All of you hush, damn it!" Preacher ordered as he came up to Corliss, Jerome, and Deborah. Jerome stood with his left arm draped protectively around Deborah's shoulders. She had both hands pressed to her mouth. Corliss stood a few feet away, glaring at them. Both of his hands were clenched into fists.

Jerome turned his head enough to look at the mountain man. "This is a private matter, Preacher—"

"Not anymore it ain't," Preacher broke in. "Not the way the two of you been bellerin' like stuck pigs. I'd say that everybody within half a mile knows exactly what's goin' on."

"I'm sorry we disturbed the camp—" Jerome said.

"What about me?" Corliss asked. "*I'm* disturbed! Hell, the way you two were going, you'd have been rutting on the ground like animals in another couple of minutes!"

Deborah gasped. "That's not true!" she said. "Jerome is a gentleman! He's never done anything except . . . except kiss me. Even though I wanted him to . . . do more."

Corliss stared at her, aghast. "You . . . you trollop!" he said when he recovered from his apparent shock.

Jerome took his arm from around Deborah's shoulders and stepped forward. "How dare you!" he said. "You can't talk to Deborah like that!"

"Why not?" Corliss asked with a sneer. "Obviously, that's what she is."

"Oh, hell," Preacher muttered. He knew what was likely to happen next, and although he tried to get between the cousins, Jerome moved faster than Preacher expected him to. Jerome's fist smashed into Corliss's mouth, rocking the larger of the cousins back a step.

Corliss caught himself and lifted a hand to rub his mouth where Jerome had struck him. An ugly grin stretched across his face as he said, "I'm glad you did that."

"Apologize!" Jerome responded as if in his rage he hadn't even heard Corliss's comment. "I demand that you apologize to Deborah!"

"Go to hell, both of you," Corliss said.

Then he launched himself in a diving tackle at Jerome.

Both men went down hard as Corliss crashed into his cousin. Preacher stood there and shook his head as they rolled on the ground, punching and gouging at each other. Deborah clapped her hands to her mouth again and let out another horrified scream as everyone else in the group came pounding up, including Jake. The boy tugged at Preacher's sleeve and asked, "What's goin' on? How come Mr. Corliss and Mr. Jerome are fightin'? And ain't you gonna stop 'em, Preacher?"

"Too late for that, I reckon," Preacher said. "They got to get out what's inside of 'em, and the only way to do that is what they're doin' now."

"Yeah, but how come they're whalin' away on each other? Somethin' happen to make 'em mad?"

Gil Robinson snickered and said, "I reckon that gal happened."

"You mean Miss Deborah?"

Preacher frowned at Robinson to keep the man from making some leering reply. He didn't like Robinson much to start with. He wasn't a hard worker, and he had caused trouble before this. Problem was, they needed him. If anything happened to Robinson, or any of the other men, they'd be short-handed. They should have brought more fellas with them from St. Louis, Preacher thought, but the Hart cousins had been responsible for hiring the crew.

And now Corliss and Jerome were responsible for the fracas going on, although Deborah had had a part in it, too, Preacher told himself. She had to bear some responsibility for this awkward situation, first because she had come along on the journey when she wasn't supposed to, and second because she had decided that she wanted Jerome instead of Corliss, the man she had promised to marry.

The whole thing was a recipe for disaster if Preacher had ever seen one.

Now they would just have to make the best of it. He turned to the others and said, "You boys go on back to the wagons. This ain't any of our business, and those trade goods don't need to be sittin' over there without anybody watchin' 'em."

"Nobody's gonna sneak up and steal the wagons with us right here," Robinson protested.

"All right, but if there's any trouble, I'm holdin' you responsible, mister," Preacher said with a hard look.

Robinson's gaze dropped to the ground. "All right, all right," he muttered. "Come on, fellas."

"Blackie, you and Lars go back on guard duty like you were before," Preacher added.

Blackie said, "Looks like we didn't do a very good job, since the lady and her two beaus left camp without us ever noticin'."

"You were watchin' for people tryin' to sneak in, not out," Preacher pointed out.

Blackie shrugged.

"Take the boy with you," Preacher went on as he put a hand on Jake's shoulder and turned him away from Corliss and Jerome, who were still brawling and wrestling, and Deborah, who looked on with a worried expression on her face as the combat unfolded before her.

"Aw, I want to stay and find out what happens!" Jake complained.

Preacher gave him a more forceful push toward the wagons. "Growin' boys need their sleep," he said.

"You think I'm just gonna go to sleep after this?"

Preacher didn't know if any of them were going to get much sleep the rest of the night, but Jake was too young to stand around and watch a couple

of men fight over a woman, with all the cussing and
frank talk that went along with that.

Blackie put a hand on Jake's other shoulder and
said, "Come on, kid. Preacher's the boss on this
trip. We all agreed to that."

Grudgingly, Jake allowed himself to be led away.
The others all went back to the wagons, too, leaving Preacher and Deborah to watch as Corliss and
Jerome continued to pummel at each other. Both
men had dark streaks on their faces now from the
blood that had welled from an assortment of cuts
and scrapes.

"Can't you *do* something?" Deborah demanded
in a ragged voice. "Can't you stop them before they
kill each other?"

"They ain't gonna kill each other," Preacher told
her. "Neither one of 'em is a good enough fighter
for that. They'll just wallop each other until they
get too tired to keep goin'."

"And what's that going to solve?"

It wouldn't solve anything, and Preacher knew it.
Even when they wore themselves out, the anger they
felt would be as strong as ever. Some things could be
settled by fighting. The rivalry for a woman's affections wasn't really one of them. Oh, one fella might
knock the stuffing out of the other, but that wouldn't
change the way anybody felt.

So maybe Deborah was right. Maybe this battle
was futile. Preacher grimaced and shook his head,
then decided that the cousins had pounded on
each other for long enough. He moved closer, waiting for the right moment, then waded into the
struggle and grabbed the collars of both men. With
the strength that packed his lean, hard-muscled

frame, he hauled them upright and held them apart at arm's length.

Corliss and Jerome both continued trying to flail away, even though they couldn't reach each other, until Preacher gave them each a hard shake and said, "Damn it, that's enough! Settle down, the both of you!"

"He started it!" Corliss accused, panting from exertion and anger. "He threw the first punch! And he stole my fiancée!"

"You forced her away from you, the way you treated her!" Jerome shot back. "You don't deserve to have her!"

"Both of you just stop, please," Deborah put in in a tortured voice. "Can't you . . . can't you see what you're doing to me?"

They both looked at her, puzzlement momentarily replacing rage. "Doing to you?" Jerome asked. "I'm trying to help you."

"And I'm trying to keep this bastard from stealing you from me!" Corliss added.

"You're tearing me apart, that's what you're doing!" Deborah put her hands over her face and began to sob into them. The sobs were so strong they shook her entire body.

Corliss and Jerome fell silent and frowned at her, obviously unsure what they should say or do next. Preacher let go of them, figuring that they wouldn't start throwing punches at each other again, at least not right away.

Jerome took an uncertain step toward her. "Deborah?" he said.

"Leave her alone," Corliss snapped. "Haven't you done enough damage already?"

"I'm not the one who did the damage. You're supposed to be in love with this woman, for God's sake. If you'd just treated her decently—"

"And if you'd kept your hands off of her—"

Preacher said, "If you fellas go to scufflin' again, I'm gonna be tempted to knock your heads together."

Corliss glared at him. "You work for us, you know. We could dismiss you."

"Yes, that would be the intelligent thing to do," Jerome said. "Dismiss our guide when we're hundreds of miles away from civilization, surrounded by untamed wilderness."

"We'd be fine," Corliss said. "We know we're supposed to follow the river. And nothing has happened to us so far, has it?"

"No, nothing except an encounter with Indians who might well have wiped us out if not for Preacher's expertise in dealing with them."

"They didn't seem all that hostile to me," Corliss insisted.

"Then you're an even bigger fool than I already thought you were!" Jerome scrubbed a hand over his face and heaved a sigh. "Look, this isn't about Preacher. It's about Deborah. What are we going to do?"

"You're going to keep your filthy hands off of her, that's what we're going to do!"

Jerome put his arm around Deborah's shoulders again. Corliss squinted at them in anger and took a step forward, clenching his fists again. Preacher was ready this time. He was going to clout Corliss if the younger man tried to throw another punch.

But instead, Corliss stopped short as he saw the way Deborah turned into Jerome's embrace and buried her face against his chest. She continued to cry. Awkwardly, Jerome patted her back with his free hand and said, "There, there, Deborah. It'll be all right."

Corliss frowned. "She used to turn to me when she was upset," he said, and there was a small, wounded sound in his voice.

"Yes, well, that was before you began behaving in such an arrogant, high-handed manner," Jerome told him. "Women are like delicate flowers—"

Deborah lifted her head, sniffled, and thumped a fist lightly against Jerome's chest. "N-no, we're not," she said as she swallowed her sobs. "But we still like to be treated decently."

Then she buried her head against him again and he continued to pat her back.

Corliss drew in a deep breath and blew it out. "All right," he said. "Maybe I *am* to blame for some of the problems. But you took advantage of the situation, Jerome. You know you did."

"That was never my intention," Jerome said with a shake of his head. "Things just . . . happened. I didn't plan to fall in love with her."

Corliss turned away. "Shut up. I don't want to hear any more about it, and I don't want to talk about it. We'll discuss this in the morning."

"Yes, I think that's a good idea. Come along, Deborah. I'll take you back to your wagon. You need to get some rest. You're distraught."

"No, I'm n-not," she insisted. "I'm just mad because things have to be so . . . so damned complicated!"

Jerome looked shocked that she would use such blunt, unladylike language, but he didn't say anything about it, which Preacher thought was probably a smart move. Deborah wasn't in any mood to be scolded about anything, and if Jerome tried, she was liable to haul off and wallop him one.

Corliss had already stalked off toward the wagons. Now Jerome and Deborah followed, leaving Preacher standing there on the prairie. He scratched at his beard, thinking that it probably would have been a good idea if he'd had a talk with Jerome when he first discovered what was going on. He could have told Jerome to leave his cousin's fiancée alone and headed this problem off.

Of course, there was no guarantee that Jerome would have followed Preacher's advice. Fellas who were in love were known for not being able to think too straight.

Preacher waited until they had reached the wagons before he moved. While he was standing there, he listened intently, searching for anything unusual in the night sounds. Hearing nothing like that, he thought about the plans he had made for tonight. As upset as everybody was, he decided it might be a good idea to postpone his scouting mission to see if anyone was following them. If another fight broke out between Corliss and Jerome, he ought to be on hand to deal with it. Despite what he had told Deborah about the two of them not being able to kill each other, he knew that such battles between close relatives sometimes *did* turn deadly. He couldn't allow that to happen here.

So he went back to the wagons instead of heading off into the night on foot. When he reached the circle, he found Jerome waiting for him. The man said, "Preacher, I'm sorry. I know I've caused a problem here, but I couldn't help it. Like I told

Corliss, what happened between Deborah and me just . . . happened."

"Yeah, I know," Preacher said. "I ain't an expert on such things as fallin' in love, but I do know that it's a mite like bein' attacked by Indians."

Jerome frowned at him. "It is? How so?"

Preacher gave a grim chuckle. "Most o' the time it comes outta nowhere . . . and if you ain't lucky, you wind up with your scalp danglin' from somebody else's belt."

Twenty-one

The atmosphere in camp the next morning was chilly, but it had nothing to do with the weather. Corliss Hart sat by himself on a wagon tongue, sipping from a cup of coffee and frowning. Anyone who spoke to him got a curt, unfriendly answer. He didn't come anywhere near his cousin Jerome or Deborah Morrigan, who sat with Jerome near the campfire.

Preacher supposed that if the worst that happened was Corliss being sullen for the rest of the journey, they could put up with it. Now that the romance between Jerome and Deborah was out in the open, they seemed to have decided it no longer made sense to try to keep it a secret. They talked together openly and smiled at each other in that special way men and women do when a bond has formed between them. Preacher thought he might have a word with Jerome about trying not to throw what had happened in Corliss's face. That would just make things worse. Also, they probably ought to clear the air about whether or not Deborah and Corliss were still engaged. Preacher figured they weren't.

Corliss must have been thinking along those same lines, because while the men were hitching the teams of oxen to the wagons, Corliss suddenly strode into the middle of the camp and said in a loud voice, "Jerome, come out here. We have to talk."

Jerome was checking the grease on one of the wheel hubs. He straightened from that task, looked at his cousin, and asked, "What do you want?"

"Just come here," Corliss insisted.

Preacher was putting the saddle on Horse while Jake stood nearby and watched him, scratching Dog's ears at the same time. They all looked around at the sound of Corliss's voice, and Jake said, "You think they're gonna fight again?"

"They'd durned well better not," Preacher replied as he finished tightening one of the cinches. He turned and strode toward Corliss, trailed by Jake and Dog.

Jerome came from the other direction and got there first. "Well, what is it?" he asked, not bothering to keep the impatience out of his voice. "There's work to do before we can get started again, you know."

"I don't care," Corliss said. "I'm not going."

Jerome's eyes widened in surprise, as if that was the last thing he had expected to hear from his cousin. "Not going? What in the world do you mean, not going?"

"Not with you anyway." Corliss's face was stony with determination. "We're splitting up, Jerome."

"Don't be insane. We're partners. We've worked together for years now. We put equal amounts of money into this venture. We can't split up."

Corliss shook his head. "I don't see why not. We'll divide the goods right down the middle and each take three wagons."

Preacher didn't like the sound of that idea. Things were about to get a whole heap more complicated if Corliss got his way.

"There's no reason to do that," Jerome insisted.

"There's the best reason in the world," Corliss countered. "My engagement to Deborah is over."

Jerome shrugged. "Well, I think that goes without saying, under the circumstances."

"That being the case," Corliss said, "I'm not going to travel with her, or with the man who stole her from me. And I'm sure as hell not going into business with you, you traitor."

"Now see here—"

Corliss poked a finger hard into Jerome's chest. "No, *you* see here. Our partnership is dissolved. We'll split the goods, like I said, and take different routes. We'll set up two trading posts instead of one."

Jerome was starting to look a little frantic. "But we can't do that."

"Why not? The frontier is a big place. There'll be room for two trading posts." Corliss shrugged. "I think I ought to get the best spot, though, just to be fair. Since you get Deborah, after all." He glanced around at the mountain man, then went on. "And also to be fair, I think Preacher should go with *me*."

That came as a surprise to Preacher, since he didn't think Corliss had much use for him. Just the night before, in fact, Corliss had been talking about dismissing him from their employment. That would have been a damn fool thing to do, of course—but then so was splitting up this expedition into two parties.

And the foolishness had gone on long enough. Preacher stepped forward and said in a growling tone, "Nobody's gonna go their separate ways. That'd be a good way to get everybody killed. This bunch is really too small already. Bust it in half and you'd all be easy targets for whatever trouble came along."

"You see, Corliss?" Jerome said. "I told you—"

"What I see is that I can't stand to travel with the two of you, knowing how you've both betrayed me," Corliss interrupted. "I don't like to admit it, but . . . it hurts too much." His voice caught. "My God, Jerome, can't you see that my heart's broken?"

Preacher didn't figure *his* heart had ever been broken, although it had come mighty close when Jennie died. But he could understand that it probably stung a mite. Still, what Corliss suggested was crazy, and Preacher wasn't going to allow it.

Before he could get back in the middle of the argument, Deborah said from behind them, "Corliss . . . your heart is broken?"

They all turned toward her, and when Preacher saw the expression on her face, he muttered a curse to himself. Deborah's eyes were shining as she stepped toward them and went on, "Losing me has hurt you that badly?"

"Of course it has," he replied, his voice rough with emotion. "I planned for us to spend the rest of our lives together. To have that taken away from me is almost more than I can stand." He took a deep breath and squared his shoulders. "That's why I can't stay around while the two of you are . . . Well,

I just can't, that's all. And since I financed this expedition in equal shares with Jerome, the only solution is to divide everything right down the middle." His mouth twisted. "Except you, of course. We can't do that. He's won."

Deborah shook her head. "No. No, he hasn't. Not if you truly love me enough so that you're heartbroken over losing me. I . . . I thought you didn't care anymore, Corliss."

Jerome said, "Excuse me, but . . . what's going on here?"

Jake looked up at Preacher and said, "I'm mixed up, too. Which one of 'em is it she likes?"

Preacher didn't know the answer to that question. He wasn't sure Deborah knew the answer.

Or maybe she did, because suddenly she stepped up to Corliss, put her arms around his neck, and pulled his head down to hers. Their lips met in a kiss.

"Deborah!" Jerome said. "What are you doing?"

"Oh," Jake said. "I get it now. Miss Deborah really liked Mr. Corliss better all along, but she thought Mr. Corliss didn't like her no more, so she took up with Mr. Jerome instead. But now that she knows Mr. Corliss still likes her, she wants to be with him again. That about the size of it, Preacher?"

"Yeah, I reckon," Preacher said, thinking to himself that he'd rather wrestle a grizzly again than have to sort out the romantic problems of these greenhorns. It was enough to make a man feel like he ought to go back to the mountains and never come out again.

Jerome looked like he'd been walloped over the head with a singletree. He stared at Corliss and

Deborah as if he couldn't comprehend what was happening right before his eyes. Preacher almost felt sorry for the poor son of a bitch . . . almost.

"There's just one thing I don't understand," Jake said.

Preacher looked down at him. "What's that?"

"How come they like to kiss that way? That can't be any fun, can it?"

"I reckon if you live long enough, you'll find out, younker."

Jake shook his head. "I'll never live long that I'd want to kiss a girl."

Preacher put a hand on Jerome's arm. "Come on. Like you said, there's work to do before we get them wagons rollin' again."

"But . . . but . . ."

"You're not gonna start up that crazy talk about splittin' up the expedition again, are you?" Preacher asked in a hard voice.

"No . . . No, I suppose not." Pain shone dully in Jerome's eyes. "But if things were different—"

"If things were different, we wouldn't be out here in the middle o' nowhere havin' to depend on each other to survive. But that's the way it is. Ever'body's got a job to do, and that's what's gonna keep us alive."

Jerome took a deep breath and watched as Corliss and Deborah walked off, hand in hand. "You're right. Of course, you're right, Preacher. I was a fool, wasn't I?"

"No more so than every other man since Adam went traipsin' through the garden."

Jerome looked around and saw that the drivers were watching them. He snapped, "What are you men gaping at? Let's all get busy. The sun's up, for heaven's sake. We're burning daylight!"

Preacher smiled as Jerome stalked off toward the wagons. The expression didn't last long. Despite the fact that things seemed to be resolved once more, he had a feeling that the trouble was a long way from over. When Corliss and Jerome had been arguing about which group he would accompany if they had split up, he had been just about disgusted enough to declare that all of them could go to hell.

But he knew he couldn't bring himself to abandon them this far from civilization.

These pilgrims wouldn't stand a chance on their own.

The tension that gripped the wagon train that morning lingered for the rest of the day, and for several days afterward. Jerome's face was set in grim, stony lines as he drove the lead wagon. He said little, speaking only when he had to, and never smiled, despite the fact that Jake rode beside him on the seat and chattered incessantly.

Deborah rode with Corliss now, perched beside him on the seat, with her arm looped through his most of the time. Occasionally, she rested her head on his shoulder. It was domestic as all hell, Preacher thought as he tried to contain his disgust with the situation. He supposed that what had happened wasn't really anybody's fault, but he wished that Deborah hadn't driven such a big wedge between the cousins, whether that had been her intention or not.

"See that blue line on the horizon?" Preacher

said to Jake one day, pointing as he rode alongside the lead wagon.

"Yeah. What is it?"

"Those are the mountains," Preacher told the boy.

Jake leaned forward, his eyes widening in excitement. "Really? I never seen any real mountains before, only just pictures in books. How long will it take us to get there?"

"Another week, maybe more. It'll look like they're only a few miles off, when really they're still a long ways away, so don't get too excited just yet."

By nightfall, however, they had drawn close enough so that Preacher's eaglelike eyes could make out the pale areas that marked the snowfields at the top of the peaks. That snow, which never melted, gleamed in the fading light and gave the Rockies their sometime name of the Shining Mountains. Preacher pointed out the snow to Jake, but he wasn't sure if the boy ever really saw it.

The next day, Jake was able to see the snow for sure, though, and so was everyone else. The feelings of anticipation grew stronger. These people were ready to reach the mountains. Even Jerome perked up a little after days of moping.

After getting sidetracked from his scouting mission on the night the trouble had broken out between Corliss and Jerome, Preacher still hadn't gotten around to it. But there had been no more gunshots from behind them and no sign of anyone following them. Preacher's mind hadn't really been put at ease—he was too naturally wary for that to happen—but he was beginning to wonder if he had been worried about nothing.

Disappointment set in among those with the wagon train as day after day passed and they seemed to get no closer to the mountains. Preacher had seen it happen again and again when folks came west for the first time. He had warned them that the distances were deceptive, but the sight of the mountains had made them forget what he'd said.

"Are we *ever* gonna get there?" Jake asked with a sigh as they sat around the campfire one night.

"If we keep goin' long enough, we will," Preacher said. "Got to, 'cause them mountains are between us and the ocean. If they weren't, we could keep goin' all the way to the Pacific."

"That's what people are going to do, isn't it?" Corliss asked. "Take wagons over the mountains to the Pacific?"

Preacher nodded. "Some already have. Most of the folks who've settled up in the Oregon country got there by takin' ships all the way around South America. Leastways, that's what I've been told. Couldn't swear to it myself since I never been on anything bigger'n a keelboat, goin' up and down the Mississippi. But plenty o' folks have traveled the overland route, startin' with ol' Lewis and Clark. I knew some o' those boys who went with 'em. They went back to the mountains to trap beaver later on, fellas like John Colter, Jacob Reznor, and the Holt brothers. Now some missionaries have gone that way, too, provin' that you can take wagons through South Pass and on over the mountains. Just a matter of time before there's a whole bunch more folks doin' the same thing, because there's land up there for the takin' and people are always hungry for land. Pert' near everybody wants to find a place where he can look around and call it his own."

Deborah smiled and said, "I think that's the longest speech I've ever heard you make, Preacher. What about you? Where's the place that you call your own?"

Preacher lifted a hand and moved it in a gesture that took in all their surroundings, north, south, east, and west. "When the sun comes up in the mornin', stand out on the prairie and turn all the way around in a circle. You'll be lookin' at it."

Deborah nodded in understanding. The whole frontier was Preacher's home.

Twenty-two

Schuyler thought the mountains were mighty fine-looking, and he couldn't wait to get there. The summer heat on the plains had grown worse over the past week. He was looking forward to the weather being a little cooler once they reached the peaks.

And of course, once they got to the mountains, they were going to kill Preacher and all the others and take those wagons and all the goods they carried.

Schuyler was looking forward to that, too. It was the first step toward being rich.

Actually, Fairfax planned to strike once the wagons reached the foothills. He wasn't going to wait until they were in the mountains proper, because it would be harder to set up an ambush once the terrain became too rugged. They sat beside the tiny fire built in a hole some of the men had dug earlier, so the flames wouldn't be visible, and figured out what they were going to do.

"The first thing is to get around that wagon train and move on ahead of it," Fairfax said. "Once we've done that, we can find a suitable spot for a trap."

One of the men said, "As many rifles as we've got, we ought to be able to kill all of 'em in one volley. They won't never know what hit 'em."

"Preacher's mine," Schuyler said.

Fairfax frowned. "You've had three shots at him and missed with all three. I think anyone who can bring that bastard down should go ahead and do it."

"Damn it, Colin! I had good reasons for missin' him those other times."

"Yes, like the fact that you're a poor shot."

Schuyler swallowed the anger he felt. He trusted Fairfax and wouldn't go against anything he decided, but all the same, Fairfax hadn't had to bring up the bad luck that had dogged Schuyler the other times he'd tried to kill Preacher. There'd been no good reason to do that.

"Preacher is too dangerous to take any chances with him," Fairfax went on. "Anyone who has a good shot at him, *take it*. I want that son of a bitch dead as soon as possible when we hit the wagon train."

Schuyler knew his partner was right, but it rankled him anyway. If he got the chance, he promised himself, he was going to take Preacher down. Then Fairfax would be proud of him.

The next morning, the gang of killers and thieves crossed the Platte River so they could begin swinging farther north and west to get around the wagon train. They had to be careful because of the treacherous mud and quicksand, but they were able to make the ford without any incidents. Schuyler was surprised when, a short time later, they came to another broad, shallow, muddy stream.

"If that was the Platte we forded back yonder, what

river is this?" he asked as he and Fairfax reined their horses to a halt and the rest of the gang followed suit.

"According to the maps I studied back in St. Louis," Fairfax said, "the Platte splits somewhere out here. That must have been the South Platte we crossed earlier, and this is the North Platte. I never noticed the split when we passed it. This river is such a maze of channels, it's hard to tell where it ends and where it begins."

They forded this stream, and then rode almost due north for several hours before turning west again. Ever since leaving St. Louis, they had held their horses back to keep from gaining too fast on the wagon train. Now the men pushed their mounts at a faster pace, and the horses responded, loping easily across the prairie toward the still-distant mountains.

During one of the times when they had stopped to rest the horses, Schuyler gazed off to the south and spotted something jutting up on the horizon. "What's that?" he asked Fairfax as he pointed at it.

"I don't know," Fairfax replied with a frown. "Let me get my spyglass."

He studied the distant landmark for a few moments, then passed the spyglass to Schuyler. When Schuyler peered through the lens, he was able to tell that the thing was a spire of rock that rose straight up into the air from a broader base.

"Chimney Rock," Fairfax said. "I remember seeing it marked on some of the maps. The trail Preacher and the others will be following goes right past it."

"Damn, it must be tall to stick up like that when we're miles away from it."

"Indeed." Fairfax closed the spyglass. "I hope Preacher and his companions are suitably impressed when they pass it." He smiled. "It may be one of the last such natural wonders they ever see."

As with everything else out here, the travelers saw Chimney Rock long before they reached it. Jake leveled an arm at it and asked in an excited voice as he pointed, "What's that?"

"Chimney Rock," Preacher explained from his saddle as he walked Horse alongside the lead wagon. "Tomorrow we'll pass Scott's Bluff, and a couple of days after that we'll be in the foothills, skirtin' around the Laramies so we can cut over to South Pass. Another week and we can start lookin' for a good place to start buildin' that tradin' post."

"Another week," Jerome muttered. "My God, is this trip *never* going to end?"

Jerome still hadn't recovered from Deborah going back to Corliss. Preacher figured that was understandable. Jerome wasn't what you'd call handsome, nor was he as big and strong as Corliss. He'd probably always played second fiddle to his cousin. For a few days, though, he'd had something that Corliss had failed to hold on to—Deborah's affections. Sure, it had been hard on Jerome when she'd slipped through his fingers through no fault of his own and he'd lost her back to Corliss.

But out here on the frontier, a fella couldn't afford to spend too much time brooding over lost loves and suchlike. There was too much work to do, and too many dangers that could come out of nowhere.

Like the war party that suddenly boiled around the base of chimney rock and galloped straight across the prairie toward the line of wagons.

Preacher saw them coming and bellowed, "Circle the wagons! Circle the wagons!" He could tell from the way the Indians drove their ponies over the grassy plain that they meant business. There wouldn't be any negotiating with these fellas.

By now, the men had had enough practice so that drawing the wagons into a circle was second nature to them. They had to keep their wits about them now, though, and perform the maneuver faster than they ever had before. There wouldn't be time to unhitch the teams and move the oxen into the protection of the circle, so some of the beasts would probably die. Corliss and Jerome had brought along extra oxen, of course, and as the wagons were circled, Preacher drove those animals into the center of the formation.

He saw Jake jump down from the seat of the lead wagon and run to the back of the vehicle. The boy reached inside and pulled out an armful of powder horns and shot pouches. He was getting ready to perform his reloading chores, and that was good.

Corliss pushed Deborah inside their wagon and told her, "Stay down!" The vehicle's thick sideboards would stop an arrow or a lance and most rifle balls, too. As long as Deborah hugged the floor of the wagon, she ought to be safe.

Gil Robinson, Lars Neilson, and Blackie all hurried to find good positions from which to fire. Pete Carey ran over to Jake and gathered up some of the powder horns and shot pouches. Rifles in hand, Corliss and Jerome crouched at the rear of their wagons. The Indians were only about a hundred yards away when Preacher surveyed the circle and gave a curt nod of satisfaction. The men had spread out so that they could defend in every direction.

The fact that the Indians hadn't started shooting yet probably meant that they didn't have any rifles, Preacher thought. That was a good thing. The fact that the wagon train's defenders were armed with good, accurate rifles would help them counter the war party's superior numbers. Preacher figured there were at least thirty of the Indians.

He swung down from the saddle, knelt beside one of the wagons, lifted his rifle to his shoulder, and set out to cut down some on the war party's numbers.

The weapon belched smoke and flame as its charge of black powder detonated with a roar. Preacher barely felt the recoil. As he lowered the rifle and began the process of reloading, his muscles functioning without conscious thought, he squinted through the cloud of smoke and saw one of the Indians lying sprawled on the ground. The others continued the attack. More shots blasted out from the defenders. Preacher heard the faint flutter of arrows flashing through the air. One of them buried itself in the side of the wagon with a solid *thunk!* The shaft quivered from the impact, no more than a couple of feet from Preacher's head.

But as long as the arrows missed, it didn't matter by how much. Preacher had the flintlock charged, loaded, and primed again less than thirty seconds after his first shot. He lifted it, drew a bead on another of the Indians as the war party split up to encircle the wagons, and fired. Once again, one of the warriors toppled off the back of a galloping pony.

The other defenders weren't as fast at reloading as Preacher was, nor were they as accurate with their shots. But with the help of Jake and Pete Carey, they kept up a pretty steady fire, and gradually their shots began to take a toll. Several more Indians fell, and a couple of the ponies collapsed when they were hit.

The attackers were doing some damage of their own. Oxen bellowed as they were skewered by arrows. Most of the wounds weren't fatal, since the beasts were protected by thick slabs of muscle, but they were painful and would prove mortal if enough of the shafts found their targets. One of the Indians came close enough to drive a lance halfway through an ox before a ball from Preacher's rifle blew half his head off his shoulders in a gory spray of blood and bone and brain matter.

That Indian was also close enough for Preacher to recognize the war paint. These warriors were Pawnee, good fighters and nearly always hostile to whites. Preacher had known there was a good possibility the expedition would run into some of them, although he had hoped they would be lucky enough not to.

The Indians were riding in a circle around the wagons now, the hooves of their ponies kicking up enough dust that it was difficult to see them. That made aiming hard, too. Bloodcurdling whoops came from their throats as they poured arrows at the wagons.

A shout of pain made Preacher look back over his shoulder. On the other side of the circle, Lars

Neilson staggered back from his position with an arrow jutting from the upper part of his left arm. The big Swede dropped to his knees, grimacing in pain. At the same time, one of the Pawnee warriors leaped his pony through the gap between wagons that Neilson had been defending. With a savage cry, he lunged his mount toward Neilson, lance poised to impale the Swede.

Preacher's rifle was empty, so he snatched the tomahawk from behind his belt and flung it. The weapon flashed through the air and struck the Indian in the forehead. The blade buried itself in the warrior's brain and drove him backward off his pony.

Still wide-eyed in pain, Neilson looked around at Preacher and managed to nod his thanks. Then Pete Carey hurried over to the Swede and helped him back to his feet. With the arrow still in his arm, Neilson picked up the rifle he had dropped. Carey took it from him and began reloading it.

Preacher turned back to his own killing work.

At least half the members of the war party were down. They must not have been expecting the men with the wagon train to put up such a stiff fight. After a few more minutes of whooping and galloping around and firing arrows at the wagons, they turned their ponies and raced off into the distance. The dust cloud they had caused gradually began to dissipate.

Preacher walked around the inside of the circle, checking on everyone. He started with Jake Brant. "You all right, son?" he asked the youngster.

Jake's face was smeared with black grime from the powder he'd been handling as he reloaded. His hands were even more stained. But he wasn't injured, and a grin broke out across his face as Preacher came up to him.

"Yeah, I'm fine," he said. "I was scared, but I just kept loading rifles and handin' 'em to Mr. Corliss and Mr. Jerome."

Preacher clapped a hand on his shoulder. "You done good work. A man who never gets scared ain't brave, he's just a durn fool. It's the fella who's scared but does what needs to be done anyway who's really got the most courage."

Jake beamed at the praise.

Preacher turned to Corliss and Jerome. "How about you two?"

"We're all right," Jerome said. He looked over at his cousin. "You shot more of those savages than I did."

"It wasn't a competition," Corliss said. "I just wanted them to go away and leave us alone." He went to the rear of the wagon and pushed the canvas flap aside. His voice was tight with worry as he asked, "Deborah? Are you all right?"

"Yes," she said as she appeared in the opening, looking pale and shaken but otherwise unharmed. "I was really frightened because I kept hearing arrows strike the wagon. A few of them tore all the way through the canvas. But I stayed down like you told me to, Corliss, and I was fine."

He reached up to help her down from the vehicle. "Well, you don't have to worry anymore. The savages are gone. Better not look out there, though. There are quite a few bodies lying around."

Deborah shuddered at the thought of the ground being littered with the corpses of the warriors.

"Don't be so sure the trouble's over," Preacher advised Corliss.

"What do you mean? The Indians left."

"For right now. Ain't nothin' stoppin' 'em from comin' back."

Corliss and Jerome both frowned. Clearly, they hadn't thought about that. Jerome said, "How likely is that? They lost quite a few of their men. Surely they won't risk attacking us again."

"Not unless they go back and get a bunch more warriors to come with them next time. As war parties go, this was a small one. They were probably just hopin' to steal some ponies from another tribe or somethin' like that. They didn't expect to run across a wagon train. They should've passed us by. They won't make the mistake of hittin' us with a small group again."

"But they might not come back at all, right?" Corliss asked.

"They might not," Preacher admitted. "You can't ever tell which way an Indian's gonna jump."

A quick check of the other men confirmed that the arrow wound in Lars Neilson's arm was the only injury the defenders had suffered. A couple of the oxen were dead and would have to be replaced on the teams. Preacher got the uninjured drivers busy tending to that while he looked at Neilson's arm.

"Take it out, yah?" the Swede asked in a voice thinned by pain.

"Yeah, but it ain't gonna be pleasant," Preacher warned as he sat Neilson down on a lowered tailgate. "I can't just pull it out, 'cause the barbs on the arrow will cause more damage that way. I'll have to push it all the way through."

Neilson's eyes widened with fear at that prospect, but he swallowed hard and said, "Do what you bane have to do."

Preacher took hold of the shaft and snapped it off close to where the arrowhead was buried in Neilson's arm. But not too close, because he had to leave enough so that he could push the arrowhead all the way through. "Hang on," he said as he took hold of Neilson's arm with his left hand, put his right hand against the arrow, and shoved as hard as he could.

Neilson screamed and jerked as the bloody arrowhead finished tearing a channel all the way through his arm and popped out on the other side. Preached grabbed it and pulled what was left of the shaft the rest of the way through. Neilson's eyes rolled up in his head. He might have passed out and fallen off the tailgate if not for Preacher's firm grip on his arm.

The ordeal wasn't over for Neilson. Preacher called for Jerome to bring over the jug of whiskey that was kept in the lead wagon for things just like this. Neilson whimpered as Preacher poured the fiery liquor through the wound. Then Preacher said, "Jake, fetch me a powder horn."

"*Gott hilfen mir!*" Neilson gasped. Preacher figured the words meant *God help me*. "What are you going to do now?"

"Got to fix these wounds so they'll heal up and not fester," Preacher explained as he sprinkled black powder around the bloody openings. Then he took an unloaded pistol, cocked it, and held it close enough to the entrance wound so that when he clicked the hammer against the flint, one of the sparks set off the powder with a flash. The stink of burned meat filled the air as Neilson yelled again. Preacher repeated the process with the exit wound.

"They ought to be all right now," he assured the shaken Neilson, "but we'll keep an eye on 'em, just to be sure."

"Them Gott-damned redskins," the Swede choked out. "This is their fault. I almost wish they would come back so I could kill some more of them."

Preacher laughed. "Well, I hope you don't get your wish, Lars." He turned to Jake. "Can you get some clean strips of cloth, wrap 'em around Mr. Neilson's arm, and tie 'em good an' tight?"

"Sure, Preacher," the boy said. He hurried off to find some makeshift bandages while Preacher went back to the other men.

"We'll be pullin' out as soon as we can," he told them.

Corliss waved a hand at the Pawnee corpses. "What about them?"

"The rest of the bunch will be comin' back to get their bodies," Preacher said with a nod. "That's one reason we don't want to be here when they do. Let's put some ground between us and them."

"That sounds like a good idea to me," Jerome said. He shuddered a little as he glanced at the sprawled bodies. "We were lucky, weren't we, Preacher?"

Preacher nodded. "Damned lucky," he said.

Twenty-three

Schuyler Mims, Colin Fairfax, and the rest of Shad Beaumont's men heard the firing to the south and stopped to look worriedly in that direction.

"Sounds like a damn battle goin' on," Schuyler said. "What do you reckon it is, Colin?"

"I don't know, but it's got to involve that wagon train," Fairfax replied with a scowl. "They might have run into some Indians, or something like that. We'd better go see about it. By God, nobody better try to steal those trade goods before we do!"

Fairfax decided that only a small party would investigate, because they would be less likely to be spotted by Preacher or any other members of the Hart expedition. The rest of the men would wait right where they were until the scouts came back.

Schuyler, Fairfax, and two other men, Burns and Loomis, rode south toward the towering spire of rock they had spotted earlier. The shots seemed to be coming from that direction. After they had gone a mile or so, the shooting gradually died away. Schuyler looked over at Fairfax and said, "Now it sounds like the battle's over."

"Yes, but we don't know what that means," Fairfax said. "Preacher and the others could have been wiped out. Someone could be stealing those wagons right out from under our very noses!"

His tone made it clear that he wasn't going to stand for that. He urged his horse to greater speed.

Schuyler hoped that they weren't riding right into more trouble than they could handle.

A few minutes later, they spotted a dust cloud moving off to the east. "Lot o' riders headed that way," Loomis commented.

Fairfax nodded. "Yes, but the wagons aren't with them. The dust is moving too fast for that."

The four men kept riding. They circled around the rock spire, which was a stark, striated reddish-brown. The broad base was the same color, but it was streaked with green on its lower levels where the grass from the plains had crawled up onto the rocky surface.

Shortly after riding around the towering rock chimney, they spotted dark shapes lying on the ground ahead of them. "Damn," Schuyler said in a hushed voice. "Are those what I think they are?"

"They appear to be bodies," Fairfax said. He kept his horse moving. When the other three men slowed a little, he looked back over his shoulder at them and snapped, "Well, come on! Those men can't hurt you. They're all dead."

"You can't be sure of that," Schuyler pointed out.

"If they're not dead, they're so close to it that they're no danger to us. You don't see them jumping up and capering around, do you?"

"Maybe all of 'em *are* dead," Burns said. "Some o' their friends could still be around."

"If they are, we'll see them coming in time to get away."

Schuyler wished he could be as sure of that as Fairfax sounded. Fairfax wasn't backing down, though, so Schuyler didn't have any choice except to urge his mount into a trot and catch up. Even more reluctantly, Burns and Loomis followed suit.

As they neared the bodies, Schuyler saw the buckskins and the feathers and the war paint. The dead men all had thick, midnight-dark hair smeared with some sort of grease. They were Indians, all right. Schuyler had no idea which tribe they belonged to. He didn't know how to identify such things. There were also a couple of dead oxen, their bodies feathered with arrows.

Fairfax rode boldly past the Indians and pointed to marks on the ground. "See the wheel ruts?" he said. "The wagons were here. It looks like they circled up, then moved out again."

"They had to stop and fight Indians," Schuyler said. "And they must've won or they wouldn't have kept goin'." He nodded toward the grisly shapes on the ground. "And all these dead fellas wouldn't still be layin' here."

"Boss, we'd better get outta here," Loomis said in a worried tone. "I don't know a whole heap about Injuns, but I know they don't leave their dead behind. If any of 'em were left alive, they're gonna come back for these bodies."

Burns nodded. "He's right, Mr. Fairfax. We need to light a shuck while we still can."

Fairfax considered the suggestion and then

agreed. "There's no sign that any members of the Hart party were killed," he said. "No fresh graves or anything like that. So we can assume that they're still at full strength and still headed for the mountains, just as they have been all along."

"So we join up with the rest of the fellas and go set up that ambush, like we figured to do all along?" Schuyler asked.

"That's right. Let's get moving."

The men turned their horses and rode back toward the rock tower. A short time later, they circled around it and continued on their way north.

Because of that, they didn't see the lone figure on horseback who rode up to the bodies of the fallen Pawnee a few minutes after the white men had gone out of sight. He studied the warriors' bodies without any sympathy in his cold, dark eyes, then hitched his pony into motion again and followed the four whites.

Scott's Bluff was a massive parapet of sandstone carved by wind and weather into bizarre, twisted shapes. It was even more impressive than Chimney Rock had been as the wagons passed by it and through an opening Preacher called Mitchell's Pass. It had taken most of two days to reach here from Chimney Rock, and Preacher intended to call a halt and set up camp as soon as they were through the pass.

Beyond it, close but still farther away than they appeared to be, were the Laramie Mountains. The trail would take the wagons through the foothills, but they would avoid the more rugged terrain, at least for now. Despite that, from here on out, they would be climbing most of the time. They had reached the end of the plains.

"I never saw anything like this back in Missouri," Jake said as the wagons rolled through the pass.

"Before you're done, you'll see a lot o' things you never saw back in Missouri," Preacher said with a grin. "There are some pretty good hills in the Ozarks, but they ain't nothin' compared to the Rockies."

Once the wagons were clear of the pass, they were pulled into a circle as usual. The atmosphere in camp that night was quiet and subdued. No one had forgotten the Indian attack the day before, and Preacher had decided that tonight, as they had on the previous night, they would have a cold camp with no fire. That made the pilgrims even more depressed. Even during summer, there was nothing like cheerful, dancing flames to perk up people's spirits.

It had bothered Deborah that the bodies of the Indians had been left behind without any sort of burial. Preacher had explained to her that the surviving Pawnee would take care of those who had fallen. Burying them in white man's fashion would have been a terrible insult. Deborah said she understood, but Preacher wasn't sure that she really did. She still seemed shaken tonight as she sat next to Corliss and gnawed on some jerky for supper. At least she didn't complain about the tough strips of dried meat, as some women would have.

The men had pulled all the arrows out of the wagons. Pete Carey had gathered them up, tied a cord around them, and tossed them in the back of one of the vehicles, along with several bows he picked up from the ground. Preacher wasn't sure what Carey intended to do with them, but throwing the bows and arrows away would have been wasteful. Preacher thought maybe he would try to teach Jake how to shoot one of the native weapons. That was a good skill for any boy to know, not just the red ones.

Preacher was musing on that when Jerome suddenly said, "I think we need to talk."

Preacher looked around in the gathering dusk, seeing that Jerome was talking to Corliss and Deborah, not him. The tension in Jerome's voice told Preacher that trouble might be about to crop up again.

"Talk about what?" Corliss asked.

"The three of us."

Corliss smirked. Now that he had won Deborah's heart back, some of his old arrogance had returned. Preacher wondered if sooner or later that would be enough to drive Deborah away from Corliss again. Not that he cared one way or the other.

"What is there to say?" Corliss asked. "We're still business partners, and Deborah is back where she belongs."

Jerome stood facing the two of them. "Let me get this straight. When you thought that Deborah had chosen me over you, you wanted to dissolve our partnership, split up the goods and the wagons, and establish two separate trading posts."

"What's your point, Jerome?" Corliss snapped.

Jerome took a deep breath. "If that was a fair reaction from you, why shouldn't it be my reaction as well? I'm just as hurt by Deborah's rejection of me as you were when you thought she had rejected you."

"Oh, don't take it that way, Jerome!" Deborah said, lifting a hand toward him. "I still think you're a fine man, and I care about you a great deal."

"Please," Corliss said with a scornful chuckle. "You tried to woo Deborah for a few days, and you think that makes what you're feeling the equal of the pain I felt when I thought the two of you were betraying me?"

Jerome sniffed. "Betrayal is betrayal, and for a heart to break doesn't require that a great deal of time be spent with the one doing the . . . breaking."

"Stop it, Jerome," Deborah said. "You know I never meant to hurt you."

"Yes, stop it," Corliss agreed. "You always were a poor loser, even when we were children."

For a second, Preacher thought Jerome was going to hurl himself at Corliss, and then he would have another fracas between the cousins to break up. Instead, Jerome controlled himself with a visible effort and said, "I want the same thing you wanted, Corliss. I want to establish my own trading post so that I won't have to see the two of you together, especially all winter."

"Don't be ridiculous. Preacher told us it would be dangerous for us to split up our party now."

"I'm not talking about splitting up the party," Jerome said. "I'll wait until we get to South Pass, as planned. I'll even give you the prime location, Corliss, because I want to see you succeed . . . for Deborah's sake. But I'm going to take three of the wagons and some of the trade goods and find a place of my own."

Corliss looked over at the mountain man. "What do you think of this idea, Preacher?"

"It don't make no never-mind to me what you folks do once you get to where you're goin'," Preacher said with a shrug of his broad shoulders. "All I'm concerned about is gettin' you there with your hair still attached to your heads and all the trade goods in them wagons." He scratched at his bearded jaw. "I'll say this, though . . . you fellas will have a whole lot better chance o' makin' it if you stick together. Split up and you'll be that much easier targets for every bloodthirsty Indian and renegade white man in this part o' the country."

"I'll take my chances," Jerome said, his jaw set stubbornly. "That's better than being constantly reminded of . . . what I lost."

Preacher couldn't understand feeling that way, but he could tell that Jerome was sincere. He would do his best to talk Jerome out of the idea once they got to South Pass. But since Jerome had said that he didn't intend to disrupt the rest of the journey by insisting on splitting up with his cousin right now, Preacher was prepared to let the whole thing ride for the time being. It could all be sorted out later, after they got where they were going.

He settled for saying, "Well, you think about it mighty hard before you make up your mind," to Jerome, then added, "Everybody might as well get some sleep, 'cept for me and Robinson. We'll be standin' the first watch."

While everyone was getting ready to turn in, some inside the wagons and some on the ground underneath them, Preacher went over to Lars Neilson and asked the Swede, "How's the arm tonight?"

"Very stiff and sore, yah," Neilson said. He flexed his wounded arm back and forth to demonstrate that he could move it. "But I bane all right. I can still use it."

"I'll take a look at the wounds in the mornin'," Preacher decided. "Got to make sure they don't go to putrefyin'. You'll lose your arm if they do."

Neilson gave a solemn shake of his head. "I do not want that."

"Neither do I, old son. Now get some rest."

Preacher took his rifle and went to one side of the circle while Robinson posted himself on the other side. Everybody was still a little on edge from the Indian fight the day before, so Preacher didn't think he had to worry about anyone dozing off while standing guard.

The night passed quietly, and early the next morning the wagon train moved on, leaving Scott's Bluff behind and beginning its approach to the foothills of the Laramie Mountains. Although not steep, the ground had a steady upward slope to it. The oxen strained against their traces to haul the heavily loaded vehicles.

"Why don't we just go all the way around the mountains?" Jerome asked while Preacher was riding beside the lead wagon at midday.

Preacher shook his head. "Too far. We'd have to swing too far north and then back to the south to hit the pass between this range of mountains and the next."

Jake asked, "Is that the South Pass you been talkin' about, Preacher?"

"Nope. South Pass, the place we're headin' for, is a heap farther on."

"How much farther?" Jerome asked, more than a hint of impatience in his voice.

"Another week, maybe two."

Jerome sighed. Preacher supposed it was because he didn't want to spend that much more time watching Corliss and Deborah act like lovebirds. Preacher didn't care about that. He just wanted Jerome to behave himself, and so far, that was happening.

The pines that grew thickly on the slopes of the foothills gave the landscape ahead of the wagons a dark green cast. Preacher could almost smell the sharp tang of the pines. It was a scent that called to him, as some men might be drawn to the smell of bread baking, or the sea, or even the smoke of industry. Any smell that meant *home,* whatever it might be, reached out to a man with strength that could not be denied. Preacher was more than ready for it when the wagons rolled through a natural saddle between two pine-covered hills and the scent washed over him for real.

The others seemed to sense that this represented a significant change from the plains where they had been traveling for the past few weeks. Even the oxen appeared to have more energy.

Their route followed the shallow valleys between the foothills. Jake cried out in joyful surprise as they spooked a herd of antelope in one such valley. The animals bounded off gracefully. They had seen buffalo on several occasions during the journey, but there was no comparison between those shaggy, lumbering beasts and the sleek, fleet-footed antelope.

They camped that night at the head of a long, grassy valley with a creek meandering through it. The stream was shallow, but it flowed swiftly over a rocky bed, and when Preacher dipped up a hand-ful of water and tasted it, it was as clear and cold as could be. Fed by snowmelt, the creek would stay cold all summer.

Preacher told the others it would be all right to have a small fire again. "We're out of Pawnee coun-try now," he explained. "They won't come up here after us."

"What sort of Injuns live around here?" Jake asked.

"Cheyenne mostly. A few Arapaho."

Jerome asked, "Are they hostile?"

"They can be," Preacher replied with a nod. "Mostly it depends on how you treat 'em. None of 'em are as bad as the Blackfoot. Blackfoot'll kill any white man he comes across, no matter what the fella does. They'll try to anyway. It was a bunch o' Blackfoot that grabbed me one time, tied me to a tree, and planned on torturin' me to death the next mornin'."

Jake's eyes widened with awe. "And you got away?"

"I'm here, ain't I?" Preacher said with a grin.

"How'd you do it? Did you get loose and kill all of 'em?"

Preacher thought about it and decided it wouldn't do any harm to tell them the story of how he came by his nickname. If they were going to stay out here on the frontier, they were going to hear it sooner or later anyway.

He put a hand on Jake's shoulder and said, "I'll tell you all about it after supper. Now, why don't you hustle up some wood for the fire?"

"Sure, but I'll hold you to that promise. I want

to hear the story." Jake hurried off to follow Preacher's orders.

Preacher started to turn away from the valley that spread out before the wagons, but then something caught his eye. The valley was a couple of miles long, and at the far end it narrowed down to a canyon where it passed between two rough, rock-strewn ridges. Preacher thought he had seen something move up there in the canyon, even at this distance.

But as he stood there for a long moment, watching the place with his keen eyes narrowed, he didn't spy anything else. He didn't think he had imagined the movement, but it could have been anything—an antelope, a moose, a grizzly bear, even an eagle or an owl swooping low to flit through the canyon. Didn't have to mean a damned thing. Taking note of it had been just a matter of instinct and habit.

Despite being aware of all that, Preacher knew that come morning, when the wagon train passed through that canyon, he would be especially watchful.

Because that was a mighty fine place for an ambush, if he had ever seen one.

Twenty-four

After Schuyler, Fairfax, Burns, and Loomis rejoined the rest of Beaumont's men, the entire group pushed on west toward the mountains, riding fairly hard. By nightfall, Fairfax judged that they were far enough ahead of the wagon train to turn back to the southwest. That would keep them ahead of the Hart expedition, but still allow them to intercept the wagons in a day or two.

Another day's travel found them in the foothills, with the snowcapped peaks looming ahead of them and an even taller range farther west that could be glimpsed from time to time. Fairfax led the group to the top of a thickly wooded ridge and called a halt there.

"All right, we'll wait here while you locate the wagon train and determine where it's going, Schuyler," he said. "Take Burns and Loomis with you. They seem like good men."

Burns chuckled and said in a dry voice, "Thanks for the vote o' confidence, Boss."

"I meant it just like it sounded," Fairfax snapped. "But I can choose someone else if you'd prefer."

All of Beaumont's men were aware of how Schuyler and Fairfax had handled themselves against the pair of burly bodyguards back in St. Louis. None of them wanted to tangle with the two new additions to the gang, so Burns was quick to say, "No, Boss, that's fine. I'm glad you've got faith in me and ol' Loomis."

Fairfax nodded, satisfied that he had asserted his authority. "We'll camp here," he said, "and you can start scouting for the wagon train in the morning."

Schuyler, Burns, and Loomis were on their way before sunrise, riding back out to the edge of the foothills. Being careful to remain in the cover of the trees, they ranged up and down for several hours, searching the approaches to the slopes for any sign of the wagons.

Around the middle of the day, Schuyler thought he spotted something. He still had Fairfax's spyglass, so he took it out, opened it up, and lifted the lens to his eye. He needed a few minutes to find what he was looking for, but then he settled the spyglass on the six wagons with their white canvas covers. The canvas was patched in numerous places. Schuyler supposed that was where arrows had torn through it during the battle with the Indians.

He closed the spyglass and said in satisfaction, "There they are."

"Yeah," Loomis agreed, "I can kinda see the wagons, too, even without that glass."

"Are they all there?" Burns asked.

Schuyler nodded. "Yes, and they don't look like they were damaged during the Indian fight. Colin's gonna be happy. I'll bet all the trade goods are just fine."

"What do we do now?"

Schuyler thought about it. He wasn't used to making decisions and giving commands. Finally, he said to Burns, "You go back and tell Colin that we've found them. Loomis and I will stay here and watch until we're sure where they're goin'."

Burns nodded and turned his horse, accepting the order without hesitation. That felt pretty good, Schuyler thought as he watched Burns ride off toward the ridge where they had left Fairfax and the others.

For the next couple of hours, the two men watched, well concealed in the pines, as the wagons drew closer. They were less than five hundred yards away when the vehicles entered the foothills, not following any trail that Schuyler could see.

But Preacher seemed to know where he was going. He rode in front of the wagon train, leading the way, and the pace of the rangy stallion the mountain man rode never faltered.

Schuyler and Loomis let the wagons get well ahead before following them. The two men stayed back and used every bit of cover they could find as they stalked their quarry. The wagon train wound through the foothills, and Preacher still rode with the confident certainty of a man who was sure of not only his surroundings, but also his destination.

By late afternoon, the wagons had come to a stop at the head of a long, shallow valley. As soon as it became obvious that the expedition was going to make camp there for the night, Schuyler told Loomis that they had better get back to the others.

He had watched the landmarks closely during the day and had a pretty good idea where the rest of the gang was.

In order to get there, though, they would have to go around Preacher and the others who were making camp.

Schuyler led the way around the far side of one of the long hills that formed the valley. Preacher couldn't see them from where he was, and they walked the horses so that the drumming of hoof-beats wouldn't be audible at the wagon camp.

But when they came to the far end of the hill, they were greeted by a sheer cliff. A man might have been able to climb the rugged rock face, but a horse sure couldn't. Schuyler and Loomis stared at the cliff for a minute before Loomis asked, "Now what?"

They could backtrack and go around the other side of the valley, Schuyler supposed, but a glance at the low-hanging sun told him it would be dark before they could do so. He wasn't confident that he could locate Fairfax and the others after night fell.

"We'll go over the hill and through that canyon," he decided.

Loomis frowned. "Preacher's liable to spot us."

"We'll have to risk it. There's nothing else we can do."

Loomis shrugged in acceptance. He followed as Schuyler urged his mount up the slope, weaving in and out of the clumps of pine trees.

They crested the rise and started down. Schuyler was nervously aware that they were where Preacher could see them now, if the mountain man happened to be looking in just the right spot. He took as many precautions as he could, using trees and boulders and thickets of brush for cover. By the time he and Loomis had worked their way down almost to the mouth of the canyon, Schuyler wasn't quite so worried anymore.

The wagons were all the way at the other end of the valley, a good two miles away. Surely not even someone with the eyes of a hawk, like Preacher was reputed to have, could see two men on horseback at that distance, especially when they were moving against a background of dark green pine trees, the brown of tree trunks, and gray, jumbled rock.

They had nothing to worry about, Schuyler assured himself. Preacher didn't have any idea that there was anybody within a hundred miles.

Stars were beginning to be visible here and there in the sky, which was turning purple and blue with the approach of night, by the time Schuyler and Loomis rejoined the rest of their group. Burns was already there, having brought back the news earlier that the wagon train had been located.

"Where are they?" Fairfax asked, unable to keep the eagerness out of his voice.

"Camped at the head of a valley about three miles from here," Schuyler replied. He had been thinking about the layout of the terrain all during the ride back here, and now he ventured to add, "I've got an idea where we can hit them."

Fairfax arched his eyebrows. "Really? Then let's hear it, by all means."

Schuyler couldn't really tell if his partner was being sarcastic or not. Fairfax hadn't had to sound so surprised that Schuyler might have a good idea, but at least he was willing to hear him out.

Schuyler began explaining about the valley and the canyon. "That's got to be where they're goin'," he said. "It's a natural path through the foothills."

"Yeah, and you can't get through to the east because there's a damn cliff there," Loomis put in. "They'll be goin' right straight down that valley to the canyon at the far end."

Schuyler was a little irritated that Loomis had butted in, but he tried not to show it. Instead he said, "The canyon is the best place to set up our ambush. Both sides are pretty steep, and there are plenty of trees and rocks we can use for cover. If we get up there tomorrow mornin' and hide while the wagons are comin' up the valley, Preacher and the folks with him won't have any idea what's waitin' for them."

"Yes, it sounds like it could work," Fairfax agreed. "I'll have to see the layout for myself, of course—"

"I'm tellin' you, it's a sure thing!" Schuyler interrupted with newfound boldness.

"Yes, so was shooting Preacher and stealing his furs when he was paddling that canoe down the river above St. Louis. And you saw how *that* worked out."

Schuyler frowned. Fairfax hadn't had to remind him of that. He'd done his best to kill Preacher that day, just as he had when they broke in on Preacher at the tavern. The fact that bad luck had caused them to fail both times wasn't Schuyler's fault.

But his partner would always blame him for those failures, Schuyler realized, until Preacher was dead—and preferably, at Schuyler's own hands.

"You set up the ambush in that canyon and you'll

see," he said, stubborn in his belief. "And you can just leave Preacher to me. This time, that long-legged son of a bitch is gonna die!"

"It sure smells nice here in the mountains," Jake said to Preacher that night as they sat beside the campfire.

"These ain't the mountains yet," Preacher corrected, "but yeah, I do like the smell o' pine. Makes a man feel glad to be alive."

Jerome came up and sat down beside them. He made a point of not even glancing toward Corliss and Deborah, who sat next to each other on the far side of the fire, but other than that he didn't seem quite as much like the gloomy cuss he had been for the past few days.

"I've been thinking, Preacher," he began. "After we reach South Pass and find a suitable location for Corliss's trading post, would you be willing to come along with me and help me decide where mine will be? I'd be glad to pay you an additional fee for your help."

Preacher frowned at him. "You ain't given up on that crazy idea yet?"

"On the contrary, I'm more convinced than ever that it's the right thing to do. And it's hardly a crazy idea. As large as the frontier is, there should be plenty of room for dozens of trading posts, maybe hundreds!"

Preacher couldn't argue with that point. The frontier was vast enough to hold just about anything.

"You really don't have to leave on account of us, Jerome," Deborah said.

Without looking at her, he said, "I believe that's my decision to make, and I've made it." Turning back to the mountain man, he went on. "How about it, Preacher? Are you willing to come along with Jake and myself?"

Before Preacher could answer, Corliss said, "Wait just a minute, Jerome. What makes you think that Jake is going with you?"

"Well, he's been riding next to me on the wagon for the entire trip. We've become good friends, haven't we, Jake?"

The boy shrugged. "Yeah, sure, I guess."

"And you didn't even want him to come along to start with," Jerome added.

"That's different," Corliss insisted. "I've gotten to know him since then. He's not as big a brat as I thought he'd be."

"Gee, thanks," Jake said.

"Corliss!" Deborah scolded. "Jake's not a brat at all. He's a fine boy, and I'd like for him to stay with us." She smiled across the fire at the youngster. "I've come to think of you almost like a son, Jake. You should stay with us. It'll be like you have a real father and mother again."

Jerome gave a grunt of humorless laughter. "Please! Corliss is hardly an appropriate father figure for anyone, let along an impressionable young lad."

"That's not true," Deborah said as she took hold of Corliss's arm. "He's going to be a fine father to our children."

"That's right," Corliss said. "So it's settled. Jake stays with us."

"It's not settled at all—" Jerome argued.

"Damn it, stop fightin' over me!" Jake burst out.

Jerome turned to him with a frown. "Really, Jake, that's not appropriate language for a boy to be using."

"I don't care what's 'propriate," Jake said as he came to his feet. "I don't like all this fussin'. And it don't matter, because I ain't goin' with either of you."

Jerome, Corliss, and Deborah all stared at him. "You're not?" Deborah said after a second. "Then where are you going to go?"

Oh, Lord, Preacher thought. He should've seen this coming.

Jake grinned. "I'm gonna go with Preacher here. He's gonna teach me how to be a mountain man!"

"Dad-gum it! I never said nothin' of the sort," Preacher protested.

Jake turned to him. "Aw, come on, Preacher. Ain't you never had a partner before? I'll work hard, I swear it."

"I ain't doubtin' that, and yeah, I've rode with partners before from time to time, but none of 'em was kids."

"You were a kid once."

"And I done what I was told, too," Preacher lied. He got to his feet and shook his head firmly, so Jake would know he wouldn't put up with any more arguments. "You can stay with Corliss or Jerome, whichever you decide; it don't make no never-mind to me. But I got beaver to trap once I'm done with these folks, and you ain't comin' with me."

Jake stared up at him for a long moment, eyes wide. Those eyes started to shine in the firelight as they filled with tears. Preacher saw that and felt like cussing, but he kept his face stony. Better to go ahead and disabuse the boy of that damn fool notion right now, he told himself.

Suddenly, with a choked sob, Jake turned around and plunged out of the circle of firelight at a run. Preacher heard the crackle of brush as Jake left the camp.

Jerome, Corliss, and Deborah all jumped up. "You've got to go after him!" Jerome cried as he flung a hand toward the darkness where Jake had disappeared.

"That's right," Corliss said. "You can't let a youngster like that go wandering around in the wilderness in the middle of the night."

"He's just a helpless little boy," Deborah said.

Even the drivers seemed worried about Jake as they gathered around the fire. Preacher looked around, saw that everyone was looking at him like it was all his fault, and said, "Jake ain't helpless. He's got a pistol and a knife and knows how to use both of 'em. Besides that, he ain't gonna go far. He's mad. Like any kid, he's gonna go off and sulk for a spell, and then he'll come back."

"What if he runs into a grizzly or some other dangerous animal?" Corliss asked.

"Or an Indian?" Jerome put in.

Those were both legitimate worries, Preacher supposed. But he thought if he went after the boy and started calling his name, Jake was liable to run even farther away from the camp to get away from him.

"Give him a minute or two to cool off, and then I'll go find him."

The others didn't look too happy with that suggestion, but they nodded grudgingly. "You're right about one thing," Jerome said. "Jake can't live with you. He needs to stay with me."

"Or Deborah and me," Corliss said.

Preacher left them there to waste time and energy on that argument if they wanted to. He picked up his rifle and started toward the edge of camp. Blackie fell in step beside him.

"I'll go with you," the one-eyed man offered. "I had me a kid once. I know how they like to hide."

Preacher nodded. "I'm obliged," he said. He wondered what had happened to Blackie's kid. From the tone of the man's voice, the youngster was dead. Or maybe it was just that Blackie had abandoned the child, along with its mother, to come west. That happened a lot, too.

With the instinctive quiet of natural woodsmen, they moved out of the camp and began searching for Jake.

Sitting on a log, sobbing almost silently to himself, Jake tried to figure out why Preacher didn't want him around. He couldn't understand it. He reckoned he just wasn't a good enough kid for anybody to want him.

A soft sound behind him made him stop crying for a second and lift his head. Somebody was back there. Maybe Preacher had come to look for him! Maybe Preacher would let him be a mountain man after all!

Jake was starting to get to his feet and turn around when a hard hand clamped like iron over his mouth and jerked him backward.

Twenty-five

The sounds of a scuffle suddenly came from the brush in front of Preacher and Blackie. Knowing that Jake was out there somewhere and that the boy could be in trouble, the two mountain men didn't hesitate. They broke into a run toward the spot where somebody was rustling around and thrashing through the thick bushes.

Before they could get there, a shape burst out of the brush and rushed toward them. Preacher and Blackie stopped and swung their rifles up, but Preacher snapped, "Hold it!" before either he or Blackie could squeeze the trigger. "That's Jake!"

He lowered his gun and stepped forward to catch the boy, who seemed to be charging blindly through the night. Jake let out a *"Whoof!"* as Preacher grabbed him around the middle with one arm. He started to flail around and yelled, "Lemme go, you damned redskin! Lemme go!"

"Settle down!" Preacher told him. "Jake, it's me, Preacher!"

The words must have gotten through to the

youngster's brain, because Jake stopped his terrified struggling and grabbed on to Preacher for
dear life.

"Lord!" Jake said. "I thought for sure he was
gonna scalp me!"

Blackie still held his rifle ready for instant use.
"You say there's an Injun out here somewheres,
younker?" he asked Jake.

"Y-yeah. I was sittin' on a log over yonder when
he grabbed me from behind. I thought he was
gonna scalp me!"

Preacher moved Jake behind him, just in case an
arrow or a tomahawk came flying out of the darkness. "You're sure it was an Indian?" he asked.

"Yeah. I twisted around and got a look at him. I
couldn't see him real good 'cause it's dark, but I
saw the feathers in his hair."

"How'd you get away from him?"

"He had his hand over my mouth, so I bit the
hell out of it."

Preacher couldn't stop a grim smile from tugging at the corners of his mouth under the droop-
ing mustache. Jake had plenty of fighting spirit,
that was for sure.

"What happened then?"

"He let go of me, and I started runnin' back to
camp. I was afraid he'd grab me again, or shoot an
arrow at me, so I ran as fast as I could."

"Made enough racket to be a grizzly bear chargin'
through that brush, too," Blackie said. "Chances are,
if there was really a Injun, he's long gone by now."

Sounding offended, Jake said, "Hey! What do
you mean, if there was really a Injun? You think I
made the whole thing up?"

"No, I reckon you didn't," Preacher said. "You've never been the sort o' kid who makes up stories all the time, like some do."

Blackie said, "Sorry, kid. I didn't mean to make it sound like I thought you was lyin'. Was there just one redskin?"

"One was all I heard or saw. But it's dark. There could have been others."

Preacher didn't doubt that. He seemed to feel eyes on him even now, watching him from the darkness.

"All right, let's get back to camp," he said. "I reckon the others are probably worried about us."

Blackie put a hand on Jake's shoulder and steered him toward the wagons, while Preacher backed away from the spot where Jake had encountered the Indian, holding his rifle ready just in case. No one followed them or took a shot at them, and a few minutes later they were back in camp, where Deborah let out a cry of relief at the sight of Jake and hurried forward to throw her arms around the boy and hug him.

Jake looked uncomfortable. He tolerated the hug for a few moments and then started trying to pry himself loose. Corliss and Jerome were both right there, too, hovering anxiously over him.

"Are you all right, Jake?" Jerome asked. "We heard shouting. Are you hurt?"

"No, I'm fine," Jake said, his voice a little muffled because Deborah still had his head pressed to her bosom. "I just got grabbed by a Injun, that's all."

"An Indian!" Corliss said.

"But I got away from him," Jake went on, "and

then I ran into Preacher and Blackie and they brought me back here."

"How did you get away from him?" Jerome wanted to know.

Jake managed to worm his way out of Deborah's embrace and explained again about biting his captor's hand. "He just grunted a little, didn't yell or nothin'. But from the way he turned loose o' me right quicklike, I'll bet it hurt him plenty."

"I'll bet it did, too," Preacher said with a chuckle. "Most fellas can't stand bein' bit."

"There was just one Indian?" Corliss asked.

"Just one that I saw," Jake said. "But there could've been a whole war party out there for all I know." He glanced down at the ground, a sheepish expression on his round face. "I reckon I shouldn't have gone runnin' off like that, just 'cause I got mad."

Deborah said, "You certainly shouldn't have. You had us all very worried, Jake. Don't do that again."

"I won't," the boy promised. "But you got to stop fightin' over me. I don't know what I'll do when we get where we're goin', but it ought to be my decision, oughtn't it?"

"You're too young to make any important decisions, like where you're going to live," Jerome said. "We're just trying to look out for your best interests, Jake."

"That's why Deborah and I think you should live with us," Corliss added.

Jerome began, "That's not necessarily—"

Preacher held up a hand to stop him. "There's been enough squabblin' tonight," he said in a tone that would brook no further argument. "You can figure out what Jake's gonna do later, after we get to South Pass. For now, let's just worry about gettin' there with our hair still on our heads and all those trade goods intact."

Jerome sighed and nodded. "You're right, Preacher. What do you think that Indian wanted with Jake?"

"They'll carry off white kids from time to time," Preacher replied with a shrug. "They take 'em into the tribe and raise 'em up like family. When they're raidin', Indians will kill youngsters, but when they grab one like that, they generally don't mean him any harm, at least accordin' to their lights. Chances are that one wouldn't have hurt Jake."

"But he would've carried me off and tried to make a Injun out of me?" Jake sounded astounded. "That'd be worse'n killin' me!"

Preacher didn't agree with that, but he didn't say anything. Everybody needed to calm down instead of rehashing what had happened. The danger appeared to be over.

For now.

When things had settled down some and most of the members of the group were sitting around the fire again, Preacher went to check on Horse. Blackie followed him and asked in a quiet voice that couldn't be overheard by the others, "You reckon there was just the one Injun?"

"No tellin'. Could've been. Could've been a whole war party out there."

"If that was true, they would've gone ahead and jumped us, wouldn't they?"

"You been to see the elephant, Blackie," Preacher said. "You know there's no way of knowin' what an Indian's gonna do. What seems right to him might not make a lick o' sense to you and me." Preacher scraped a thumbnail along his jaw. "But I got a feelin' there was just the one warrior. Don't know why, but that's what my gut tells me."

"What'd he want with Jake?"

"Don't know . . . but if he tries again, maybe we'll find out."

Schuyler didn't feel all that confident about leading Fairfax and the others back to the canyon in the darkness. But he just had to get them close to it, he realized. The wagons wouldn't be making their way up that long valley until morning, and it would take them a couple of hours at least, probably longer, to reach the canyon. Plenty of time after sunup for the ambushers to find the place and get into position.

That was what happened. Schuyler was able to get the gang within half a mile of the canyon, and then as the gray light of dawn began to spread, he got his bearings even more and led them the rest of the way, assisted by Loomis and Burns, who had also been there.

As the sun began to peek over the eastern horizon, Colin Fairfax surveyed the scene and nodded in approval. "You were right, Schuyler," he said. "This *is* a good place for an ambush. Everyone spread out. I want men on both sides of the canyon. Find good spots with plenty of cover, where you can fire down on those wagons as they come through. *But*," he added, "nobody fires until I give the word. Is that understood?"

Nods of agreement came from the men.

As they fanned out over the rocky, wooded slopes

that formed the canyon, Schuyler came up to Fairfax and said, "Don't forget what I told you last night. Preacher's mine."

Fairfax grunted. "You're welcome to him. Just don't miss this time. The quicker he dies, the better."

Schuyler nodded, so anxious to settle the score at last that he didn't even take offense at Fairfax's reminder of his previous failures. He was in total agreement.

The sooner Preacher died, the better.

Because of Jake's encounter with the Indian, everyone was especially watchful the rest of that night, but nothing else happened and the wagon train was ready to move on the next morning with a minimum of fuss.

Before starting out, they refilled the water barrels from the creek. The oxen had enjoyed the water and the thick grass. This was probably the best grazing the animals would have for a while, Preacher thought. There would be enough grass along the way to sustain them, but the pastures between here and South Pass weren't as lushly carpeted as this valley.

Jake seemed to be none the worse for wear after his experience the night before, and now that he had recovered from his fear and the adults had stopped fighting over who he was going to stay with, he was back to being his usual cheerful, inquisitive self. He was asking Jerome questions about running a trading post as Preacher loped past on Horse, with Dog trotting alongside.

Since the open sweep of the valley made everything in it visible, Preacher rode farther out in front of the wagons than he usually did, letting the stallion stretch his legs for a change. The wagons dropped back a mile behind him, then a mile and a half as Preacher approached the canyon at the far end of the valley.

He hadn't forgotten about that fleeting impression of movement he had seen in the canyon late in the afternoon of the previous day. After what had happened to Jake, Preacher had to wonder if what he had seen was that Indian lurking around. As he drew closer now to the canyon, his eyes scanned the slopes carefully, searching for any sign of trouble.

And as he searched, he rode closer . . . closer . . .

"I can hit him!" Schuyler whispered to Fairfax as they crouched behind a pair of boulders, peering through the tiny gap between the rocks. "I know I can!" Schuyler started to lift his rifle.

"Wait, damn it!" Fairfax whispered back as he grabbed the barrel of Schuyler's rifle and forced it back down. "He's still too far away! And even if you did hit him, those wagons are still more than a mile back down the canyon. The shot would just warn them, and they'd stop before they're in the trap where we want them!"

Schuyler grimaced. He hated to admit it, but he knew Fairfax was right. As much as he wanted to blow a hole through Preacher, opening fire now would be a mistake.

"What's he doin'? How come he ain't back with the wagons?"

"He's worried," Fairfax said. "His instincts tell him this is a good place for an ambush." He frowned in concern. "I hope everyone has enough sense to stay down and keep hidden, damn it. The last thing we need is for someone to get overeager and give the game away."

Like he had almost done, Schuyler thought. He took a deep breath to settle his nerves and pushed his desire for Preacher's death to the back of his mind.

That time would come soon enough, he promised himself. Just a little while longer, and Preacher would be right in his sights.

Preacher didn't see anything unusual about the canyon, so after a few minutes he turned and rode back toward the wagons. A continuing feeling of uneasiness rode with him, though.

When he reached the lead wagon, he held up a hand in a signal for Jerome to stop. Jerome hauled back on the reins and brought the lumbering oxen to a halt. "What is it?" he asked. "Is something wrong?"

Preacher jerked his head toward the far end of the canyon. "I got a bad feelin' about that place up yonder. As slow as these wagons are, we'll be easy targets while we're goin' through it, and there are plenty o' hidin' places on those slopes where somebody could be waitin' to ambush us."

"Indians, you mean?" Jerome asked with a worried frown. Preacher saw that Jake was starting to look a mite concerned, too.

He gave Jerome an honest answer. "I don't know. Could be Indians or renegade whites or nobody at all. Could be I'm just imaginin' trouble where it ain't. But I've lived out here too long to just ignore what my gut's tryin' to tell me."

"And I don't want you to," Jerome answered without hesitation. "What do you think we should do?"

Preacher thought it over, then said, "Not much we can do except keep goin'. It'd take too long to turn around and go back. Anyway, this route has the best grass and water. But keep your eyes wide open. Be ready for trouble. Jake, first sign of it you see, I want you to hop back there in the wagon bed and get your head down. And stay there until somebody tells you it's all right."

"I can fight, Preacher," the boy said. "It'd be better to give me a rifle and let me be ready to shoot if I need to."

Preacher mulled that over for a few seconds before shaking his head. "It ain't that I don't trust you," he said. "I do. But you're a kid, Jake. You don't need to be fightin' and maybe killin'."

"What about you?" Jake insisted. "You fought British soldiers at the Battle o' New Orleans when you weren't that much older'n me. I'll bet you killed some of 'em, too."

"How'd you know about that?"

"Blackie told me. He said you were a mountain man by the time you were fifteen, and everybody out here knew that."

"That ol' boy talks a mite too much once he gets warmed up," Preacher said. "Do what I told you, Jake."

"Yeah, sure," the boy said with a sigh, but Preacher wasn't convinced he would follow orders.

There was nothing he could do about that except hope, so he moved on down the line of wagons, warning all the other members of the party. He gave Deborah the same orders he had given Jake—in case of trouble, get in the back of the wagon and stay down. Unlike the youngster, she nodded in quick agreement, having already come through one battle unharmed that way.

Then, having done all he could to get ready for the potential danger, Preacher wheeled Horse around and rode toward the far end of the valley once more. Because of the steepness of the high slopes, not much sunlight would penetrate between them until later in the day. The canyon lay dark and gloomy as it waited for Preacher and the wagons that followed him.

"All right," Fairfax breathed. "This time you can kill him."

A cruel grin stretched across Schuyler's face as he lifted his rifle to his shoulder and nestled his beard-stubbled cheek against the smooth wood of its stock. His thumb hooked over the hammer and pulled it back. He rested the barrel against the side of the boulder to steady it, and drew a bead on the buckskin-clad mountain man leading the wagon train into the canyon.

"Let them get a little farther," Fairfax whispered. "I'll tell you when to fire. That will be the signal for everyone else."

Schuyler heard the pulse pounding in his head. A killing lust coursed through his veins. He settled the rifle's sights on Preacher's broad chest. All that was lacking was the slightest pressure on the trigger.

A sound whispered behind them, the soft scuff of leather on rock. Fairfax heard it, and started to turn toward the other boulders clustered behind them on the slope.

With a shrill scream of anger and his knife upraised in his hand to kill, Antelope Fleet as the Wind launched himself from the top of the rock behind the two white men.

Twenty-six

Preacher heard the cry, followed a second later by the boom of a gun from somewhere up on the slope to his right. He wasn't sure what was going on up there, but the sounds were proof enough for him that the wagons had been rolling right into an ambush, just as he had feared.

He whirled Horse around and lifted his rifle over his head, using it to motion the wagons back toward the mouth of the canyon. "Turn around!" he bellowed. "Get the hell out of here!"

But while it was possible to turn the wagons in this narrow canyon, it was going to take time . . . time they didn't have. More shots roared from both slopes. Preacher heard the wind-rip of heavy rifle balls passing close beside his head. He saw Jake diving back into the bed of the lead wagon, and was glad that the boy was doing as he had been told. He hoped that Deborah was doing likewise.

One of the riflemen concealed on the slope was careless and edged out from behind the boulder where he had been hidden. Preacher whipped his rifle to his shoulder and pressed the trigger. As smoke plumed from the weapon's barrel, Preacher saw the man fly backward as the ball tore through his body. He hit another rock, bounced off, and flopped forward lifelessly.

A howl of pain made Preacher jerk his head around. He saw Jerome Hart sagging on the seat of the lead wagon, his right hand clutching at a suddenly bloody left arm. Jake scrambled back over the seat, grabbed the reins, and started trying to haul the oxen around. Preacher gave the boy credit for guts, but he didn't think Jake was going to be able to make the team do what he wanted.

As another ball whipped past his ear, Preacher heeled Horse into a run. He saw Corliss struggling to get the second wagon turned around. There was no sign of Deborah, so Preacher assumed she was inside the wagon where she was supposed to be.

On the third wagon, Gil Robinson bolted to his feet on the driver's box and doubled over with both hands pressed to his stomach. Crimson flooded over his fingers. Gut-shot, he toppled onto the backs of the oxen in his team, spooking them. Robinson managed to scream as he slipped off their backs and fell to the ground under their hooves. The oxen weren't moving much, but enough to trample Robinson's body into the dirt as his shriek was abruptly cut off.

That meant the third wagon wasn't going anywhere. Neither was the fourth, because Pete Carey clapped a hand to his thigh where a ball ripped a deep gash.

The storm of lead pouring down from both sides of the canyon told Preacher there were at least two dozen killers hidden up there, maybe more. There was no way to save the wagons, but maybe he could keep anybody else from getting killed. He waved a hand and shouted over the din of gunfire, "Leave the wagons! Get out of the canyon!" He veered Horse toward the lead wagon. "Jake! Climb on!"

Jake hesitated, but then reached out to grasp Preacher's arm as the mountain man lifted him from the wagon seat and placed him on Horse's back behind the saddle.

Still clutching his wounded arm, Jerome said, "We can't abandon the wagons and all the goods!"

"It's that or get killed!" Preacher told him. "Come on, damn it! Get down from there and run!"

Jerome had no idea how badly the idea of running stuck in Preacher's craw. When the Good Lord had made the mountain man, He hadn't included any back-up in Preacher's nature. But Preacher could be pragmatic when he had to, and he knew that if they stayed here in the canyon, they would all be wiped out.

Jerome must have understood that, too, because he half-climbed, half-fell from the wagon seat, caught his balance, and hurried toward the canyon mouth. "Come on, Corliss!" he shouted at his cousin. "Where's Deborah?"

"I'll get her!" Corliss said, wide-eyed with fear. He waved Preacher, Jake, and Jerome on.

Lars Neilson had dropped to the ground from his wagon and run forward to give the wounded Pete Carey a hand. They made an awkward pair, the short, squat Carey and the tall, burly Neilson, but nonetheless, they were moving fairly quickly with one of the Swede's arms around Carey's waist, supporting him.

Blackie was on the ground, too, squinting through his lone eye over the barrel of his rifle as he drew a bead on one of the bushwhackers. The gun roared, and Blackie turned to Preacher with a grin on his weathered face. "Got the son of a bitch!" he exulted.

Then he staggered as he was hit. Preacher didn't know how bad it was, but he reached down and grabbed hold of Blackie as he passed, straining to lift the man and drape him across Horse's back in front of the saddle. Horse was carrying three riders now, but he was big enough and strong enough to maintain that for a short distance, and that was all that was required to get out of the canyon where they would be safer.

Horse lunged out from the narrow space between the steep slopes a moment later, carrying the triple burden. Preacher reined in and turned to see the others running after him. Neilson helping Carey, Jerome stumbling along, Corliss behind him . . .

Where the hell was Deborah Morrigan?

The scream was the most bloodcurdling thing Schuyler had ever heard. He twisted around and saw the Indian hurtling through the air toward him. The savage's red, painted face was twisted in an expression of pure hatred. Schuyler's brain had only an instant to register that fact as he tried to bring his rifle to bear on the Indian.

Too late. The warrior crashed into him and drove him back against the boulder before Schuyler had time to pull the trigger.

But at least the barrel of the rifle struck the Indian's arm and knocked the knife aside before he could bury the blade in Schuyler's chest. The knife hit the rock instead, and the unexpected impact tore the weapon's grip out of the Indian's hand. The savage's other hand flashed toward Schuyler's throat with fingers hooked to close around it and choke the life out of him.

The next instant, Fairfax's pistol boomed, so close and loud that the roar nearly deafened Schuyler. But the Indian's weight pressed against him was gone suddenly. Schuyler straightened, and saw that the warrior had fallen, driven off his feet by the ball from Fairfax's pistol that had struck him in the side.

The Indian didn't stay down long. He was up a second later, leaping to his feet despite the wound in his side that welled blood. Schuyler tried again to draw a bead on the redskinned varmint, but the warrior was too fast, bounding away among the rocks.

"Let him go!" Fairfax said, and as Schuyler heard his partner's raised voice, he realized that guns were going off on both sides of the canyon. The other members of the gang had taken Fairfax's shot at the Indian for the signal to begin the ambush.

"We have more important things to worry about than one crazy Indian!" Fairfax went on. "Kill Preacher before it's too late!"

Schuyler turned back to the business at hand. He saw that the drivers of the wagons were trying to turn them around and escape the trap, but they weren't having much luck at it, despite Preacher's urging. Schuyler brought the rifle to his shoulder, and settled the sights on the mountain man as Preacher rode toward the lead wagon.

Preacher veered his mount toward the wagon and

reached out to grab the kid from the seat just as Schuyler pressed the trigger. Even before the smoke from the barrel began to clear, Schuyler knew he had missed Preacher yet again. Bitter curses tumbled from his lips. That damned mountain man had a lucky angel riding on his shoulder, looking out for him.

So did the rest of the members of the Hart expedition apparently. One of the drivers fell, mortally wounded, and some of the others were hit as the bushwhackers continued to pour lead down into the canyon for the next couple of minutes, but they were able to flee from the ambush even though they had to abandon the wagons to do so.

"Do we go after them?" Schuyler asked as he reloaded after firing several shots. The attack seemed to have been going on for a long time, but he knew that wasn't really the case.

"We'll secure the wagons first," Fairfax said. "That's more important than whether or not the rest of those bastards get away."

Schuyler frowned. "We need to make sure Preacher's dead. I don't want that son of a bitch on my trail."

"He's just one man, and he'll be saddled with wounded men. He must realize by now how outnumbered he is, too."

Fairfax didn't sound too concerned. Schuyler didn't share that attitude. He didn't think anything good could come out of allowing Preacher to escape.

What did it take to kill that man anyway?

"When I get down, climb up here in the saddle and hang on to Blackie!" Preacher told Jake. "Don't let him fall off!"

Then he swung down from the stallion's back and ran to meet the four men from the wagon train. Corliss was bringing up the rear. Preacher shouted at him, "Where's Miss Morrigan? Damn it, Hart—"

Corliss stopped short and stared at Preacher for a second, then jerked around to stare back toward the canyon mouth. "She was right behind me," he said. "My God! Deborah!"

Preacher had had other things to distract him during the attack, like the rifle balls whizzing around his head, but he didn't recall seeing Deborah at all once the shooting started. He sure as hell hadn't seen her following Corliss out of the canyon. Corliss was engaged to her and was supposed to love her. Surely, he hadn't yelled for her to follow him and then taken off running, assuming that she would do so. Hadn't he looked back even once to make sure she was coming?

Even as Preacher asked himself those questions, he had a sickening feeling that that was exactly what had happened. Corliss had panicked and left Deborah behind in the wagon. With all the shooting going on, she had probably been too scared to follow him, if she had even heard him tell her to do so over the din of the assault.

That meant Preacher had to go back for her, but first he wanted to get the others to a place of relative safety. A gully cut across the valley about three hundred yards from the mouth of the canyon. That would give them some protection from the occasional potshot that came winging their way from the slopes of the canyon.

"Move!" he told them as he waved them toward

the gully. "Get back yonder and stay down! Jake, can you ride?"

"A little," the boy replied, sounding scared.

Preacher didn't blame him. "Then hang on and get Blackie into that gully with the others." He turned back toward the canyon. "Come on, Dog!"

With the big, wolflike cur at his heels, Preacher ran toward the wagons. He still hadn't had a chance to reload his rifle, but he had two loaded, charged, and primed pistols behind his belt.

Of course, a brace of pistols against two dozen or more bloodthirsty renegades was pretty damned bad odds. Preacher found out just how bad when the bushwhackers opened fire on him again, forcing him to launch into a low dive that took him behind a pine log just to avoid being riddled. Dog hunkered beside him, growling with rage.

Preacher felt like doing some snarling and growling himself, but he knew it wouldn't do any good. As balls thudded into the log, throwing pieces of bark and splinters of wood into the air, Preacher felt the trunk shivering under the impacts and knew that if he stood up, or even stuck his head up, they would ventilate him. He and Dog were pinned down here, pinned down good and proper.

He twisted his head to look back toward the gully, and saw Neilson helping Pete Carey down into it. They were the last ones still visible from Preacher's position. As soon as Carey was clear, the Swede dived after him. The now-riderless Horse had trotted far off to one side, pretty much out of the line of fire for now.

Preacher heard shouts from the bushwhackers as some of them emerged from their cover and started down toward the wagons. The words were in English, which came as no surprise to him. When that many gunshots had rung out, he knew the attackers had to be white. The Indians who lived in these foothills had a few rifles, but he doubted that any of the bands would have been able to muster that many firearms at one time.

When he heard a woman's scream from the canyon, it took all of his willpower to keep his head from popping up so he could take a look. He was willing to bet that at least a few of the bastards still had their rifles trained on this log where he had taken cover. They would be just waiting for another shot at him.

"Deborah! Oh, my God, Deborah!"

The furious, agonized shout came from Corliss Hart. Preacher looked around to see Corliss climbing out of the gully. Immediately, some of the riflemen on the slopes of the canyon opened fire on him. He would have been hit if Lars Neilson hadn't reached up with a long arm, snagged the back of his shirt, and yanked him back into the gully.

"Stay down, blast it!" Preacher yelled at the men in the gully. "Gettin' yourselves shot full o' holes ain't gonna help anything!"

He lay there, seething in anger and gritting his teeth against the flood of curses that welled up inside him, as Deborah screamed again and then fell silent. With a creaking and screeching of wagon wheels, the heavy vehicles lurched into motion again. Preacher heard that and knew the thieves were driving the wagons on through the canyon. The shooting started again. The men peppered the log, and also fired at the gully where the others had taken cover, keeping the group pinned down until the wagons were gone . . . taking Deborah with them.

"Burns, Loomis, take half-a-dozen men with you and circle around on horseback so you can come in behind Preacher and the rest of that bunch," Fairfax ordered. "The rest of us will go on with the wagons. You can catch up quickly enough when you've killed all of them."

"Can't I go with them?" Schuyler asked.

Fairfax shook his head. "I want you to stay with me. Anyway, you haven't had any luck where Preacher's concerned. If you're jinxed when it comes to him, maybe it'll be better if you just steer clear of him until he's dead."

Schuyler didn't like that, but he supposed Fairfax probably had a point. Anyway, Burns and Loomis were good men. They could handle the job of disposing of Preacher and the others while the rest of the group pushed on with the stolen wagons.

And the woman.

That was a stroke of good fortune. None of them had known there was a woman along on the Hart expedition, especially not one so young and pretty. After gagging her, tying her up, and stashing her in one of the wagons, Fairfax had ordered that she be left alone otherwise. Once they reached South Pass and set up the trading post, the woman could be sent back to Beaumont with the men who would be returning to St. Louis. When they got there, she would be turned over to Beaumont, who would surely be able to figure out some way to turn a profit on her. If she came from a wealthy family, she could be held for ransom. If not, she could be put to work in one of the whorehouses Beaumont owned. Either way, it was important for now that she remain unharmed, so Fairfax's orders to that effect had been firm.

He and Schuyler tied their horses on behind the lead wagon and climbed to the driver's seat. "Take the reins," Fairfax said. Schuyler felt a sense of satisfaction as he grasped the leathers. They might not have succeeded in killing Preacher—yet—but by God, the wagons and all they contained now belonged to them!

Behind them, as the wagons rolled on through the canyon, more shots rang out as a handful of men kept Preacher and the others pinned down while Burns, Loomis, and the rest of their handpicked killers circled around on horseback to get behind them and wipe them out.

Preacher heard hoofbeats coming from the trees and figured out what was going on. It didn't surprise him that the thieves didn't want to leave anyone alive behind them. If they knew who he was, they would know that if he survived, he would never rest until he'd tracked them down.

He shouted, "Behind you!" and then rolled over and lifted the rifle he had reloaded earlier, while he was trapped here behind this log. As riders emerged from the trees and thundered toward the gully, Preacher settled his sights on the man in the lead. He snapped, "Go get 'em, Dog!" then pressed the trigger.

The flintlock roared and sent a heavy lead ball

driving into the chest of the lead rider. The impact swept him backward out of the saddle like a punch from a giant fist.

At the same time, Dog broke from cover and dashed toward the attackers, darting back and forth so that the men on the slope couldn't draw a bead on him. Shots kicked up dust behind the big cur, but didn't come all that close to him. Dog leaped the gully and then leaped again, crashing into one of the attackers and knocking him off his horse. Man and dog went down in a welter of dust and flailing arms and legs. Screams mixed with growls and snarls as sharp teeth flashed and rended.

While that was going on, the men in the gully were putting up a fight, too. Pete Carey couldn't stand on his wounded leg, but he propped himself up at the edge of the gully and fired a brace of pistols at the oncoming horsemen. Corliss, Jerome, and Neilson each had a pistol, and fired those weapons as well. Jake poked the barrel of a rifle over the edge of the gully and squeezed off a shot. Preacher took all that in with a glance as he reloaded his own rifle. He didn't see Blackie and wondered if the one-eyed man was dead.

The gunfire from the gully took a toll. Two more of the attackers went down, tumbling off their mounts. But they had been shooting, too, as they charged, and Lars Neilson was thrown backward as two pistol balls smashed into him. He rolled to the bottom of the gully and lay motionless.

Preacher fired again and saw blood spray from the head of another man as the ball bored through his skull. That left just one man on horseback. He wheeled his mount to flee, knowing that the attack had backfired on them. The move came too late, as Jerome put a pistol ball in his back and toppled him off the horse.

Instead of wiping out the survivors from the wagon train, the thieves and killers had been wiped out instead.

Preacher heard more hoofbeats and ventured a look. Three or four men rode through the canyon and out the far end, galloping after the wagons, which had disappeared by now. No more shots came from the slopes of the canyon. The men who had just fled must have been the ones posted up there to keep Preacher and his companions trapped while the others circled around. They rode out of sight, and silence settled down over the valley.

"Preacher!" Jerome called. "Preacher, are you all right?"

"Yeah," Preacher replied. "Keep your heads down. I ain't sure they're all gone."

But after a quarter of an hour had gone by, Preacher felt certain they were. He stood up and trotted over to the gully to see how bad things were there.

Someone had rolled Neilson onto his back, so that the Swede's eyes stared sightlessly up at the morning sky. After everything that had happened, it was difficult to believe that it wasn't even mid-morning yet.

Preacher was sorry to see that Neilson was dead, but relieved when he saw Blackie sitting up with his back propped against the side of the gully while Carey tied some makeshift bandages ripped from a shirt around his torso.

"How bad is it, Blackie?" Preacher asked as he hunkered on his heels beside the gully. Dog came up beside him and nuzzled his shoulder. Preacher scratched behind the big cur's ears.

"Reckon I'll live," the one-eyed man said. "That shot dug a chunk o' meat outta my side, but Carey's patchin' it up."

Carey had a bandage tied around his wounded leg already. He glanced up at Preacher and said, "Blackie and me ain't gonna be too much use in a fight for a while."

"That's all right," Preacher told him. "You two can sort of take care of each other and Jake, while the rest of us go after those damned thieves."

"They took Deborah," Jerome said. Anxiety twisted his face and voice.

"We have to rescue her," Corliss added.

Jerome turned to his cousin and snapped, "If you hadn't left her there for those bastards to capture—"

"I swear, I thought she was right behind me!"

"You panicked!" Jerome accused. "You abandoned her!"

"That's a damned lie!"

"Both of you shut the hell up!" Preacher roared. "We ain't got time for—"

He stopped as Jake climbed out of the gully and tugged on his sleeve. "Uh, Preacher," the boy said, and when the mountain man looked in his direction, Preacher saw that Jake was staring toward the canyon.

Preacher turned his head to see what the youngster was looking at, and was almost as surprised as Jake seemed to be at the sight of a bloody, buckskin-clad figure limping and staggering toward them.

"It . . . it's a Injun," Jake said.

"Yeah, it sure is," Preacher said as he straightened to his full height. "That's the Arapaho chief we met a while back. Antelope Fleet as the Wind."

Twenty-seven

As the Indian hobbled closer, Preacher could tell that Antelope Fleet as the Wind was badly hurt. His buckskins bore dark bloodstains in several places, he had his left arm pressed hard to his side, and his face was drawn in tight lines that told Preacher he was trying not to show just how much pain he was really in. As Antelope stumbled and almost fell, Preacher leaped forward to grab his arm and steady him.

"Preacher, be careful!" Jake called. "I ain't sure, but I think that's the Injun who grabbed me last night!"

"I don't reckon he means us any harm," Preacher said. "Otherwise, he wouldn't have come walkin' up to us out in the open like this."

The Arapaho chief gave a weary shake of his head. "Antelope . . . friend," he said in English.

As Preacher helped Antelope sit down, Jake said, "Ask him if he's the one who tried to kill me."

Antelope smiled through his pain. "Did not try to kill . . . young one . . . Antelope wanted to . . .

talk to boy." The warrior held up his right hand and showed them the bite mark encrusted with dried blood. "But boy is like . . . badger . . . fights when you try to . . . catch it."

"You spooked him," Preacher said as he hunkered beside Antelope. "He didn't know what you wanted."

"He wanted to scalp me, I'll bet," Jake said. He scowled in obvious distrust at the Indian.

Antelope shook his head again. "Preacher and his friends . . . are Antelope's friends." With a trembling hand, he pointed toward the canyon. "Preacher's enemies . . . are Antelope's enemies."

"You're the one who jumped them as they were about to ambush us," Preacher guessed.

Antelope nodded. "They killed the warriors in my hunting party . . . all but Antelope and . . . Eagle Flies High . . . who rode for help while . . . I followed them." The chief was hunched over against the pain of his injuries, but he straightened and squared his shoulders as he went on. "There must be vengeance."

"So you tracked those sons o' bitches while your pard Eagle went to fetch the rest of your warriors?"

"That is right. But when I saw them about to attack you . . . I knew I could not let them do that . . . could not let them kill Preacher and his friends . . . You treated Antelope and his people fairly."

That was the way it was with Indians, Preacher reflected. They could be your friend one time and try to scalp you the next, or they could be your friend for life. There was no predicting it. Preacher squeezed Antelope's shoulder and asked, "How bad are you hurt?"

Before the chief could answer, Jerome said, "I hate to intrude, Preacher, but those men are getting farther away with each minute that goes by."

"You ought to know by now that those wagons don't move very fast," Preacher said. "When we're ready to catch up, we will."

"On foot?" Corliss asked.

Preacher gestured toward the horses that had been ridden by the men who had circled to attack them from behind. The now-riderless animals had drifted a hundred yards or so down the valley and were cropping contentedly at the grass.

"We'll catch some of those mounts when we're ready to go," Preacher explained. "First, we need to patch up Antelope here, then bury Robinson and Neilson, I reckon."

"You're going to give that savage medical attention?" Corliss sounded like he couldn't believe it.

"That savage is on our side," Preacher snapped. "We'll have a better chance o' gettin' Miss Morrigan back and settlin' the score with those bastards if he's along with us."

Jerome asked, "What about those other men? Are we going to bury them, too?"

Preacher snorted. "With this gully handy to toss 'em in? I don't figure to waste time and sweat on varmints who were tryin' to kill me just a little while ago."

That decision met with nods of approval from Blackie and Pete Carey. The one-eyed man said, "Anyway, there are wolves around to take care o' them."

A little shudder ran through Jerome. Even after

everything that had happened, he was still a civilized man, with a civilized man's squeamishness.

Preacher got busy tending to Antelope's wounds. The Indian had been shot three times, but two of the times, the rifle ball had just grazed him, leaving behind bloody but relatively shallow furrows. The third wound was more serious. The ball had passed through his side at an angle, exiting from his back. Preacher went into the trees to scout up some moss, which he used to pack the holes. Then he bound them up with strips of cloth torn from Neilson's shirt, since the Swede didn't need it anymore. Antelope's chances weren't very good, Preacher thought, but he had done all he could for the Indian. And Antelope seemed to be a little stronger, at least for now.

Since they didn't have any shovels, they couldn't dig graves for Robinson and Neilson, but Preacher and Corliss carried the bodies into the gully, placing them under one of the banks where it bulged out. They were able to collapse the bank over the bodies, then piled rocks on top of the fallen earth. It was the best they could do. Jerome said a prayer, and then they were ready to move on.

There was no question that they were going to go after the men who had taken the wagons and stolen Deborah as well. Even though they were outnumbered by more than three to one . . . even though four of them were wounded and one was just a boy . . . the need for vengeance burned inside all of them. Preacher hadn't quite figured out yet how they were going to accomplish it, but they were going to rescue Deborah.

And the sons of bitches would pay for what they had done.

* * *

When the men who had been left behind to take care of Preacher and the others caught up to the stolen wagon train, there were a lot fewer of them than Schuyler and Fairfax expected.

"What the hell happened?" Fairfax demanded, anger making his voice shake slightly.

"Preacher and them others put up more of a fight than they ought to've been able to," one of the men explained. "They killed Loomis and Burns and the boys who went with 'em."

"So Preacher is still alive?" Schuyler asked.

The man nodded. "I'm afraid so."

Fairfax grabbed the front of the man's buckskin shirt and shook him. "Damn you! You had good cover in the canyon! Why didn't you stay there and make sure they were dead before you left?"

The man pulled loose and glared at Fairfax. "We was runnin' low on powder and shot, and anyway, Preacher and the others were hunkered down where we couldn't get a good shot at any of 'em. Besides, we figured you needed to know what happened to Burns and Loomis and the others."

"You mean you were afraid of Preacher once the odds were closer to even," Fairfax said in a scathing tone. He sighed. "Well, the damage is done. Were any of Preacher's companions killed in the fighting, at least?"

"Hard to say for sure, but it looked like one of 'em was hit pretty bad. He's probably dead."

Schuyler said, "There can't be more than half a dozen of them left, Colin. Not even Preacher will be foolish enough to come after us with such a small group . . . will he?"

"I don't know," Fairfax said, "but if he does, we'll finally wipe him out for sure next time. God! How does that bastard keep escaping?"

"He's Preacher," one of the men said, as if that explained everything.

And to the dismay of Schuyler and Fairfax, it just about did.

The horses were skittish, so it took Preacher a while to catch six of them. Once he did, though, there was a mount for each of the six men plus one for Jake, since Preacher was riding his own stallion.

He had to help Carey, Blackie, and Antelope into their saddles. The Arapaho wasn't happy about not riding bareback, but he refused Preacher's offer to remove the saddle from one of the horses. As bad a shape as Antelope was in, anything that would help him stay on the back of a horse was probably a good idea.

Jerome had rigged a sling for his wounded arm, which was stiff and sore, but didn't hamper him too much in mounting and riding. He wouldn't be able to handle a rifle, though.

Before they set out, Preacher gathered all the pistols, powder horns, and shot pouches from the dead men. He left the extra rifles behind because they would be too cumbersome to carry. The group was well armed now and had plenty of ammunition, but they were still heavily outnumbered.

Preacher had to figure out some way of whittling down the odds against them. An attack out in the open wouldn't accomplish anything except to get all of them killed and to doom Deborah Morrigan to whatever fate her captors had in mind for her.

Because of the wounded men, they couldn't go too fast, but even so, Preacher knew they were moving at a quicker pace than the wagons would be able to. They rode through the canyon where the ambush had taken place. If they had been deeper into it before the shooting started, they would have been wiped out, he thought. They would have been shot down before they could have reached the canyon mouth. So in a way, they had Antelope Fleet as the Wind to thank for their lives. His attack had caused the ambush to be launched prematurely.

"What do you know about those men?" Preacher asked as he rode alongside the Arapaho.

Antelope gave a curt shake of his head as he replied in his own tongue. "Nothing, except that they are white . . . and evil. There are two men who lead them. This I learned as I followed them, after they killed my warriors. One chief is tall, the other short. They are not men of the mountains and plains. They have spent much time in cities. This I can tell."

Preacher frowned. "Tall and short, eh?" He recalled the men he had searched for in St. Louis following Abby's death. "The tall one wouldn't happen to wear buckskins, would he? And the short one's got a suit and a beaver hat?"

Antelope looked sharply at him. "How do you know these things, Preacher?"

Preacher caught his breath. "You mean it really is them?"

"The two men are as you say. Are they known to you?"

"If they're who I think they are, I don't know their names," Preacher replied. "But I know they're sorry sons o' bitches. Evil men, just as *you* say, Antelope. I ain't sure what they're doin' out here so far from where they came from, but I reckon fate takes some odd turns sometimes."

"The ways of the Man-Above are mysteries to those who live in this world. We can only accept them."

Preacher nodded in agreement with that statement. He just hoped the Good Lord saw fit to give him another shot at those two killers.

They emerged from the canyon and followed the wagon ruts along a twisted path that wove in and out of the heavily wooded foothills. It was rare to be able to see more than a couple of hundred yards up the trail before it took another sharp bend. That tortuous route had its advantages. The thieves wouldn't be able to see Preacher and his companions following them.

Around midday, they found a spot next to a creek where the wagons had stopped for a while to give the teams a rest. The droppings heaped on the ground told Preacher that much.

He found something else on the ground—the bundle of bows and arrows that Pete Carey had placed in the back of one of the wagons after the battle with the Pawnee. As Preacher picked them up, Carey asked, "Why'd they throw those out?"

"Didn't figure they had any use for them, I reckon," Preacher replied. He smiled. "But we do."

"Why on earth do we need such primitive weapons?" Corliss wanted to know. "We have guns, and plenty of powder and shot."

Preacher lashed the bundle behind his saddle. "You'll see when the time comes," he said. He was starting to put together a plan in his mind.

They allowed their mounts to rest for a short time, then pushed on. Antelope's face was gray, and Preacher worried that the Arapaho might pass out and topple off his horse. Antelope hung on with grim determination, though, as if nothing was going to sway him from his mission of vengeance.

Preacher understood the feeling. He felt the same way himself.

Corliss and Jerome were both worried about Deborah, as well they might be. Preacher figured that her captors wouldn't molest her, at least not for a while. Most men on the frontier, even hardened killers, would leave a decent woman alone. But there might be some renegades in that group who didn't care about such things, and anyway, restraint had its limits in any man. The sooner they got Deborah out of the hands of her captors, the better.

Preacher called another halt at mid-afternoon. He got one of the bows and a handful of arrows and carried them over to Jake.

"I been meanin' to show you how to use one o' these things," he told the boy. "Now's as good a time as any, I reckon."

Jake's eyes lit up. His normally cheerful face had started to show the same lines of fear and worry and strain as everyone else's, but as Preacher handed him the bow and one of the arrows, he became a kid again.

"Really? You want me to shoot this arrow?"

Preacher pointed. "Yeah. See if you can hit that tree over there."

Awkwardly, Jake fitted the arrow to the bowstring, then raised the bow and pulled back on the string. When he let the arrow fly, he yelled, "Ow!" as the string hit his left arm. The arrow didn't go anywhere near the tree.

"A child of my people with two winters could do better," Antelope said, managing to smile despite the pain he was in.

Jake rubbed his arm where the bowstring had hit it and asked, "What'd the Injun say?"

"He said you're holdin' it wrong," Preacher said. "Here, let me show you."

He worked with Jake for about a quarter of an hour, and by the end of that time the boy could hit the tree trunk with most of the arrows he shot.

After disparaging the weapon, Corliss began to show a surprising interest in it. "Let me try," he suggested. Preacher gave him another of the bows and several arrows.

Corliss was strong enough that he had no trouble drawing the bowstring taut. When he fired, the arrow flew fairly true and glanced off the tree trunk.

"Not bad," Preacher told him. "Try again."

Corliss picked it up quickly, hitting the tree with several arrows. The flint heads penetrated deeply enough into the wood that Preacher grunted with effort as he wrenched them loose.

"You got the makin's of an Indian," he said to Corliss.

"Hardly. But I do seem to have a natural talent for archery."

"Think you could put an arrow through a man?"

Corliss's face hardened. "If he was one of those bastards who took Deborah, I believe I certainly could."

"You may just get your chance," Preacher said.

"Deborah wouldn't *be* a prisoner if it wasn't for you, Corliss," Jerome snapped.

Corliss surprised Preacher by nodding and saying, "You're right."

That wasn't what Jerome had been expecting either. He frowned and said, "I am?"

"Yes. I really did think that Deborah was following me, but I should have made sure. I never should have left the wagon without knowing that she was with me. It's completely my fault, and if anything happens to her, I'll never forgive myself."

"Where did *that* come from? I've never known you to try to be noble."

"There's nothing noble about it," Corliss said. "I've just had some time to think today, while we were riding, and I've decided that it's time for me to grow up, Jerome. You've always been the sensible one. I've been slothful and concerned only with myself."

"Yes, well, that's true."

"I know it is," Corliss said with a nod. "That's why I'm going to change. If we can save Deborah, you'll see, Jerome. I'll do what's best . . . even if it means giving her up and letting her be with you."

"She doesn't want to be with me. She wants you, Corliss." Jerome nodded. "That's really all she's ever wanted, don't you see? Her brief flirtation with me came about only because she thought you didn't care about her as deeply as she cares about you."

"I know." Corliss put an arm around his cousin's shoulders, being careful not to hurt Jerome's wounded arm. "I've got a lot of fences to mend. I just hope I have the chance to mend them."

Antelope looked at Preacher and asked in Arapaho, "Do those two always talk like a flowing river about nothing?"

"Yeah, I'm afraid so," Preacher replied, trying not to grin.

"Gimme some more arrows," Jake said. "I want to shoot that tree some more."

Preacher knew that traveling by horseback, they could have caught up to the wagons before the day was over. He didn't want to do that, however, so he kept the group moving at a deliberate pace that ate up the ground yet didn't bring them too close to their quarry. Whatever they did, it would be better to wait until after night had fallen to make their move.

Darkness settled quickly over the rugged landscape once the sun dipped behind the peaks to the west. Even though it was mid-summer, the elevation was high enough for a cool breeze to spring up. It blew from the west, down from the mountains, and that was good because it would carry their scent away from the thieves' horses, Preacher thought. As they reined in at the edge of some trees that ran along the top of a rise, he caught a faint tang of wood smoke on the air, carried by the breeze from a camp not too far ahead.

"Blackie, you and Pete and Jake will stay here," Preacher said.

"Hell, no," the one-eyed man shot back. "Pete's too crippled up to do any fightin', but I ain't. I can still squeeze a trigger, dad-gummit!"

"So can I," Carey insisted. "I want in on whatever you're plannin', Preacher."

Preacher shook his head. "With that wounded leg, you'd have to do your fightin' from horseback, Pete, and the sound of hooves would give us away. Anyway, I don't intend to fight a pitched battle tonight. I just want to spook those bastards and cut down the odds a mite while I'm doin' it." He turned to Jerome. "You'll stay here, too. Corliss and Antelope and I are the only ones goin'."

Jerome looked like he wanted to argue, but after a second he gave a reluctant nod. "You know what you're doing, Preacher," he said.

"Let's hope so," Preacher replied with a chuckle. "Corliss, get one o' them bows and about half-a-dozen arrows."

"I can shoot a bow," Jake piped up. "Pretty good, too. You said so yourself, Preacher. Let me come along."

"Not this time, younker. You may get your chance later, though."

Jake grumbled about it, but accepted Preacher's decision. A few minutes later, Preacher, Corliss, and Antelope were ready to leave. The stars had come out overhead, but the moon wasn't up yet, so the night was still quite dark.

Preacher led the way as the three men advanced on foot. The day of riding had been tiring for Antelope, but the Arapaho was able to walk now. The wind had died down some, but a whiff of wood smoke drifted to Preacher's nose from time to time, enough so that he knew he was going in the right direction.

They climbed a hill, moving as silently as possible. Before leaving the others, Preacher had stressed the need for stealth to Corliss. Being quiet might be a matter of life and death before the night was over.

When they reached the top of the slope, they crawled over and looked down into a hollow where the wagons had been drawn into a circle. A campfire was blazing in the center of that circle. Men moved around it, coming between the flames and the three stalkers on the hill. Preacher tried to count them and estimated their number to be around twenty-five.

His eyes narrowed as he spotted the two men Antelope had described as the leaders of the gang. Even though he couldn't be sure, he felt like there was a good chance they were the same men who had tried to kill him back in St. Louis and murdered Abby instead. How they had come to be out here, stealing the cousins' wagons, Preacher had no idea. What he did know was that he was close enough to kill them with his rifle.

But that wasn't what he had set out to do tonight, so he pushed that tempting thought aside. Instead, he let his keen eyes search the darkness for the sentries that the thieves were bound to have posted. It took him a while, but he finally located three men spread out around the camp, well out of the circle of light cast by the fire.

Silently, he pointed them out to Corliss and Antelope, and then they waited as time dragged by and one by one the men down below turned in for the night, crawling into their blankets that were scattered around the camp. Only when everyone except the guards appeared to be asleep did Preacher reach over and tap Corliss and Antelope on the shoulder.

The Arapaho didn't need to be told what to do. He crawled off toward one of the guards. Preacher motioned for Corliss to take the nearest man; then he headed off to his left to dispose of the guard in that direction.

When he was close enough, Preacher stopped, came up on one knee, and nocked one of the arrows he had brought with him to the bow. He drew the string taut, aimed at the patch of deeper darkness that marked the guard's location, and let fly. The only sound was a faint whickering as the feathered shaft flew through the air.

Then he heard the soft thud as the arrow drove through the sentry's body. The man let out an almost inaudible groan as he fell to his knees and then slumped forward on his face. A savage smile tugged at the corners of Preacher's mouth. The man had died without making much noise, just as Preacher had planned.

He hoped that Corliss and Antelope had disposed of the other two guards, but he didn't wait to find out.

Preacher crawled forward, straight into the camp of the enemy.

Twenty-eight

The whisper of steel against leather as the knife came out of its sheath couldn't have been heard more than a foot away. Preacher's left hand clamped hard over the sleeping man's nose and mouth, shutting off any sound at the same time as it jerked his head back and drew his throat taut. The knife in Preacher's right hand swept across that throat and cut deeply. Preacher felt the hot gush of blood across his fingers as the man bucked and spasmed, arching his back off the ground for a second, then died.

It was cold-blooded murder and nothing less, Preacher knew, but these bastards had called the tune when they ambushed the wagon train, killed Gil Robinson and Lars Neilson, and kidnapped Deborah Morrigan. He wasn't going to waste any sympathy on them or lose any sleep over their deaths.

They had it comin'.

The fire had died down to a faint red glow, so Preacher was able to crawl from sleeping man to sleeping man without much risk of being discovered unless someone just happened to wake up at the wrong moment. But he knew his luck would run out sooner or later, and so it did after he had slit the throats of four of the men. One of them kicked out as he thrashed around in his death throes, and even though Preacher's hand over his mouth kept him from crying out, his foot hit something and knocked it over with a clatter.

Preacher didn't waste any time. He leaped to his feet, bounded over a wagon tongue, and sprinted off into the darkness as men woke up, realized something was wrong, and started shouting questions. Those questions turned to bellowed curses as the bodies were discovered.

"Over there!" somebody yelled, and several rifles boomed. The shots didn't come anywhere near Preacher. He grinned as he ran through the night.

Those bastards would be even more shocked when they found the bodies of the sentries with arrows in them. They would realize that the enemy had been right there among them, and that it could have been any of them who had died. That would be as unnerving as all hell to them.

That was just what Preacher wanted.

He reached the spot where he had left Corliss and Antelope. Both men were there waiting for him. "Let's go," Preacher said. He led the way down the far side of the slope.

"Will they come after us?" Corliss asked. "They're bound to come after us."

"Not tonight, they won't," Preacher said. "They'll be too spooked. They'll build up the fire and then sit around it all night, too nervous to go back to sleep, wonderin' when death is gonna come for them . . ."

"It had to be Preacher!" Fairfax stormed. "By God, it had to be that bastard!"

Schuyler felt like his blood had turned to cold water in his veins. "What are we gonna do now?" he asked, trying to keep his voice from shaking as he looked at the seven dead men who had been laid out on the ground inside the circle of wagons. Half-a-dozen men were on guard now, standing beside the vehicles as they peered out fearfully at the night.

"We're going to find him and kill him, that's what we're going to do," Fairfax said. "We'll leave the wagons here with a few men to guard them, while the rest of us hunt him down!"

Schuyler shook his head. "No."

Fairfax frowned at him for a moment, then demanded, "What did you say?"

Schuyler summoned up his courage and said, "That's just what he wants us to do. While we're gone, he'll slip in here and take the wagons back, along with the girl. You'd see that, Colin, if you weren't so mad that you ain't thinkin' straight right now."

"Damn it, Schuyler, I'm the one who does the thinking around here!"

"Yeah," Schuyler agreed, "but that don't mean you're always right. And now you ain't."

For a second, Schuyler thought his partner was going to strike him. Fairfax was red in the face and shaking with fury. But then, with a visible effort, Fairfax controlled himself. "Maybe you're right," he admitted. "Preacher knows we outnumber his group, even after he slipped in here and killed half a dozen of us. It'd be to his advantage to split us up somehow."

Schuyler nodded. "That's what I'm talkin' about."

"All right. Come morning, we'll push on toward South Pass. We'll be more alert than ever, and we won't let Preacher pull a trick like this again. But if we haven't dealt with him by the time we get where we're going . . ."

"Then we hunt him down and kill him," Schuyler said.

Antelope Fleet as the Wind was breathing hard by the time he and Preacher and Corliss Hart reached the hill where they had left the others. Corliss put a hand on the Arapaho's arm and said, "Let me help you," but Antelope shrugged him off.

"Antelope needs no help from a white man," the chief said in a weak but haughty voice.

"I'm white," Preacher said as he took hold of Antelope's other arm. "And you lost a lot o' blood the past couple o' days."

"Preacher's skin may be white, but his heart is that of a true human being," Antelope insisted. "Antelope will let you help."

Corliss said, "Suit yourself. I just figured, now that we've fought side by side against the same enemies . . ."

Antelope hesitated, then put out a hand. Corliss grasped it and moved up on his other side. Between him and Preacher, they supported the Arapaho chief on their climb up the hill.

"What do we do now?" Corliss asked before they reached the top.

"Keep an eye on the wagon train," Preacher replied. "If those varmints come after us like I'm hopin', then we can get around them and grab the wagons back before they know what's goin' on. If they're smart enough not to fall for that, then we'll keep harassin' 'em until they don't have any choice but to come after us. Otherwise, we'll whittle 'em down to nothin'."

"Either way, we have to kill the rest of them."

"Yeah," Preacher said. "Either way we kill the rest of them."

Antelope was badly winded by the time they reached the crest. The moon had risen by now, and Preacher saw Jake and Jerome step out of the trees to greet them. "Thank God you're back," Jerome said. "Is everyone all right?"

"As all right as we were when we left," Preacher replied. "Except for Antelope bein' a mite wore out. He needs some rest—"

Preacher would have gone on, but at that moment, unable to contain himself, Jake burst out, "Preacher, somethin' happened! There's Injuns, a whole bunch of Injuns!"

Preacher didn't need Jake to tell him that. He had already spotted the shadowy figures drifting out of the cover of the trees, arrows nocked to their bowstrings, ready to kill. Dozens of them.

"I see 'em, Jake," Preacher said. His voice was calm. There was no need to panic now, because if those warriors were hostile, then it was too late for him and his companions to do anything except die.

* * *

By morning, the members of Shad Beaumont's gang who were still alive had settled down considerably, since nothing else had happened during the night and it was easier not to be scared when the sun was up. They buried the men Preacher had killed—nobody entertained the slightest doubt that Preacher was responsible for their deaths, although it was possible he might have had help—then prepared to get the wagons rolling again.

The woman refused to eat when Schuyler tried to give her some breakfast. He knew her name was Deborah Morrigan. She had admitted that much before falling stubbornly silent. So now he said, "Miss Morrigan, you've gotta eat. You'll die if you don't."

She gave him a look that seemed to say that was exactly what she wanted.

Schuyler kept at her. "What can I do to talk you into eatin'?"

"Let me go," she said.

"I don't reckon I can do that," he replied with a shake of his head. "My partner wouldn't like it."

"You mean that bald little man who gives all the orders?"

"Yeah."

"Then tell me what you're planning to do with me."

Schuyler was glad she was talking again, even if she wasn't eating. "Nothin' bad is gonna happen to you," he promised. "We're gonna take you back to St. Louis and let our boss decide what to do with you."

"And just who is this boss of yours?"

Schuyler opened his mouth to answer the question, then thought better of it. He didn't know if

Shad Beaumont would want him telling people that Beaumont was really responsible for what had happened to the wagon train. Just in case things didn't work out.

"Go away and leave me alone," Deborah snapped when she saw that Schuyler wasn't going to answer her question. "I wouldn't believe anything you told me anyway."

After a few minutes, Schuyler gave up. When he left the wagon where Deborah was being held prisoner, Fairfax asked him if he'd had any luck getting her to eat. Schuyler shook his head.

"She'll cooperate when she gets hungry enough," Fairfax said with a smirk. "She'll do anything we say when she realizes that she's not going to get away."

"She probably thinks Preacher's gonna come to save her."

"Well, we won't let that happen, now will we?"

The wagon train got under way again. It was a beautiful, crisp, high-country morning. Schuyler could tell, though, that they would soon be working their way down out of the foothills and back onto the flats before the next range of hills and mountains rose. That was the one where South Pass was located, according to the maps he had seen. That was where they were headed.

The trail took a downward slant before Schuyler was expecting it. The wagons rolled around a hill and then started down a gentle slope, at the bottom of which the terrain flattened out into a broad, grassy plain.

Also waiting at the bottom of that slope was a line of buckskin-clad, feathered-decorated, painted figures mounted on nimble ponies. There were at least forty of the warriors. They made no move to attack, simply sat there blocking the path of the wagons.

"Oh, hell," Schuyler said from the seat of the lead wagon as he hauled the team of oxen to a halt. He glanced over at Fairfax, who was even paler than usual. "Oh, hell, Colin."

"Take it easy," Fairfax grated. "Maybe they're not hostile."

"Not hostile? Look at them!" Schuyler had never seen a more bloodthirsty-looking bunch in his life.

Fairfax swallowed hard. "Maybe we can bargain with them."

One of the warriors suddenly edged his pony forward a couple of steps. He sat stiffly, and if Schuyler and Fairfax had been close enough, they would have seen how gray and strained his face was underneath the streaks of war paint. Antelope Fleet as the Wind had endured a great deal to reach this moment alive. The burning deep inside him told him that he didn't have much more time remaining. So he was going to take savage pleasure in what happened next.

"See?" Fairfax said, never recognizing the man on the pony. "That must be their chief. He wants to negotiate."

The Indian carried a rifle. He thrust it into the air over his head, cried out a command, and swept his arm forward.

The rest of the war party charged, the hooves of their ponies thundering as they raced up the slope toward the wagons.

For these evil men who had fouled the frontier with their presence, there would be no negotiation, only death.

* * *

Preacher burst out of the trees on Horse as the shooting started. Dog raced along after him. Corliss and Jerome Hart, Pete Carey and Blackie all followed as well. They were to one side of the wagons, launching a flank attack. Closer than the Arapaho warriors led by Antelope Fleet as the Wind, they would reach the wagons first.

They had traveled all night to get ahead of the wagon train and set up an ambush of their own. Preacher intended to leave the bulk of the fighting to the Arapaho war party that had been brought back by Eagle Flies High. His own goal was to strike quickly, get in and out, and bring Deborah Morrigan to safety. If along the way they could kill a few of the bastards who had taken over the wagon train, then so much the better.

With the attention of the thieves focused on the attacking Indians, Preacher and his companions were within a few yards of the wagons before anybody noticed them. One of the men let out a yell of alarm and wheeled his horse toward them, raising his rifle as he did so. Preacher was close enough to use one of his pistols, firing before the man did.

The pistol was double-shotted this time, unlike back in St. Louis, and both balls ripped through the man's body, shattering bone and spraying blood as they drove him from the saddle. Preacher swept past the now-riderless horse. Behind him, the others opened fire, too. Clouds of powder smoke filled the air as Preacher veered the stallion toward the lead wagon, figuring that was the most likely place for Deborah to be. He had already spotted the two men he most wanted to meet again on the driver's seat of that wagon, too.

The tall one stood up and raised a rifle to his shoulder. It belched smoke and flame from its muzzle, and Preacher felt a stunning jolt as the ball struck his left arm, causing him to slew halfway around in the saddle and almost fall off the lunging stallion. He caught himself, and guiding Horse with his knees, he brought up the pistol in his other hand.

"I hit him!" the tall man in buckskins shouted as he stood there on the driver's box. "I actually hit him that time!"

A second later, Preacher blew him off the wagon with the pistol. The man somersaulted through the air and crashed to the ground in a limp, bloody heap, a pair of fist-sized holes in his chest where the balls had struck him.

The one in the beaver hat leaped to the ground and disappeared in the chaos that was spreading around the wagons. Choking, blinding clouds of dust and powder smoke filled the air. Preacher let the other man go and brought Horse up next to the wagon. "Miss Morrigan!" he shouted. "Deborah! You in there?"

The canvas flap was thrust back, and she stuck her head out. "Preacher!" she screamed.

Corliss flashed past Preacher and reached out to grab Deborah, lifting her from the wagon and cradling her in front of him. "I've got you," he told her. "I've got you, and I'll never let you go again."

She wrapped her arms around his neck and hung on tight.

One of the renegades on horseback suddenly loomed up behind them, a shotgun clutched in his hands. He swung the weapon's twin barrels toward them, but before he could pull the triggers, a shot blasted out and the man's head jerked back as a black hole appeared over his right eye. He toppled from the saddle.

Gasping in surprise, Corliss looked at the dead man, then looked around at Jerome, who sat his horse nearby with a smoking pistol in his hand. After a second, Corliss smiled and gave his cousin a nod. Jerome returned it, then ducked aside as Corliss shouted, "Look out!"

One of the thieves had run up behind Jerome and swung an empty rifle at him like a club. The blow missed because of Corliss's warning. With one arm still firmly wrapped around Deborah, Corliss drove his horse forward and lashed out with the pistol in his other hand. The barrel crunched against the skull of the attacker, laying him out cold.

By now Antelope Fleet as the Wind and the rest of the Arapaho war party had reached the wagons, and although the renegades put up a fight, they were no match for the warriors swarming around them. It was a massacre. Preacher and his party rode away to leave the Indians to their bloody work. One of the riders who had been with the wagons broke away from the fight and tried to escape, riding hard for the trees where Preacher and the others had been concealed earlier. Blackie lifted his rifle to draw a bead on the man, but before he could fire; an arrow whistled out of the trees and caught the fleeing renegade with a perfectly timed shot. The man tumbled to the ground with the shaft sticking out of his chest. Jake stepped to the edge of the trees, bow in hand, and waved and grinned at Preacher.

It was all over in a matter of moments. Preacher made sure that none of his companions had suffered any new injuries, then rode back to the wagons. He found Antelope Fleet as the Wind sitting propped up against a wagon wheel. The chief's wounds had broken open again, soaking his buckskins with blood. But he smiled and lifted a hand in greeting as Preacher dismounted.

"It was a good fight," Antelope said in the Arapaho tongue, "but I wish there had been more of the enemy to kill since this will be my last fight."

Preacher knelt beside him. "We could not have won without you and your men," he told Antelope. "You saved us all."

"Preacher is a good man. You know . . . what is important and what is not. Do not let those who come after us . . . ruin this land."

"I'll do what I can," Preacher promised, but he knew that wouldn't amount to much against the inevitable forces of civilization. Already, there were signs that an entire way of life would eventually be coming to an end. True, the settling of the frontier would be a new beginning as far as the forces of civilization were concerned . . .

But Preacher knew the whole truth. For each new beginning, something else was lost forever.

A long sigh came from Antelope Fleet as the Wind. His eyes looked into the distance but saw nothing. His spirit ran in the next world, as fast as the beautiful animal for which he was named.

From behind Preacher, Eagle Flies High said, "We will go now. Our warriors will respect the friendship that our chief felt for you, Preacher, so you and the others may travel on in safety."

"At least as far as the Arapaho are concerned, eh?" Preacher said as he came to his feet.

"Yes." A grim smile touched Eagle's mouth. "But I can only speak for our people. Others may not feel the same way. Be careful, Preacher."

They nodded to each other; then the Indians mounted their ponies and rode away, taking Antelope and their other dead with them. Preacher waved for Corliss, Jerome, and the others to come on in.

They still had a long way to go before they reached South Pass.

Twenty-nine

One week later

"This is it," Corliss said. "This is the place for our trading post."

Jerome nodded as they stood looking over a broad, grassy park at the foot of the slope that led up to South Pass. The meadow had a creek for water, plenty of grass for livestock, and trees for logs with which they would build a large, sturdy trading post. An uneasy truce between the cousins had grown into acceptance and the beginnings of friendship again. There had been no more talk about splitting up.

For one thing, since the deaths of Robinson and Neilson, they were short-handed. It was going to take everybody to make a success of this enterprise, including Jake, who had agreed to stay with the cousins, at least until the next spring.

"But the next time you come by here, Preacher," the boy warned the mountain man, "you're gonna have to take me with you. I'll be 'most grown by then."

"We'll see," Preacher said with a grin as he got

ready to ride. He had packed some supplies on Horse and was anxious to get on up into the mountains, where the beaver were just waiting for him to trap them.

The rest of the journey had passed without incident. Preacher and Jake had both been forced to handle one of the teams, a job that Preacher didn't like. He had managed all right, but if he never saw another ox's rear end, that would be just fine with him.

Jerome, Blackie, and Pete Carey were all healing from their injuries. Blackie and Carey were going to stay on and help build the trading post; then Carey planned to continue working there while Blackie went back to trapping.

Everyone gathered around to say good-bye to Preacher. Deborah hugged him, and so, after a second's hesitation, did Jake. "Thanks for bringin' me along, Preacher," the youngster said. "Even with all the fightin', I like it a whole heap better out here than I did in St. Louis."

Preacher grinned. "I sort of feel the same way, son," he said.

"Hello!" Jerome said. "Someone's coming."

They turned to see a rider headed toward them, leading a packhorse. After a moment, Preacher recognized the man, who wore a coonskin cap with the tail dangling in front of his shoulder.

"Don't worry," he told the others. "It's a fella I know named Bouchard, another trapper."

Bouchard reined in and raised a hand in greeting. He stared at the wagons for a second, then said, "*Sacre bleu*, Preacher, what is this? The beginnings of a new town?"

"You never know," Preacher said. He waved a

hand at the others. "These folks are settin' up a tradin' post."

"*Oui*, I think I heard something about that. And a good thing it is, too, because there is a wagon train full of settlers about three days behind me." Bouchard poked a thumb back over his shoulder as he spoke. "They will be needing supplies, I imagine."

"Three days?" Jerome said. "We can't build a trading post in three days!"

"So we'll sell to 'em out of the wagons," Corliss said with a grin as he put an arm around Deborah's shoulders. "You wouldn't happen to know if there's a minister with that wagon train, would you, M'sieu Bouchard?"

The bearded trapper nodded. "I believe there is."

"Good." Corliss beamed down at Deborah. "I think we're going to need to have a wedding." Deborah smiled. Corliss glanced over at Jerome and added, "That is, if there's a best man available."

"There is," Jerome said. Then he clapped his hands together. "Let's get to work, everyone! There's a lot to do before those wagons get here!"

They were all so busy, they didn't even notice when Preacher and Bouchard rode away. Jake realized they were gone and looked around quickly, spotting the two men just as they disappeared into the trees as they climbed toward the pass.

He lifted a hand and waved anyway, not caring whether Preacher could see him or not.

As they rode, the Frenchman said, "It is unusual to see you with greenhorns such as those, Preacher. You guided them out here, *oui*?"

"Yeah," Preacher said. "I seem to keep gettin' roped into that sort o' thing."

"Any trouble along the way?"

Preacher thought about everything that had happened and then shook his head. "Nope. Not too much."

Something *was* still bothering him, though. They hadn't buried all the bodies of the men that had attacked the wagon train and kidnapped Deborah, but Preacher had checked all the corpses before the wagons rolled on westward.

The man in the beaver hat hadn't been among them.

The fella had either been wounded and crawled off somewhere else to die, Preacher told himself, or else he had slipped away during all the confusion of the battle. But either way, he was a dead man, because Preacher didn't figure there was any chance somebody like that could survive out here on his own, so far from civilization. If a grizzly didn't get him, a wolf would, and if somehow he escaped from those predators, the elements or the Indians would take care of him.

Still, Preacher would have liked to know for certain sure that the bastard was dead.

But you couldn't have everything, he told himself as he rode on toward the mountains with Bouchard. Looking at the wild, magnificent landscape around him, he thought again that no, a man couldn't have everything . . .

But a fella who lived out here on the frontier came mighty damned close to it.

* * *

Two months later

Shad Beaumont stared in amazement at the gaunt, filthy scarecrow of a man who had been brought into his study in his big house on the outskirts of St. Louis. The beaver hat was long gone and the clothes were in tatters, but Beaumont recognized the man despite that. But only barely, because Colin Fairfax had changed a great deal.

He looked like a man who had been to hell and back.

"What happened?" Beaumont demanded.

Fairfax was swaying with exhaustion. He had to put a hand on Beaumont's desk to steady himself as he leaned forward and croaked, "*Preacher* . . . Preacher happened. Killed poor Schuyler and ruined everything. Nearly killed me." A cackle of laughter that sounded like it was touched with insanity came from the tortured throat. "But he didn't. I made it back. The animals didn't get me, and neither did the Indians. And you know what kept me going?"

Beaumont could only shake his head as this crazed mockery of a man.

"Preacher kept me going," Fairfax whispered, and despite everything, the light of hatred burned brightly in his sunken eyes. "I knew I had to live so that someday, somehow . . . I can kill that damned Preacher."